The Girl Who Ate Kalamazoo

Also by Darrin Doyle

Revenge of the Teacher's Pet: A Love Story

The Girl Who Ate Kalamazoo

Darrin Doyle

ST. MARTIN'S GRIFFIN
NEW YORK

This is a work of fiction. All of the characters, organizations, and events portrayed in this novel are either products of the author's imagination or are used fictitiously.

www.stmartins.com

Library of Congress Cataloging-in-Publication Data

Doyle, Darrin, 1970–
    The girl who ate Kalamazoo / Darrin Doyle.—1st ed.
        p. cm.
    ISBN 978-0-312-59231-8
    1. Problem families—Fiction.   2. Young women—Fiction.   I. Title.
    PS3604.O95475G57 2010
    813'.6—dc22

                                                        2009033863

First Edition: January 2010

10 9 8 7 6 5 4 3 2 1

For Simon and Charlie

Acknowledgments

The author would like to acknowledge the following people and places:

Sara Crowe and Vicki Lame for the faith and hard work.

Christine Schutt for the encouragement.

Jason Ockert for the mad tennis skills.

The grounds crew at Miami University of Ohio for the beautiful landscaping, which provided an idyllic setting for writing a portion of this novel in my notebook.

The city of Kalamazoo for the inspiration.

Courtney for everything.

And of course, McKenna Mapes for finally letting us in.

A Note from the Editor

Many rational people will question the decision to bother the marketplace with another Audrey Mapes book. Certainly, the "Mall City Muncher" has well exceeded her fifteen minutes. Her wonderfully mystifying act—indeed, her life itself—may be remembered less for the benefits to the city of Kalamazoo than the way it turned people off from reading. This is regrettable, but who could blame the common book buyer for running, screaming, from the printed word when the 2000 *New York Times* bestseller list was choked, week after week, with nonfiction and fiction titles all dealing with the same little Midwestern bombshell?

No doubt we all recall the torrent of pseudo-biographical, pseudo-scientific, and pseudo-historical accounts of the 1997–1999 Swallowing of Kalamazoo: Maverick Burns's *The City That Wasn't and Then Really Wasn't (and Then, At Last, Was)*; Cecil Rocheport's *Audrey Mapes: Chewing the Doors of Infamy*; Dr. Ellen Morose's *The Mother (and Father) of all Eating Disorders: The Mapes Family Tragedy*.

Mercifully, those floodwaters have receded. And yet, even if they hadn't—even if dozens of Audrey Mapes books were at press *right now*—I would rush this into print. You see, the book you hold is an entirely different animal than every one that has come before it and any that will likely follow.

A bold statement, to be sure. The truth? Read on.

Like your fellow Americans, you probably didn't hear about the sale of a private residence last spring. The press never covered it.

Why would they? Well, the home stood at 219 Moriarty Street, in Grand Rapids, Michigan. Yes, *that* Moriarty Street. Yes, *that* house. The last occupant moved out, taking with her only a medium-sized suitcase and a 5' × 7' storage crate. She provided instructions with the family attorneys that everything else, the remnants of the estate, be sold at auction and the proceeds given to an undisclosed charity.

The auction received scant attention. The house was left nearly full; only the attic was empty. Little that remained was of monetary value—furniture, dishes, children's clothing, a set of barbells, lamps, and a tool bench. As everyone knows, the Mapeses weren't rich. Even after Audrey became a worldwide phenomenon, they never ascended from their lower-middle class station. Almost nothing in the house could even be described as the type of personal effect that would attract fetishistic collectors of "Mapesorabilia." All of the photographs, scrapbooks, baby books, kids' drawings, and so on, had evidently been removed—if they ever existed at all. With one momentous exception, what populated 219 Moriarty were the ordinary possessions of an ordinary American family.

Still, if the auction had taken place five years ago, the bidding would have been legendary. A Mapes toaster would have fetched $1,000. A handful of crumbs from the trap: at least fifty bucks, by my reckoning. But now the public has had enough.

There was, however, one curious item on the auction block. Labeled simply, "container of handwritten miscellanea," it was a nondescript cardboard box, slightly wider and deeper than a case of copy paper. Bidding began at twenty dollars. Within two minutes, it was sold for forty to a Mr. D. M. Doyle. An estate facilitator had rifled through the box just enough to properly designate it, but no more. It was filled with notebook paper—much of it dog-eared scraps, yellowed, torn in two, stained with liquids. Readily identifiable were grocery lists, "To Do" lists, phone numbers, reminders of bill payments. Every sheet featured the same cramped, slanted handwriting.

But no one dug beneath the surface.

Thankfully, Mr. Doyle read every word. What he found among those thousand pages was an undiscovered window, one most thought would never exist: a view into one of the most reclusive and talked about families in modern American history. The surviving Mapeses, of course, are legendary for their fiercely guarded privacy. Not a single interview exists on record. No family photographs have ever been leaked to the press or appeared on the Internet.

Mr. Doyle pored over the papers for more than a year. What began as the self-described "voyeuristic romp of a guy with too much time on his hands" evolved, at last, into a labor of love. For he fell in love with the woman behind the words—her personality, her thoughts, her wit, her maddening contradictions, her élan vital.

But unfortunately there was no cohesion to the random jottings. No story. So Mr. Doyle sculpted it, trimmed it, molded it. Gave it an arc. Found the major conflicts. Attached a suitable epigram. Like Dr. Frankenstein, he stitched together the necrotic segments in order to breathe life into the rantings of this decidedly melancholy and plain woman. He rearranged and pruned so that we could *understand*. The original scribbling remains intact, including the writer's beguiling decision to refer to herself in the third person (most of the time). And so, from this ragged chicken scratch a narrative unlike any other has emerged.

With great pride, I present here the first Audrey Mapes story told by a Mapes—more exactly, Audrey's older sister, McKenna.

I do not claim to provide the "definitive" story of Audrey and her family. It is ridiculous to suggest, in fact, that such a version— one safeguarded against the distortions of guesswork, playfulness, subjectivity, mirth, regret, and so on—is even possible. All readers are well-advised to never approach a text—from *The Little Engine that Could* to the Bible—as if it were an indisputable account of an event or, more especially, of a human being.

Let there be no doubt, however, that the author of the work you now hold in your hands is the sister of Audrey Mapes. The sheets of paper were lab-tested and certified, the handwriting was analyzed, DNA was collected, and matches were confirmed. The reader can "read easy," as the phrase goes, knowing that the incidents in this volume have been painstakingly, even painfully, researched—not through interviews and public documents, as has heretofore been the case, but through McKenna's first-hand life experiences.

However, please be advised that a few critical moments of the narrative do enter into Audrey's mind, whereupon you will be boldly submerged into the clouded waters of that beautiful young "monster's" thoughts. . . .

. . . These should be taken as earnest attempts by McKenna to reconstruct (and perhaps to resurrect?) her remarkable sister with the only tools she possesses—her imagination. Rest assured, though, that in every instance of the kind mentioned, McKenna probably had good reason to infer what Audrey was thinking at the given moment.

Kalamazoo, both of us will do a fadeaway.
I will be carried out feet first
And time and the rain will chew you to dust
And the winds blow you away.

—"The Sins of Kalamazoo," Carl Sandburg

Part One

Disappointing Children

1.

The story of Audrey Mapes begins with butter. Actually, Imperial margarine. The Mapeses couldn't afford real butter.

She rubbed sticks of Imperial on her elbows, forearms, shins, and knees. Not always, not every day. Not even every other day. But it felt like always, it felt like every day. Let's say that four times a week, Audrey the footless toddler slid in a blur across the kitchen floor. She barreled into the wheeled caddie, toppled tin canisters, ignited powdery explosions.

Nobody yelled at her. She was never told, "No." One of her parents—or, more often, one of her eight-year-old siblings—or, even more often, the meeker, kinder of the twins, McKenna, would dutifully take up broom and dustpan, careful not to mutter any profanity loudly enough that Audrey could hear while she swept away Audrey's mess and erased the Imperial glaze with a wad of paper towels.

On other days—the in-between ones when she wasn't lubricating the linoleum—Audrey gave herself a toothpaste mustache and lurched through the house on crutches while reciting the Pledge of Allegiance in the voice of Groucho Marx, who she'd never actually heard but who her daddy imitated in the basement when he was in the best of moods. This was a preschooler, mind you. She had the makings of a star, even then.

Another source of fun for Audrey was filling her right ear with cream cheese and letting Snoodles the basset hound puppy lick it clean. An hour later, still half-deaf, Audrey would slap her cheeks with handfuls of baking soda before climbing, confident as a shirpa, onto her daddy's lap.

"Gah!" he would say. "My bank statements. Get off!"

They weren't bank statements. Murray Mapes was seated on the couch, surrounded by papers—notes, drawings, schematics, the occasional hardware store shopping list—all hand-scrawled in blue ballpoint and legible only to his eyes. He had trained himself to call any important piece of paper a "bank statement" to kill any interest his children might have in what he was doing. He wanted, above all, to be left alone with his equations and crude sketches. Whereas the twins had learned, from nearly a decade of practice, to respect this dream of their father's, Audrey had only learned how to eat dirt, Play-Doh, crayons, and paper. That and how to walk on flattened soda pop cans.

Audrey would kiss her father's face, persisting through his weak objections until his light-blue work shirt was speckled with powder and his three-day scruff was white as the snow on the front lawn (more accurately, "front patch of grass"—five-minute mow time).

"Why do you hate me?" Audrey would ask, after he'd calmly gripped her shoulders, lifted her, and set her back onto the carpet.

"I don't hate you. I hate the idea of you." He pretended to return to his papers, but it was easy to see that his sideways glance was trained on Audrey's legs, on the careful rigging of straps, mounts, and clamps designed to stabilize the two Dr Pepper cans upon which his three-year-old precariously balanced.

Unflappable, Audrey mounted her dad again, stepping with her aluminum feet upon his thighs. The patches of baking soda made Audrey's cheeks resemble skin grafts, or the makeup attempts of an ill-trained clown. She gripped Murray's shoulders, mimicking what he'd done to her. She shook him, gently (in a silly way, no threats—even at such a young age, she recognized her provider).

She pouted. "Am *I* a bad idea?"

"You're a wonderful *thought*," he answered, licking the sweat from his lip. "An amazing gesture. A spectacular plan. A perfect theory."

(It's disingenuous to imply that this dialogue actually occurred when Audrey was three. It's true that Murray uttered these exact lines, but only once, many years later, moments before a furious, split-lipped, twenty-year-old Audrey, employing a dramatic high-step she'd learned by observing high school color guard practice from the sidelines, marched through the living room on her nationally recognized $30,000 prosthetic feet [designed by MIT graduate students], out the screen door, across the front patch of grass, and to the street, where she tossed her tortoise shell suitcase into the trunk of her Porsche and sped away to ingest the city of purple-capped lumber yards and railroad tracks.)

Normally, when Audrey asked, "Am *I* a bad idea?" her father answered:

"Your eyes are burnt matches. Your hair is a scented galaxy where time stands still. Your mouth can't be real, unless God, who doesn't exist, has performed a miracle and sent to Earth not a bearded savior but a pair of strawberry lips and teeth as crookedly perfect as wave-battered rocks under a maizy sun where no man could fear death. Now get the hell off my lap! I've got work to do."

2.

The ugliest stain left by this disaster—beyond the loss of an irre-
proachable young woman barely out of her teens and millions of
dollars in damage, both property and psychic—is the bilious stain
that spread over time and still colors us. It's a stain of narrative, of
story: the collected, steady drip of untruth from the lips of small-
minded busybodies—women, if I may be frank, who found a vo-
cation in slandering strangers over steaming cups. Through their
dentures they whispered predictions and slurped their chamomile
tea. All geezers are certain, but these particular geezers weren't
certain that Audrey Mapes—at the time just a preschooler living
in a rundown house and not yet experiencing functional, nonthreatening feet—wouldn't grow up to perform some monumen-
tal act so insensitive and selfish and *evil* that she would be
exposed as the devil she was. They predicted that Audrey—yes,
that Antichrist who drifted off to dreamland clutching a stuffed
rhinoceros—would alter the world forever, causing misery, horror,
and perhaps even a dangerous chemical spill or two.

These arthritic Nostrodami also added assurances that the only
folks who would come out looking good after the ordeal (Aside
from the victims. Of course.) would be the ones who'd had the pre-
science to see it coming, those who'd warned the world even while
this monster was still a sweet lily cup in a pink dress sticking out
her tongue for Polaroids. Nightly, their clawed hands patted each
other's hunches before they crawled alone between tightened bed

sheets to pray rosaries for one more day of lung power, one more
meatloaf sandwich, one more chance to trash a child they barely
knew.

The stain, of course, is that they were right. The geezers called
it. That's the sticker.

However, I hereby assert that none of these psychic busybodies,
and in fact, no one on Earth—not Audrey's half-paralyzed prophet
of a mother; not her half-deaf, wannabe-inventor father; not her
bulging brother or misunderstood sister—ever envisioned Audrey
growing up to devour an entire city. Not even a crumb like Kalamazoo.

3.

McKenna and Toby, five-year-old fraternal twins, stood with aching arms held above their heads. Each was battling bravely to keep Misty's assigned leg aloft. Misty lay undrugged and pale on the queen-sized bed, bearing down. Thick vines of sweat-heavy hair gave her head the appearance of an unpruned plant. Murray slid ice chips between her lips, toweled her brow, looked bored and distracted even during her contractions.

The midwife Sheenie, a freckle-ridden redhead with a stout body and man-hands, gave encouragement. "That's a good girl," she said. "You're doing it, honey. We're gonna get that baby out of there." She repeated her mantra every ten minutes, every two minutes, every ten seconds. The contractions rose again and again. Misty bucked on the mattress. Sheenie monitored the baby's heart rate when she could, but mostly she bustled—never rushed, never harried—from one end of the bedroom to the other, her hips and buttocks bumping McKenna and Toby's shoulders as she brought warm compresses and Styrofoam cups of ice. She rubbed lavender oil onto Misty's naked belly. Every half-hour, Sheenie reached three fingers inside to "move things around." Misty screamed like a raw brake.

McKenna, gripping her mother's calf, couldn't stifle her own yelp. Her weakness embarrassed her. She looked down at her socked feet.

Blood vessels branched over Misty's cheeks. Then branches

formed atop the original branches. Eventually, she was the color of an eggplant.

When McKenna and Toby could take no more, as their arms began to burn, tremble, and collapse, as they began to fear that their mother's face was literally going to explode . . . just then, a swirl of matted yellow hair appeared between Misty's legs. Then a whole head. A squished face. A gush of blood and water that rusted the twins' tube socks.

Like magic, Audrey was a reality—the baby sister the twins had envisioned for so long.

There she was: a slick, glistening body; a crying mouth; tiny legs bicycling.

Legs with no feet attached.

The midwife hurried the footless infant onto Misty's bare chest. Murray cooed, smooched the bloody cheek. He allowed his index finger, which to the newborn was the size of a baseball bat, to be grabbed. McKenna and Toby stepped around Sheenie as she scissored the cord. They leaned, straining to see inside. Perhaps the feet were still on the way.

No such luck.

"You'll need to help out around here," Murray told the twins, days later. "You're old enough to pitch in. No more free lunch."

This news caused McKenna so much anxiety that she messed her pants. Toby smelled it. He glared.

Their father didn't seem to notice. He kept talking, flapping like a bird as he tried halfheartedly to take flight from the front cement steps and over the Bader's dilapidated two-story across the street. Murray had strapped on the latest prototype of his Man Wings—this particular untested pair built from wax paper, tin foil, and eight hundred melted-together plastic Sporks.

"McKenna, you're in charge of baths. Three a week. Don't get soap in her eyes, and pay special mind to the stumps. Be gentle but firm, dig into those crevices like you mean it, and don't let her drown." He paused long enough to ignite a Kool 100 and kick his flip-flops onto the lawn, for less ballast. He resumed flapping, the white cigarette hanging from his lips. He was doing a dry run, a "flap check," trying to get a feel for the wings and how they responded to his body before the Actual Launch Date. (The Actual Launch Date never came. FYI.)

McKenna and Toby stood on the grass near the steps. Toby, like a Wimbledon ball-boy, sprinted to retrieve the discarded flip-flops. McKenna watched her father, anticipating with each swoosh of the wings that he might actually rise off the stoop, take to the sky, and never return.

Murray continued with his instructions: "And space them out, okay? Or else it won't count. Like for example Monday, Wednesday, Friday. That's not a rigid schedule, understand? Just a 'for instance.' Nobody's trying to lock you into anything. No contract except the one you draw up in your own head. I trust you. Pick different days! Have fun with it! You're a smart girl. You'll figure it out."

McKenna hated her sister's stumps, the little knobs of skin where the feet were supposed to be. Like drawstring purses cinched tight. The mere mention of them upset McKenna's stomach.

Later that night, she tried to get Toby to switch jobs.

McKenna's eyes had adjusted to the darkness, and she could see in the adjoining bed that Toby was also awake, studying the ceiling, perhaps imagining, as McKenna was, two-week-old Audrey walking acrobatically on her hands, ascending a flight of stairs, entering Heaven for all eternity.

McKenna tried to make her whisper sound casual, conversational—any way but desperate: "Baths are so easy. And you love the water."

"I love *swimming*," Toby answered. "Not water. No way I'm washing Stumpy."

"You *want* to change her diapers? That's nasty!"

"They can't smell as bad as you."

It was a low blow. McKenna had no response. She felt her face blushing. Despite being triple-wrapped in Bounty and sprayed with Misty's patchouli oil, the soiled underwear McKenna had stashed behind her dresser (until smuggling it to the toilet before bedtime) had filled the room with rank. Her neck itched with perspiration. She tried to sleep. Toby snored for hours.

4.

Murray Mapes wanted to give his new daughter the feet she'd forgotten to carry out of the womb. By his own estimation, he'd been an inventor for twenty years at the time she was born. He liked to tell the story of how, at age five, he'd transformed three plywood boards, a handful of nails, and four industrial-sized rubber bands into a gun and turret mounted on a Radio Flyer wagon. The weapon could launch screws and nails up to twenty-seven feet.

In the following decades, Murray filed dozens of patents (the first at age twelve), including, but not limited to, the Clock Hat, the Squeezable Survival Kit, the Hood Wiperz, the Detachable Shirt Collar, the Hot Dog Pouch, the Pencil Pachyderm, the Collapsible Ukulele with Hairbrush, and the Moldproof Towel Organizer.

Murray's habit was to pursue each new idea with an intensity approaching madness. Once a brainstorm hit him, he spent every free moment in the basement, from which issued clanks and buzzes, scrapings and explosions, celebrity impersonations, paroxysms of laughter, and, now and then, weeping. He pretty much drained his emotional well down there. If Misty and the twins saw Murray ten minutes each day during an invention jag, they felt blessed.

Then, three months after the idea first took shape in his mind, Murray would ascend from his dungeon. He would kick open the basement door, his clothes and hair covered in sawdust and metal shavings, bearing his new baby. He would promptly demonstrate the gadget to his wife, children, mother-in-law, and a few select neighbors, to varying degrees of applause.

That's as far as Murray took any one idea. The fury of his initial passion left him exhausted and listless, and he was unable, or unwilling, or a combination of both, to actually thrust his inventions into the public sphere. Try as he might ("might" being the operative word) he could never find an investor to fund the production of his goods. And of course, there wasn't enough money in the Mapes's bank account to make the inventions anything more than conversation pieces in a future attic museum.

Daily bread found its way to the table because Murray worked the line at Hanson Mold, a factory that made plastic injection molds for automobiles. It was a thankless, noisy existence. Murray hunched hour after hour in the shadow of the 300T Castmaster press, far from natural light and fresh air. By age forty, half of his hearing would be gone, causing him to shout for his salt and pepper. Red trenches from the safety goggles would become permanent circles around his eyes. His palms would thicken with calluses from repeated burns. His fingers would chap and split.

But that was years later. And on the plus side, Hanson Mold was the type of repetitive, mindless, union-protected work that allowed a man to daydream. While the radio rocked "Running on Empty" and "Point of Know Return" for the hundredth time in a month, and while his coworkers bickered about the pros and cons of low-cal shortening substitutes as a way of diverting their attentions from their indignation over the latest infringement on personal rights (Article 4.9.4 of the Standard Operating Procedures now stipulated that all mustaches had to be "well-groomed"), Murray lived somewhere else, sketching in his mind (and during lunch breaks, on McDonald's bags), the perfect pair of prosthetic feet for his breathtaking new daughter.

Audrey was a comely baby; this much is indisputable, no

matter how twisted and grotesque people try to make her in legend.

Henri Rousseau said, "To see something as beautiful is to see in it the promise of happiness."

Notice that the "promise of happiness" is all it takes. No actual happiness is necessary.

Audrey was beautiful like the fever that kills a virus. Like a vivid dream of an ex-lover. Like a perfect beach moment just before the carnation horizon is swallowed by a night so complete you forget pink is a color. Like a fat, barn-red apple straddling the line between ripeness and rot.

Audrey stole the breath of all passersby who happened to glance into the stroller Misty piloted to the supermarket. Half a dozen times a day, a bespectacled old retiree leaned in, blew kisses, and tried to stammer out a verbal appraisal of Audrey's intense splendor. An impossible task. Misty smiled, her eyes flashing a crumb-sized speck of doubt, or maybe exhaustion, and offered a quiet, "You're sweet to say so," or, "She takes after her daddy," before bustling away.

McKenna and Toby trailed behind, kicking pebbles.

5.

The twins were midway between five and six when Audrey was born, so in theory they were able to help in the ways their father wanted them to help. But the only skill they'd mastered thus far was sprinting through the house in *Dukes of Hazzard* underwear, spitting water at lampshades.

Toby was eight minutes older than McKenna—a fact Toby kept filed in his mental reserves and brought out as a way of settling certain profound disagreements, such as who would eat the last cookie, who would sit in Daddy's TV chair when Daddy was working in the basement, who could belch the loudest, who would end up married first and to a more beautiful wife (he always said "wife," no matter how much McKenna protested), and who would be crowned heavyweight boxing champion of the world.

According to the baby books, McKenna and Toby were physically identical in nearly every visible way for their first four years: Long, narrow feet and hands; tiny rumps; wide ears flat to their heads; fair skin; green eyes; mud-brown hair, cut by Misty into "bowls"; and prominent rib cages and spinal cords.

"Gangly kids," according to their parents.

"Gangly if skeletons are gangly," according to their maternal grandmother.

Grandma Pencil possessed authority on the issue of malnourishment, having been on a death march in the Philippines when she was a child. If she found herself outside arm's reach of a food source, she became uncomfortable to the point of itchiness. She would snatch at invisible flies, her wrinkled forehead worming with sweat. Nonsense words like "mag-mag" and "riddle kidder" fled her throat at six per second until Misty raced to her side and inserted a disc of summer sausage into her mouth. Breathing and temperature returned to normal; no more riddle kidders.

To avert such a crisis, Grandma Pencil stocked her purse with peanuts and American cheese. However, fear of robbery prevented her from taking her purse anywhere unless "absolutely necessary," which meant the post office or bank. The Mapes home, therefore, was Snack Food Central. Bowls were positioned in a dozen strategic locations: Pringles on the buffet; roasted almonds on the bookshelf; Hershey's Kisses on the end table; Corn Nuts on the telephone stand; sunflower seeds on the kitchen counter beside the toaster. As most people know, Grandma Pencil lived five houses down the street. She visited often.

Perhaps because of this gratuitous access to food, the twins rarely felt hungry. At dinner, they carved frowny faces into their mashed potatoes or flicked chunks of hot dog into Snoodles's mouth.

Murray and Misty had grown used to the twins' eating habits: "If they're skinny, they're skinny." All a parent could do was put food on the table—the rest was beyond their control. If the twins were indeed "adults-in-training," as Misty called them, then they would never, *never*, learn to be adults unless allowed to make their own decisions, which meant making a few mistakes along the way. Clever sound bites filled Misty's arsenal, and she lobbed these like grenades at Grandma Pencil as well as at the nosy kindergarten teachers who attributed the twins' lack of appetite to, among other things, their late and inconsistent bedtimes. "Nothing earned means nothing learned," was Misty's reply. And "Boners make geniuses of men." She meant "mistakes." This last one might have been a red flag for the nuns, come to think of it.

But Misty's grenades were tossed with pins unpulled. Neither she nor Murray was a fan of confrontation. Not with each other, not with their kids, not with anyone. They were mellow, pragmatic young adults quick to remind anyone who would listen that they were good listeners. In 1972, while stoned and drying the dishes, twenty-year-old inventor Murray had invented a simile that served him and his twin-pregnant nineteen-year-old wife for the next two decades: parenthood was like bowling. You gave your ball a hearty push in the best way you knew. Then all you could do was wait. You stood anxiously, shouting with glee when your ball toppled ten pins, or shedding a tear as it thudded into the gutter.

Grandma Pencil tried to fatten up the twins. She took them on the No. 7 GRATA bus to the movie theater at North Kent Mall. She bought tubs of buttered popcorn. At dinner, she told them a fairy would visit their bedsides with a train of solid silver if they would eat two whole hot dogs ("Without buns, even!") and just a "fistful" of macaroni and cheese. She melted lard into their oatmeal, hoping they wouldn't notice.

And then, when she was especially ornery—when not only were Toby and McKenna hurdling her legs in a mockery of the slaughter of the Native Americans, but their father was also filling the house with a blinding turpentine reek—at times like these, Grandma Pencil pulled out the heavy artillery.

She would cry. Softly at first. A whimpered coo, a morning dove. When the twins didn't notice, or when their notice consisted only of timid glances in her direction, Grandma's volume and urgency increased until they approached, heads down, index fingers idly exploring nostrils.

"Are we being too loud?" McKenna would say. Always McKenna.

A long pause.

"That's not why I'm crying," Grandma Pencil answered. Sniffle. Sob.

"You hate to see Indians getting chased, don't you?"

"Anyone with a heart would pity the red man," she admitted. "But tears won't help his plight."

"You want us to put on pants," Toby would say. "No chance!"

She dabbed her eyes with tissue. "It's your house. You may do as you please."

As the twins turned to resume their chase, Grandma would freeze them in their tracks by launching into a detailed account of how she, as a girl, had watched a pretty young woman collapse in exhaustion after walking twenty-seven hours in 104-degree heat without food or water. "And what did this woman get for falling to the ground? A bullet to the nose. Boom. Face explosion. Bits of face on every leaf."

Grandma then nodded at Toby's nose-digging finger and described how her own mother had done the same thing, except instead of flicking her goblins away or rubbing them under a chair, "Mummy" had saved them between her toes so that little Pencil could have something, anything, in her belly at the end of the day.

Then came the story of her shoes swamped with pus and blood. And the noises that rang through the darkness, the moans of children dying of thirst, the shrieks of girls being violated. And the cold night winds that made you wish your toes had been chopped off. And the monkeys that laughed from the trees. And the bats that landed on your chest and nibbled at you because you were too weak to shoo them. Then the recurring dream of cutting into your own leg with a knife and fork, and how the dream made you deliriously happy, causing you to wake in a puddle of drool (that you eagerly lapped up, sharing with no one).

At about this time, McKenna would sprint to the kitchen. She would squat beneath the table, sobbing, squeezing her sphincter until coaxed out by Misty with promises that she wouldn't have to eat Grandma's leg or anything else she didn't want to eat.

6.

McKenna had to bathe baby Audrey. Three times a week, she hugged shampoo, towel, washcloth, and soap to her chest and walked through the dining room to the kitchen, where she arranged the supplies on the counter. She could hear coos and gurgles resonating through the house from somewhere unknown, most likely Mother's arms, most likely Mother's bed upstairs, where Audrey was being rocked, sung to, and loved behind closed doors. McKenna dragged the collapsible stepladder from the space between the refrigerator and wall and spread it open at the foot of the sink. Following her father's instructions (pinned by magnet to the refrigerator, "just in case" McKenna's memory faltered [it never did]), McKenna climbed the stepladder. She unfolded the towel across the countertop. She filled the sink with two inches of "tepid" water. She submerged the washcloth, swished it, let it drink.

She pulled open a drawer and withdrew the silver bell, which was smaller than her five-year-old fist. Using three overhead arm motions, as deliberate as a lion tamer cracking a whip, she rang it. The high-pitched sound, her father had said, would ascend stairs, drift around corners, pass through doors and walls. The special curvature, along with the pea-sized, felt-covered clapper, allowed the bell to be audible from one hundred yards away, and most importantly—this was Murray's big selling point—at a consistent volume. In other words, to a person standing two feet from the bell it would be no louder than it was to a person two hundred

19

feet away. The patent was for The Tap-on-the-Shoulder Handheld
Alarmer Bell.

Only one such bell was ever produced, and it remains in Mc-
Kenna's possession, tossed carelessly into the bottom of an un-
labeled box in the attic.

Since the birth of her sister, McKenna had noticed that Audrey's tiniest squeals were audible from almost any location in the
house. Not always at the same volume, to be sure, but what did
that matter? McKenna rang the bell and wrestled with the notion
that her father's invention—and by extension, her father—was a
crock.

Still, the bell did summon her mother every time. So perhaps
it worked. Perhaps Murray was as brilliant as he claimed. Mc-
Kenna wanted it to be so.

Misty padded barefoot into the kitchen and placed Audrey,
stripped to her skivvies, onto the towel. McKenna ascended the
stepladder. Her sister was the size of a doll. She unpinned the cloth
diaper and began the bath. Misty stood watch the first few times,
offering tips for scrubbing the hair and neck. Once satisfied that
Audrey was in no danger, she patted McKenna's head, offered a
"Thanks, buckaroo," and retired to the living room for a nap.

McKenna hated cleaning the monster. Audrey's bald head
made her resemble Grandpa Mapes in his coffin. Red bumps that
Mom called "baby acne" speckled Audrey's forehead. Her un-
wieldy head lolled as if her neck had no bones. Instead of a thingy,
there was a tidy slit between her legs.

McKenna could get past the lack of a thingy. She knew about
anatomy. She understood that she herself had no thingy, and Mom
had no thingy, and that no matter what Toby said, this didn't
make them any less of a person.

The baby kicked. Her legs resembled broken branches.

But without feet, can they still be called legs? Without ball
peen and claw, is it still a hammer? Without tines, is it still a
fork? Is a spoon without its bowl still a spoon?

By the end of the first week of washing, the stumps ceased to frighten McKenna. They became sad. They made her feel as if a heavy blanket were smothering her chest, suffocating her. Part of McKenna wanted to protect this crippled, sweet-smelling girl; this big-headed angel with the plump cheeks and curled swath of blond hair and nipples no bigger than periods. At the same time, she wanted to lift her by the throat and stuff her into the garbage disposal.

What made Audrey a monster was her mouth. Always needing to be filled. The mouth opened wide, enormously wide, as she lunged at any object in her path. Her own fingers were a typical target, but when these were restrained, she craned and twisted until her gums hit pay dirt: McKenna's hands; the washcloth; the rubber duck; the faucet tap. Audrey's eyes, pulsating like Kmart blue lights, registered no recognizable emotion. She resembled the hatchlings on *Wild Kingdom* that probed the air blindly with their beaks, ready to swallow whatever dropped into their dark holes.

7.

In 1977, the year Audrey was born, none of the Mapeses had heard of Johann Zimmermann. He was moderately famous in his native Germany, having performed for nearly a decade at circuses, fairs, and European talk shows. His stage name was Herr Essenalles, which translates roughly to "Mister Eat Everything." He devoured drinking glasses, light bulbs, chains, eyeglasses, and chainsaw blades. He ate a shovel.

Once, he ate a shopping cart. He took his time with this one, as you might expect. It was a plodding, meticulous process that sucked away every drop of urgency and excitement.

Kind of pathetic, really. Like a poodle trying to put away an elephant carcass. Makes you want to yawn and cry. For live demonstrations, Herr Essenalles generally consumed the smaller items—snow globes, whistles, screwdrivers—for quick applause. A ten-inch TV took him twelve hours. First, he crunched the VHF dial. Then the antenna, divided by hacksaw into inch-long segments. Then the UHF dial, which he worried like a stale cookie until it was soft enough to swallow. Then the TV's plastic shell, broken by mallet into potato-chip-sized pieces. And finally, the cathode tube, also smashed into bites. Sometimes his mouth bled, but never seriously.

Audrey, as we all know, needed no hacksaws or mallets.

The doctors studied Herr Essenalles and found that the lining of his stomach was unusually thick. His stomach acids were also stronger than normal. Aside from these qualities, he was a regular, healthy guy. A fine swimmer, near-sighted, a mediocre conversationalist, a chess aficionado. Short-tempered but otherwise balanced. Sexual function = just dandy. Attracted to women his own age. That was the story, anyway.

8.

A doctor examined the children's mother regularly. Grandma Pencil babysat the twins every Wednesday from two to four so Misty could go to her "health appointments." McKenna and Toby, infatuated with their mom, created and maintained the delusion that she was attending beauty school—not the kind where beauticians are trained, but rather where Misty taught other women how to look and act like princesses, where adoring attendants preened and primped her into the immaculate image they'd grown used to seeing around the house.

Deep down, they knew the beauty school wasn't real. They'd seen the shadow that settled over their mother's face. They'd noticed her naps getting longer—two, three, sometimes four hours a day. They'd seen her drift through the house in her canary-yellow nightgown from morning to night, speaking rarely, floating from room to room with an expectant face as if around the corner would be the unnamable something—a person?—that would ignite her insides and make her happy again. Each twin wanted to be that person. They stumbled over one another trying to make her smile.

Misty never held a job. Her estranged father, a Grand Rapids businessman, believed that the very notion of a woman working outside the home was unseemly, akin to letting a baby suckle a sweat sock.

But what did this matter to McKenna and Toby? They knew

nothing of their maternal grandfather or his attitude. Their mother loved being a mother—the twins felt that this had to be true. They couldn't picture Misty doing anything else. She'd raised them. She'd stayed home with them all these years. Hers was the face they fell asleep picturing, the face they sought out when they awoke.

But they also understood that things had changed. They were "big kids" now. The new baby was here. The twins played together. They depended on each other. Audrey kept Mommy busy. Audrey kept her happy.

Yes, at times Misty was happy. She sang. She played Candyland. She read books to them. She kissed their cheeks, one twin at a time, before turning out the light.

9.

"It's a medical record," Toby said, on the eighteenth day of measuring. "For science."

He scribbled numbers. He was irritated, indignant at being questioned. He promptly closed the notebook, snapped a thick rubber band around it, and thrust it under a pile of pants in the bottom drawer of his dresser.

This was a young boy trying to justify his obsessive need to compare every one of his and his "little" sister's body parts during the summer after their kindergarten year. Kindergarten had made Toby a king, and he needed to make it clear that he was the *only* king of this household.

He forced the drawer shut with his foot and said, "If you touch it, you're dead."

"Why would I touch your crappy book?" McKenna answered from her seat at the card table, where she doodled a woman robot melting a man's head with an optical laser beam. She, too, was indignant. But she'd never felt indignant before, and because she was unused to managing this particular emotion, she'd actually said, "crammy book." She hoped Toby hadn't noticed.

"You'll change the numbers," Toby answered. "You hate that I'm bigger than you."

"Three centimeters? Big whoop."

The height difference was one of seven documented disparities between the twins. The yardstick measurements had shown that

Toby's hands, feet, kneecaps, waist, spinal cord, and skull were ever-so-slightly longer and/or wider than McKenna's. McKenna's only advantage was neck length, but these results were circled in red crayon because Toby claimed that Mom had fudged the figures so McKenna wouldn't cry again.

McKenna hated the ritual, but even worse than enduring the ritual was being called a coward, so she succumbed to the weekly assessment, standing pole-straight and facing forward. She studied the crude Winnie the Pooh mural her mother had painted on their wall. Misty held the yardstick and yawned into the back of her free hand. Toby recorded the data, smug, satisfied.

Audrey, the footless one-year-old, crawled with confidence along the carpet in the middle of the bedroom, searching for something, anything, to stuff in her mouth.

Dad stood at an assembly line eight miles south, his feet aching, earplugs and safety glasses pushing the world away while the dust of steel and iron slipped into his nose with each breath.

10.

Long before Audrey Mapes ate Kalamazoo, and long before Herr Essenalles ate his first light bulb, medical literature was rife with stories of people devouring coins, buttons, laundry detergent, screws. We can all agree that these are disgusting, if somewhat imaginative, dinners.

There's more, too. Bed sheets. Chalk. Rust. Folks who can't stop swallowing wooden toothpicks are so common they've earned their own nickname (I mean, medical term): xylophagians. Look it up. Compulsive swallowing is a condition that affects about as many people as are killed annually by falling out of bed.

Here's a story from the archives:

A hardy man in Tucson by the name of Garry Tranquility ("Garry" pronounced with a short *a*, incidentally, because it rhymed with "starry") once fit a Webster's dictionary, hardcover and all, into his stomach. It took him a full business week. His body rejected the dictionary the next day, in an unsettling series of pulpy expulsions, but what no doubt carried him through this unpleasantness and made him feel worthy and strong was the memory of the hundreds of local folks who'd cheered him on. Somewhere between eight and ten of these people even sent flowers, dictionaries, and cards with yellow smiley faces and praise like, "You are first-place wild man!" (a Japanese tourist) and "My dad thinks you're nuts!" One woman from the audience was so impressed with Garry's gustatory abilities that she proposed marriage. Garry accepted her proposal, effectively ending his burgeoning rock-n-roll career. That's the '60s for you! One minute he's Garry Tranquility, front man for The Splendid Knights, the next he's plain old Bertram Trank again, guitar instructor at Rainbow Music and future footnote in *The New England Journal of Medicine*.

My point is that while Audrey Mapes was unquestionably talented when it came to her craft (and you'll find no bigger fan than this writer), precedent had already been set. She was the first in many categories—perfecting the footless Moonwalk, for instance—but she was not really a pioneer in gastronomical exploration.

I can hear the whining already: "Screws and cigarette butts and dictionaries are weird and flavorless, but an entire city?! You can't even compare the two!"

I agree in principle. Certainly, even a city as culturally bankrupt and magnetic to clouds as Kalamazoo contains hundreds of thousands of bed sheets, millions of buttons and coins, metric tons of dictionaries, canyons of laundry detergent. Not to mention all that brick, wood, steel, and concrete—31,000 homes, hundreds of apartment buildings, a public university, a liberal arts college, a luxury hotel, ten motels, two root beer stands, five bowling alleys and five cemeteries (coincidence?), forty churches, three malls, miles of chain link fence, armfuls of doghouses, handfuls of cathouses, a children's museum, a restored theater, a railroad station, a factory for guitar chords. And so on.

Certainly, it's difficult to compare Audrey to even the most extreme compulsive swallower. I'll just answer this way: Audrey was never a girl to go at a task without full commitment.

In fact, none of the Mapeses were (or are). Some people see this as a fault.

11.

Audrey grew. By her third birthday in January of 1980, she was an average height of forty inches (without feet, mind you). She was a spunky child, full of vim, with eyes like blueberries and ringlets of shoulder-length blond hair inherited from a recessive gene not seen in a Mapes since Great Uncle Tilbert, who died in 1947 at the ripe old age of one hundred. She mastered all the skills that would earn her applause and adulation. She recognized her ABCs (upper and lower case), could count to forty, and was able to write the first name of each person in her family (except Grandma Pencil). She could spell a handful of words like *STOP, NO,* and *OFF.* She'd memorized the Pledge of Allegiance, the lyrics to "Somewhere Over the Rainbow," and the entire Life cereal commercial with Mikey. She could, and often did, eat upward of a dozen Crayola crayons without getting an upset stomach.

But her Dr Pepper feet were a disaster. Honestly, they'd never worked. Walking in them, she looked like she was constantly traversing a tightrope. Had she been an actual tightrope walker, though, she would have died thousands of times.

"She's learning!" Murray used to yell, not even glancing up from his *Popular Mechanics* to see the fallen girl cradled in Grandma Pencil's arms. "Toddlers tip. You'll be okay, sweetie."

"Feel these," Grandma demanded. She fondled with disgust the set of four straps that connected Audrey's left "foot" to the plastic

30

band choking her thigh, just above the knee. "She's standing on a goddamn see-saw."

Murray ignored all criticism on the subject. For a year he did, anyway. He would kiss Audrey's boo-boo, hug her to his chest, set her upright again, tighten the straps, and send her on her way.

There was a profound allure to the way the children's dad so stingily dispensed his scruffy affections. On the rare occasion that he was home from work and not in the basement, Murray's eyes were pointed at a book, a joist, a schematic, or a can opener that he quietly manipulated to study the movement of its parts. In those even rarer moments when he met one of the children's gazes, they fell in love. His round-the-clock intensity, which in later years they would understand was only a screen for insecurity and pain, fooled the children into believing he was doing everything humanly possible, at every waking moment, for them and them alone—in the very way, for example, that he faced the bookshelf, scratched the top of his nappy head, yawned, and threw a handful of cashews into his mouth.

When he perched on the toilet for an hour with a notebook in his lap, hollering a string of invented curses at a mathematical equation that hadn't panned out the way he'd planned ("Knuckles!" "Fist YOU, piehole!" "Pinto beans!" "Oh, rip my stick, buckwad!"), McKenna and Toby, studying phonics in the dining room, could feel his energy like a pulse in the air. The twins faced each other across the table, and they shared a glance that meant they both understood. They understood that Murray's fury was inflamed because the equation he'd toiled over had failed and would therefore not better the lives of his wife and children. They understood that this failure drove their father into the kind of rage a gorilla feels when his baby, or his banana, is eaten.

When Murray knelt between their beds to kiss the twins goodnight (every three weeks or so), his body odor, textured like one of Grandma Pencil's exotic cheeses, clouded the air for hours after his departure. His gamey stench wasn't an offense. It was a signal—a primal scent encoded by God and designed to narcotize his children, to tether them to him chemically so that they would never, not even far in the future, abandon him when he was sick and feeble and dying. He needed their love like he needed air. He needed their love to make him whole. The children knew these things. Toby and McKenna dreamed of him. They woke in the middle of the night thinking he was still by their bedside. They reached out to touch him, but he wasn't there.

So this explains why three-year-old Audrey never disliked her shabby aluminum feet. She was only a child. She hadn't known any other way. She'd worn the cans for a year without complaint. Even McKenna and Toby thought the junky things were miraculous. They bragged to their third-grade classmates at St. Monica's about the wonders of their dad's mechanical mind.

Meanwhile, the feet were destroying Audrey's legs. The bruises above her knees darkened from purple to black. Her stumps swelled as if bitten by a rattlesnake. When McKenna bathed Audrey, now in the regular tub, she dabbed at the stumps with the washcloth, fearful that the skin might simply burst. Rigidly, Audrey sat, clutching a ducky, staring up at McKenna with her sad, round eyes, an invitation to love, or pity, or something else, perhaps, a question or a plea, something that made McKenna confused and afraid.

McKenna never spoke to anyone about Audrey's legs, just as she'd never spoken to anyone about the way the suds when Audrey was an infant had slid so perfectly into her folds. She'd never spoken of Audrey's arms, thinner than candy bars. Or the way Audrey giggled when she got splashed. Or the way McKenna let Audrey suckle her finger, and how the insistent, rhythmic pull—almost painful—made McKenna flush with shame.

McKenna never spoke of Audrey's damaged legs. But neither did Toby, and neither did Misty. It was a fact of life that the Mapeses bore without worry, without reflection. They believed steadfastly in the father, believed he would never allow them to experience pain. It was merely a matter of time, he said, of adjustments, of settling in.

As everyone knows, Murray finally removed the Dr Pepper feet. What most readers don't know is that this only happened after Grandma Pencil stopped her scolding and threatened to inform Child Social Services.

12.

Even though their parents were atheists, McKenna and Toby were sent to St. Monica's Elementary. One of the Mapeses' Christmas rituals was to join hands in a circle and have a moment of boisterous laughter in honor of all the suckers who were kneeling in a cold church instead of at home in their pajamas, sipping hot cocoa and unwrapping presents in front of the tree. Murray called religion "the opium of the people" and a "mass neurosis," digging up well-worn sound bites from Marx and Freud to make his plebian purposes sound intellectual.

What Murray ignored, or willingly forgot, or never read, was the line that preceded Marx's opium quote: "Religion is the sigh of the oppressed creature, the heart of a heartless world, and the soul of soulless conditions."

Murray hated and mocked all organized religion, but he skewered Christianity in particular. His jokes had earned him official reprimands at Hanson Mold, which wasn't a Christian company, according to Murray, but was a company that nevertheless "puckered up for the two zealots on Line Six." Murray was responsible enough not to risk losing his job over such a trivial matter. Or, looking at it another way, he was too cowardly to stand by his convictions. Whichever the case, he began to tell his jokes exclusively at home, where the only resistance came from his mother-in-law.

Murray: "What's the difference between Jesus and a picture of Jesus?"

Twins: "I don't know."

Murray: "It only takes *one* nail to hang up the picture."

Guffaws from Toby and McKenna. Giggles from Misty. Tongue clucks from Grandma Pencil, followed by her exit to the bathroom.

Murray: "An Iranian man dies and arrives at the Pearly Gates. 'Hello,' says Saint Peter. 'How can I help?' 'I'm here to meet Jesus,' answers the Iranian. Saint Peter turns his head and shouts, 'Jesus, your cab is here!' "

Knee-slaps from the twins, who don't know why they're laughing but know that Dad's voice is funny. A chuckle and nod from Misty. No reaction from Grandma Pencil. Feigned sleeping, perhaps.

Murray: "Hey, honey?"

Misty: "Yes, my love?"

She sometimes called him "my love." Hearing the phrase always gave McKenna a little stab, a sort of nerve pinch in her chest.

Murray: "How does Jesus masturbate?"

Misty: "Why don't you tell me?"

Murray places his open hand, palm-first, against his groin. He moves the hand like he's patting the front of his pants in slow, rhythmic motion. Misty groans, and then covers her mouth in laughter.

This visual punch line, viewed by McKenna and Toby as they finger-paint at the table, won't make sense for three more years, when they learn about stigmata.

Misty was less pointed in her criticism of religion. In fact, she never claimed to be an atheist. She was a spiritual being, she said. When pushed for an exact definition of her dogma, Misty described a belief in humanity, in the cosmos, in the interconnection between all living things. Grandma Pencil was unsatisfied by such vagaries. She pushed: "How can you tell your problems to some quack with ink blots, but you won't tell the One who created you?".

The twins sometimes thought an argument would break out, but Grandma's provocations were only answered with halcyon smiles and the dusty 1967 compendium *Myths from Around the Globe*, which Grandma Pencil always accepted with a smirk and then inevitably "forgot" on the coffee table, under a planter, or once, in the bathroom trash can.

Grandma Pencil bore Murray's jokes by crunching pretzels to drown out his punch lines. If no pretzels were handy, peanuts worked. The fingers-in-the-ears method was always available as a last resort. Murray's mouth formed a satisfied grin when his jokes made Grandma Pencil change the subject or turn to ask Toby why he was doing pushups and sit-ups in the corner there, was it for a special game?

Undoubtedly, Murray's dream was to see Grandma stand from her chair, wag a gnarled finger like she did at the neighborhood "no-goodnicks" with their boom boxes, and hobble furiously out of the house, so consumed by indignation that she forgot to grab her hat from the rack. But Grandma never gave him this satisfaction. It was a psychological war between bully and victim. Or better yet, fisherman and bass. Day after day, bait was dangled before Grandma's face, tempting her to bite and be dragged to the hostile surface . . . but the metaphor stops there because what Murray did was far worse than inviting her into an argument.

He threatened her core, her spiritual foundation, that bubble of peace into which she'd climbed decades ago—since the Philippines—and risen to a place of calm high above the nightmare of her father's brutal murder.

In April of 1977, on a day when the rain rattled the windows as if the Almighty Himself was getting impatient, Grandma Pencil strolled unannounced through the front door. Without wiping her shoes, she crossed the room and handed Murray a one-inch stack of fifty-dollar bills. Her hands were wet and dripping. Murray stood with one slippered foot propped on the coffee table, taking a brief respite from pacing to tap the air with his index finger (his invisible calculator).

"The twins will be given a Godly education," Grandma said.

She knew what she was doing. Undoubtedly, she had planned this encounter detail by detail for months, maybe years. Possibly even for a decade, beginning when Misty had first brought home the dry-skinned, scrawny kid with the flattop and horn-rimmed glasses and introduced him as "Murray. My man." It's likely that Grandma saw the future at that moment and had planned accordingly, chucking away a dollar or two a week into some secret, secure place—the bottom drawer of her dresser?—waiting patiently for the chance to regain control.

Such an idea wouldn't be tough to believe. Grandma Pencil knew the virtue of farsightedness. She was all about the long haul. She also knew the perils of complaint. She knew the value of the human ability to suppress instinct, to control urges, to mentally leapfrog the miserable present and land in the future, where a better day waited.

She arrived in early evening, after dinner, with money in hand and a glint in her eye. Her timing was precise. She entered while Misty napped, Toby changed Audrey into pajamas, and Murray paced the living room, mumbling random ideas to the air.

Murray took the cash from Grandma Pencil. He studied it, turned it over, mocked it with his eyes as if it was a primitive ashtray sculpted in a child's art class.

McKenna looked up from the circus train she was pushing on the carpet. She watched the exchange.

"You will enroll them in Saint Monica's," Grandma said. "It is nearby enough that they can walk. They will get exercise of the body, mind, and soul. Free of charge for you. Everyone is happy."

Murray scratched his earlobe, frowning. "Do you know what I could do with this much money?" he asked.

"It's enough for one year's tuition," Grandma answered, turning. "Next year, I'll bring another stack, and the year after that, another."

"This isn't funny," Murray said, to her backside.

"AND SO ON!" she screamed, as the door slammed.

13.

Audrey was a momma's girl. Always nursing. Always nestled in Misty's arms or in a sling fitted against her breast. Misty pacing the dining room, unhurried, her expression blissful, a Nature Mother in a field, cool grass caressing her toes, stepping so gently not even a floorboard squeaked. Murray at Hanson Mold, being molded. Midafternoon, McKenna and Toby home after a half-day of kindergarten, Toby with an ice cream sandwich in the living room, watching *The Courtship of Eddie's Father*. McKenna, if not stolen away by Toby to race laps around the house, would be sitting at the table, assembling a puzzle. Misty making her rounds, lulling McKenna with her humming, her gentle sway, "Rock-a-bye Baby" flowing like water.

McKenna closed her eyes so that she herself was being rocked, being serenaded.

Now and then, the spell was broken by Misty whispering, "What will you be, sweetheart? What will you be? Audrey the audacious. Audrey the awesome. Audrey the automatic garage door opener. You can be Audrey anything."

You forgot Audrey the awful.

"Mom, I need help," McKenna said.

Misty stopped behind McKenna's shoulder. Still swaying, still humming. "What is it?"

"I can't find this piece." There was a hole in the puzzle, a gap in the center of the swimming pool.

"You know what goes there, right?" Misty said.

"Yeah, but . . ."

"It's water. Just blue. Fill it in with your imagination. That's what I'd do." She patted McKenna's head the same way she patted Snoodles.

Whenever Audrey got the chance, she bogarted Misty's lap, curling up on it like a kitten, refusing to budge. She purred, "Sing to me, Mommy."

Even years later, when Audrey and Misty had their epic battle of Flute vs. Drum, it was obvious that beneath the tears, nasty words, obsessive tapping, and flute chomping, Audrey felt unwavering love. Mommy, Mommy, Mommy. No one else called Misty "Mommy." No one even tried.

And it worked both ways. Audrey was the baby of the family, Misty's clear favorite.

Oh sure, Misty never said it. She couldn't. Wouldn't. Not in words. "Do you think I love my pinky more than my ring finger?" she said once, after McKenna, age eight, asked why Audrey always got away with stuff, why everyone had to clean up after her, why Misty loved Audrey the most. Misty held out her hand. "If I lost any of my fingers, my hand would never be the same. When you're a mother, you'll understand."

McKenna couldn't sleep that night. Even as a third-grader, she was skeptical of the analogy. In the dark, she felt the fingers of her right hand. Clearly, the pointer was the most useful, with the best reflexes. Much more nimble than the others. And what about the thumb? Was that part of the analogy?

The next day, McKenna tried performing ordinary activities without her thumb. She struggled to brush her teeth, tie her shoes, braid her hair. Writing was nearly impossible.

Was every finger equal? Did McKenna love everyone the same? Not even close.

From that day on, McKenna noticed whenever Misty gave

Audrey a special smile, or she bought Audrey a new dress at a yard sale, or praised the wonderful job Audrey did in brushing her teeth without swallowing any paste, or lifted Audrey and said, "Gosh, such a *big* girl," or brushed Audrey's hair, or took Audrey to the dentist, or told Audrey to "Please stop banging the table," or folded Audrey's socks in front of the television.

From that day on, McKenna noticed everything about Misty and Audrey. Noticing, McKenna realized, or decided (she couldn't tell which), was her special talent. It was the one thing she did well, the thing she did best, and so she chose to do it often. And often. And often. And often.

14.

What could a Catholic education mean to two kids who thought "Noah's Ark" was some old man's forty-day piss stream?

Not much, truth be told. But for better or worse, it got them out of the house. Preschool hadn't been offered; the twins never heard that word until they came to kindergarten. (They would learn a number of valuable words and phrases at St. Monica's—*covenant, forgiveness, only begotten, transubstantiation, Body of Christ,* and *sin.*)

Toby was thrilled. Among other children, he flourished. School became his first obsession, and in many ways it lead to his second obsession—body measurements—which undoubtedly was the springboard for his greatest obsession—body mass.

Each day before sunrise, Toby dressed in the dark. He kicked McKenna's mattress until she opened her eyes. Perhaps he knew she had been awake for hours. Perhaps this is why he kicked so hard.

The children slurped milky spoonfuls of Froot Loops or Honey-combs. They heard their father emerge from the master bedroom, where Misty and Audrey slept. They heard his loud ablutions, his bathroom routine of light switch snaps, water hisses, cupboard slams, gargles, and toilet flushes.

After twenty minutes, he stomped down the wooden stairs into the dining area wearing steel-toed boots and an untucked work shirt. His face was smooth, his hair parted flat to his head with a wet brush. The twins teased that he looked like a teenager. Eyelids puffy, he waved away their insults like mosquitoes and joined them in crunching a bowl of sweet cereal before heading out the door with a mumbled, "See ya." Outside, the Catalina roared to life.

In the half-light, their backpacks like turtle shells, the twins left the house, carrying lunchboxes—Toby's *Six Million Dollar Man* and McKenna's *Planet of the Apes*. They climbed the hill to Coit Avenue, crossed. They walked five blocks, passing North Park Elementary, where the public school children were deboarding buses. Then it was six blocks up Elmdale hill, into the "good" neighborhood (Grandma Pencil's term), past the row of "nice" houses (Misty's term) with their manicured bushes and sprinkled lawns. At the thicket of trees that obscured Ascendance Lake, McKenna liked to step off the sidewalk into the brush, inhaling the fecund leaves and soil, hoping to see a robin, stooping to catch a glimpse of the calm water hidden between branches like a treasure. Toby marched onward without pause, turning left onto Assumption Drive, which inclined even farther upward until reaching another road, one narrow as a driveway that sloped downward into the church parking lot.

Beyond the lot, a one-story brick structure crouched in the shadows of sycamore trees. The yellow lights inside revealed barren classrooms waiting to be filled.

McKenna didn't feel welcomed by the lights. Nor by the wash of warm air upon opening the door. Nor by the scent of ammonia and floor wax, nor the prickly rose perfume of Principal Potterman, who arrived early and always left a robust cloud hovering at the entrance like some ghost self. The empty hallways filled McKenna with dread. The loneliness and abandonment were palpable. Every morning, she fought the urge to turn and flee, to sprint all the way home and jump back into bed, a bad dream averted.

Kindergarten, come to think of it, was a pretty accurate snapshot of McKenna's entire life.

Each half-day was four hours of sensory assault. Kids vomited on desks, spilled blood from fat lips, and over-picked noses. They smeared McKenna's shoulder with paste. They jabbed her backside with pointy Elmer's bottles. During lunch, they lost muffin chunks down their shirts before finding them later and throwing them at McKenna. Boys and girls alike screamed. Not endearing, helpless screams like Audrey's. Rage, desperation, ecstasy—each fought for supremacy in those caterwauls, and frankly, they were upsetting.

McKenna retreated. She didn't realize it at the time, but she was behaving exactly as her father did at Hanson Mold. While her fingers painted, or her mouth recited the alphabet, or her feet danced the hokey-pokey, her mind ran through a languid play-by-play of the washing of Audrey's body parts: the wrinkled hands; the fingers like twigs, the nails like paper; the folds of neck spread carefully and soaped; the stumps at the ends of the legs, each bearing a soft pebble of skin she longed to pinch; the umbilical cord like a gnarled black root, hard as bone, that McKenna dabbed with the sudsy cloth until one day, like a loose tooth, it quietly detached, exposing Audrey's navel, freeing her. *There's no going back now*, McKenna had thought, and it struck her as a defining moment. Audrey was locked forever out of the only home where she could be safe and warm, always.

By the time McKenna entered kindergarten, she'd learned how to handle Audrey's mouth. Once something was inside it or attached to it—a rubber duck, a washcloth, a rattle—the mouth was satisfied; Audrey was satisfied. As time passed, the mouth's urgency began to please McKenna. It *needed*, purely, and McKenna could fill that need, and it felt good to fill it.

As for Toby, he loved kindergarten. Not so much the learning and structure, but the being out in public and announcing his existence to the world. His assimilation was instantaneous. He rolled on the carpet in beet-faced tantrums, whipped muffin chunks at McKenna. He quickly established himself as a leader, a conqueror, a man among boys. All year he looked forward to June's Field Day, when he could earn honest-to-goodness ribbons that would quantify the superiority of his body in shiny blue magnificence.

15.

I'd like to share Misty with you, construct a living Misty before your eyes. A tree house of sentences high in the branches, barely visible from the ground. You need to shimmy up the trunk, squint into the leaves. Ahh, there she is. A sturdy structure, but one that isn't so finished or vivid that it precludes imagination. I want you to help create her. That way you can visit her anytime, in your own mind.

Envision a short woman, five-four, well-proportioned and trim. She walks barefoot through the house, except in winter when wool socks warm her toes. Her feet are compact, gorgeously curved, arches never touching the floor. "Bright colors are me," she likes to say, and her wardrobe reflects this: lemon skirts to mid-calf, peach scarves, shirts the color of cartoon skies. She even owns a pair of green panty hose, popular with the teenagers in the late 1970s. Murray says to Misty, "You aren't a ditz, but you dress like one."

She pretends not to hear, or in fact doesn't hear his words but rather the music of his voice. Her bliss is her beauty.

Light brown hair, a self-inflicted haircut, bangs draping her brow while the back and sides rest upon her shoulders. Breasts moderate, unremarkable. Hands long-fingered and thick-knuckled. Low-slung face, not pretty in a chiseled way. Jaw broad and defined, tending toward mannish, but her lips—"supple" is a good word—remove all doubt that this is a woman. She has soft, heated hands, one of those people whose skin radiates warmth in spite of her lack of body fat and in spite of always complaining of being cold (so much that McKenna has to run to the hall closet for a blanket every time Misty watches *Dallas*).

But other than her great gift of touch—which isn't to be downplayed and in fact communicates haystacks of words in the smallest of cheek caresses—Misty is not an emotional person. Her children never see her cry.

They also never see her thirty-seventh birthday.

Toby, a technical adult, is proud to stand with five other men (none of whom are their father) in dark, ashen suits. They carry Misty in her closed coffin up the aisle of St. Monica's church. They set her on a rack at the foot of the steps leading to the altar. After the service, the men bear the coffin outside, slide it into the hearse. Toby watches the door slam shut. He leans over and whispers to McKenna: "You look like a bag of sticks, Kenny."

It's a spectacular April day, with the sun staring through a hole in a bank of clouds amassed in the east, a columnar pattern of clouds, which, if studied closely by a person with an artistic eye, resembles a door. The sun is the knob.

16.

Imagine you're eating a hamburger. Better yet, go to a nearby fast food restaurant and buy a hamburger. It'll cost you eighty-nine cents. You go. I'll wait.

Ready? Now lift the burger as you normally would, by the buns. Bring it to your mouth. Take a bite—not huge, not tiny. Bite as if you weren't being watched. Rend as much meat, cheese, tomato, and bun as is comfortable for your particular mouth. Now chew. Concentrate on what happens inside there. Notice how the food shifts naturally, without conscious thought, from one side to the other? First, it's kept near the front, dancing over the middle of the tongue. Those bumps—called papillae—each one of these bumps has taste buds on it. And the buds themselves are wearing wigs—microscopic microvilli, sensitive hairs that describe to your brain what you're chewing: salty, grilled, fleshy; sour, tangy, sweet; metallic; ashy; acidic like bile; flavorless as glass.

Within seconds, your teeth do a decent job of pulverizing your bite. Enough so you can swallow, anyway. Your neck convulses as the wad of Burger King breeches the back of your throat. This morsel drops into your tummy for one last disintegration, the acid bath, which will transform it like a fairy tale prince into a frog of basic nutrients—vitamins, carbohydrates, fats, minerals. These will course through your tissues and blood. They will help you live.

But wait! Don't let that bite go so fast. Bring it back up. With a slight flex of the epiglottis, a gesture similar to making yourself

48

belch, and with an additional heaving motion, a tightening of the back of your throat to kick-start the gag reflex, you can rescue that masticated bun and burger, welcome it into your mouth again. Ahh . . . there we go.

Chew it some more. You weren't finished. It's quite soft now, more pliant than gum. Spongy, to say the least. Ten, twenty more chews.

Then swallow.

But wait! Don't let it go. Bring it back up. Run it through the courses a third time. Your saliva enzymes are doing their job. The mush is nearly liquid now, but you don't discriminate. Ten chews. Slow ones. Swallow.

You've been holding the burger for five minutes. The teeth marks in the bun indicate you've only taken one bite. Your family is looking at you. You're working on it. You haven't finished chewing yet. They need to mind their own business.

17.

Audrey gummed her first ball of Play-Doh under big sister McKenna's supervision. It was purple. McKenna didn't try to stop her as she stuffed it into her mouth. Audrey was delighted, squealing. The Play-Doh softened, and baby Audrey drooled some of it onto the carpet. She swallowed the rest. Her gums turned the color of an eggplant. McKenna saw the joy it brought Audrey and began sliding pea-sized bites between Audrey's lips when no one else was around.

Their mother had given instructions on this exact topic. She'd sat down with McKenna and Toby after Audrey was born and said, "Babies like to put things in their mouths. That's how they discover the world. But she shouldn't eat things that aren't food. She could choke. You need to be big for Momma and tell me if you ever see her putting something bad in her mouth."

At eight months, Audrey was crawling with confidence, a military-style dragging of her lower body, using her forearms. She investigated all corners, her yawning hole leading the way. *Nothing bad in her mouth nothing bad in her mouth.* This phrase spun like the hamster's wheel in McKenna's head.

Audrey grabs one of Murray's mechanical pencils: "No, Audrey."

Audrey grabs a candle: "Yucky, Audrey."

An Army man: "Not for babies, Audrey."

A spool of thread: "No, Audrey."

She would feed Audrey a couple of nibbles of Play-Doh to tide her over. Then the phrase returned: *Nothing bad in her mouth nothing bad in her mouth.*

By the time Audrey was one year old, McKenna was tired of saying "no." Audrey had been eating Play-Doh for months with no ill effects. One afternoon, McKenna found her baby sister on the floor of McKenna and Toby's room. Audrey's hair was a mass of tight yellow coils that reached her shoulders. Her oral cavity was packed with black goo that had once been a Crayola. Rather than prying open her jaws, reaching in to pull out the foreign material, calling for help, watching Audrey's face collapse into a confused jumble of sadness and betrayal, hearing the paroxysm of wailing that blamed McKenna and begged her for a return to pleasure—rather than performing any of these actions, McKenna decided to sit on the carpet and see what happened.

Audrey swallowed the goo. Then she crawled to a nearby book (one of the Choo-Choo Charlie series, if memory serves—which it does, again and again) and tried to eat a page. McKenna wrapped her arms around Audrey's gut and repositioned her so she faced the open door. Audrey crawled out of the room, slapping her hands on the wooden floor, joyous, wanting McKenna to chase. She did.

The rest of the day, McKenna waited anxiously, expecting her sister to die. Bites of Play-Doh were one thing, but a crayon, paper and all, was frightening. And what awful timing. Dad was almost finished with the top secret feet that he never discussed but that he spent every night in the basement perfecting, the new feet for Audrey, an entire year's labor, an entire year of neglecting his twins. This would be the worst time for Audrey to die, before she could even try the feet, before she could walk upright and make Daddy smile. McKenna's stomach kicked like an angry kangaroo. She watched Audrey crawl around the house. She held Audrey's hands and helped her do a wobbly stump-walk into the living room.

After six hours passed and Audrey continued to breathe, McKenna decided that she wouldn't die. No, she would become a vegetable. McKenna had seen a TV movie titled *Who's Killing the Stuntmen?* in which a mustachioed guy with a gentle demeanor and seaweed-green eyes not unlike McKenna's, jumped from the top of a skyscraper. But somebody had tampered with his air cushion. It didn't properly break his fall. The stuntman became a "vegetable" in a hospital bed. His face was expressionless. Tubes snaked out of his arms and throat. His wife, despondent, held his hand. She talked to him, but he wasn't there.

A person could be alive in body while dead in mind—a horrific revelation. During McKenna's intense mental probing of the subject, she could think of no reason that eating a crayon couldn't also turn a person—especially a baby, so vulnerable—into a pale, lifeless thing that only stared, blinked, and breathed.

Four hours later, Audrey lay asleep in her crib. Misty scuffled into the living room to watch *Dallas*, easing into the recliner without a word about Audrey's black gums. Hadn't she noticed? Did she even care? McKenna was finally able to relax . . . sort of.

From that day on, she spent a portion of her allowance at the corner drug store. Packs of forty-eight crayons cost $1.99. When she caught a moment alone with Audrey, McKenna would pull one from her sock and hand it to her sister, her stomach aching with nerves and another sensation, unfamiliar but not unpleasant, located in the same area of her gut. Audrey's hand, attached to a wild, jerky arm, reached for the crayon. Her brow scrunched in concentration. When at last the waxy stick was in her grip, she would "AHHHH AHHHH," showing all five of her teeth and punching herself in the legs with excitement. McKenna wanted to know what Audrey was experiencing, so she once took a few nibbles. It tasted similar to the overcooked carrots Misty served. McKenna doubted there was any difference in color-flavor, but for some reason, Audrey had an affinity for black. McKenna became skilled at cleaning the evidence during baths, and Audrey never complained about the soap in her mouth.

18.

The years at St. Monica's were marked by prayers, beatings, and halitosis. In fourth grade, it was Sister Peter Verona, a wisp of a woman whose habit framed a sullen, heavy-browed, fuzzy-lipped face. P.V., as the students called her, weaved prayers throughout the day. Mornings started with an Our Father, a Hail Mary, a Gloria, an Apostles' Creed, and an Act of Faith. Schooldays ended with the same, but in reverse order and with an added Memorare and Prayer for the Pope. But it was after recess when P.V. truly got the children to reach for God. Fifteen solid minutes of invocation, including a song lead by her delicate falsetto: "I have been a naughty child/Naughty as can be/Now I am so sorry Lord/Won't you pardon me?"

McKenna felt sure that she hadn't been naughty. She'd been, in fact, a model child compared to Toby. She'd resisted the pressure to take a hit from the Kool cigarette Toby had stolen from Murray's jacket pocket and invited a circle of boys to smoke in the woods behind the baseball diamond. McKenna's refusal had been mocked, while Toby, eyes narrowed, self-assured in his corruption, dared McKenna to nark on him as he dragged deeply.

McKenna was a good daughter, and a damn good one at that. She obeyed her parents without fail, even her father's nonsensical demands.

"Cut the yard after dinner, McKenna, but son of a Band-Aid,

don't be so noisy about it," Murray said. "I'm trying to concentrate downstairs, with power tools."

Having cut the grass a half-dozen times, McKenna couldn't recall any volume knob on the lawnmower. Toby smirked from across the table, bit a green bean.

Misty scooped potatoes onto her plate. "What your dad means is that maybe you could wait to cut the grass until he's done working."

"That's not what I mean, Mist. Don't speak for me, please."

"I want a *cold* meatloaf," Audrey said. She sat poised on her knees in a grownup chair. She two-handed a plastic glass of milk to her mouth and drank deeply, with noisy gulps.

"Just don't rev the damn thing, McKenna. And when you turn a corner, don't raise the blades off the ground." Murray stabbed a hunk of loaf with his fork. "The sound gets really loud when you do that. Think about it."

"Don't rev the mower, dummy," Toby said.

"I want a soap," Audrey said.

Misty frowned. "Your sister is not a dummy. Say you're sorry."

"Sorry, dummy."

McKenna cut the grass with hedge clippers. It took two hours, but it made no noise. Crickets jumped at her hands. The neighborhood was veiled by twilight. The air was chilly. She snipped away, on her knees. Now and then, she looked up at the house. On the second story, a light glowed behind the curtain in Audrey's room, and McKenna wondered if she should be saving the grass clippings.

So McKenna hated to sing the naughty child song. She also hated the way P.V. thrust her face five inches from hers when visiting desks to check homework. "Do you really think *Michigan* is the second biggest state?!" The raw blast of onions, coffee, bologna, boiled cat—Who knew what went in that slit of a mouth?—choked McKenna. She tried not to inhale. And there was another

odor, too, one that she'd also detected on Grandma Pencil's breath.
A sweet, curdled stench.

Perhaps it was food caught in her teeth. Perhaps it was the de-
cay of her gums. Perhaps it was the rot of heart, lungs, stomach—
that general wind of death that stirs inside every old person.

In private, the kids called P.V. "Muck Mouth," "Garbage Pail,"
and "Sewer Breath." They imagined what was hidden beneath her
veil. They envisioned a crew cut, a scarred, dimpled piece of head
fruit. They tried to understand how, even in an afterlife of pillowy
clouds and golden loving forgiveness, this woman could ever stand
close to God. With her foul insides, hidden disfigurements, and
cruel eyes, surely she would be cast out and left to flop like a fish
upon the hard dirt of damnation.

P.V., and all of the nuns at St. Monica's, took great pleasure in
humiliating the children; in separating them into groups (the
"fast," the "average," and the "slow"; the slow group banished to a
table in the back of the classroom); in slapping the boys on the
ears; in quivering with rage while dragging a troublemaker like
Toby to the front of the room and forcing him to sit on the carpet,
facing the chalkboard. The nuns took pleasure in demanding an
apology and, when not receiving one, pummeling his spine and
shoulder blades with an open hand, the dull thumps echoing off
the chalkboard, the globe, and the poster of the girl handing the
wheelchaired boy an apple, with the caption, *The fruit of kindness is
the sweetest fruit.* The air was forced from Toby's lungs in shallow
expulsions. His face crimsoned, and his cheeks jiggled. He fought
back tears. His lips formed a smile—one without happiness but
certainly with pleasure.

Sister P.V. was followed by Sister Michael, Sister Maximillian,
Sister Pat, and Sister Robert Ann. All sadistic, all on missions to
uncover evildoers. Like a squad of superheroes whose special powers were never bending to another's will, never apologizing, and
living to the age of one thousand. The nuns were a ruddy, sexless

creature of one mind. They had traded individuality and woman-hood for unfettered power. They were gnarled trees, eyesores that nobody could chop down. Axes would shatter; saw teeth would break loose and twinkle upon the ground in the winter sunlight.

19.

The house is a two-story (three if you count the unfinished basement; four if you count the attic, carpeted with insulation). It was built in the 1920s. The white paint has aged to oatmeal gray. A narrow cement path connects the sidewalk to the front stoop. Climbing the four stairs, which are cratered like a teenage boy's face, one will meet a white, universal hinge, crossbuck metal storm door. Open it and you'll be standing inside a screen-enclosed porch. This 6' × 12' area is littered with junk—a metal gas can; a dozen empty ceramic planters; a hoe and a rake; a bucket filled with screws, nails, washers, and bolts; a ten-pound bag of salt; oil-spotted washrags piled in a corner; empty Faygo bottles; and so on. The porch screens are a dense weave and let in little air or light; a few of the bottom corners of the screens have been torn open by squirrels who want warmth, muffin crumbs, or a sniff of the oily rags.

The door shrieks when you walk into the house. There is no mat to wipe your feet on. You stand in a narrow foyer on hardwood the color of baked bread. In front of you is a staircase with a polished, peat brown banister. To your left is a coat rack mounted on the wall. Turn to your right and view the living room, which is not large and feels even smaller because of the cramped arrangement of furniture. There is a loveseat and a dumpy sofa. A glass coffee table covered with *Popular Mechanics* magazines. A mustard recliner in the shadow of a skinny floor lamp. A low bookshelf holds books and a 12" television. To your left is the dining room, where a rectangular table is surrounded by six wooden chairs. Beyond the table are the swinging saloon-style doors to the kitchen.

Push through these doors, go to the kitchen sink, and peer out the window. You'll see that the backyard is a 15'×15' square, bounded on three sides—on your right by a one-car garage, badly flaking; in the middle by a six-foot wooden fence (a section of which leans precariously inward); and on the left by a row of bushes sheared roughly level with the fence.

Many are already familiar with this yard, this house (the exterior, anyway). These people hail from all quarters of the United States and the world—Kansas City, Tampa Bay, Phoenix. Athens, Georgia and Athens, Greece. Pamplona, Spain and Knob Lick, Kentucky.

In first gear, their rented Plymouth Grand Voyagers ease down the hill of Moriarty Street, two-thousand pounds of steel rivaling the top speed of a riding mower. The wife squints out the passenger window, searching for house numbers. She points, excited. Her husband parallel parks two feet from the curb and stomps the emergency brake to the floor. On such an incline, he won't take any chances. Hesitantly, they deboard the vehicle, scoping out the surroundings, surprised at the neighborhood, surprised that *This, really?* is the landmark they've read about. They clutch their pocketbooks and cameras in two-fisted grips, "boip-oip!" the locks, and then double-check, just to be safe, by tugging on the handles.

When they spot Oscar Foster raking his tiny yard a few houses up the street, they relax a bit. Oscar is in his seventies, widowed—a nonthreatening man. Although he's not exactly high society in his flip-flops, black socks, and ratty bathrobe, Oscar is Caucasian. His roundness, moreover, isn't vulgar (more of a Santa-esque shape, not unlike their own). His presence assures them that although the neighborhood is not glamorous, they will probably not be jumped by dark-skinned hooligans before they snap a couple of digital photos of the infamous Mapes home.

Perhaps when they are showing these pictures at a cocktail party, an observant friend will lean in, squint, and say, "Is that a person? In the upstairs window?"

On closer inspection, it does look like a face. Or maybe it's only a reflection, a trick of the light. Yes, it has to be. "After all," they say, "we rang the doorbell five times."

Long before this day, however—three presidents ago—when peering out the kitchen window at the backyard bounded by garage, fence, and bush line, you would often see Audrey Mapes, a pretty three-year-old in a yellow cotton dress, squatting near the garage, holding a plastic shovel.

She digs at the soft earth where the grass is thin. She works languidly, now and then sifting through piles of soil with her fingers, now and then taking a handful to her lips. She chews without expression. On her right, a robin has lighted atop the wooden fence. The robin studies her. Audrey imagines that the bird, with its expression, is asking, "Why eat dirt? Not even I eat dirt. Try a worm, Audrey."

Audrey doesn't want a worm. In fact, when she feels movement on her palm and looks down to see a wriggling, soil-caked earthworm, she startles.

She throws the handful of dirt against the side of the garage, where it rattles loose a few chips of white paint. Candy.

20.

Some people—the geezers especially—have called it a destruction of Biblical proportions, like Sodom and Gomorrah or the Big Flood. That's retrospect talking, hindsight making things 20/20 when actually a little blurred vision is exactly what we all need.

The first point of contention: Kalamazoo was no den of sin, not even in the late 1990s. So the idea that the citizens were being admonished with destruction is ridiculous. Second point: God had already cleaned house in 1980 with a tornado that danced down Main Street and decimated the city to the tune of twenty million dollars. How much sin can redevelop in less than two decades? Rebuild first, sodomize and whore later—that's the general rule.

In short, don't buy the Biblical punishment theory. Unless, of course, God has evolved since the days when the Bible was written, and He now cares less about sex and gambling than irresponsible pollutants and a dearth of culture, entertainment, and employment options. Which is certainly possible.

However, I prefer to think of Audrey's feat as the slowest disaster ever recorded, the rare case of a natural force exhibiting a measure of personability. She was a tornado that lollygagged, that took extended cigarette breaks, that played Parcheesi with the folks whose lives were being erased. She was the atomic bomb, except this time the Hiroshimites gathered around the fireball as it swelled, set out lawn chairs, donned radiation-proof goggles, sipped hot sake, and commented upon the Armageddon between stifled yawns. She was the gentlest earthquake, the softest tsunami. The loveable time-lapse hurricane.

The main difference is that ultimately, Kalamazoo asked for this disaster. In writing.

21.

Toby's transformation was a wonder to behold.

Both twins grew, of course. Their bones stretched. Hair sprouted. Feet strained against shoes. Pencil marks on the wall beside the bedroom door crept upward like the rungs of a ladder.

By age eleven, Toby needed a longer bed. Between fourth and seventh grade, his height increased by nearly a foot. McKenna grew a "measly" five inches. Toby's weight doubled, to 170 pounds. He was quick to point out that it wasn't fat. It was muscle. McKenna weighed eighty-nine pounds, just six pounds heavier than she'd been at age ten.

Toby was clearly Grandma Pencil's favorite. While she defended and babied McKenna—doted on her, pitied her, coddled her like a puppy—she worshipped Toby. Here was a fine, robust young lad who could finish three cobs of corn, two helpings of mashed potatoes, and a pile of roast beef, and still have room for apple cobbler. Grandma's memories of Toby as a finicky child, being bribed to eat his hot dogs, had long been forgotten. At age five, around the time physical measurements became an obsession, Toby had begun to love food. Or, if he didn't actually love food— the taste of it, the sensuality of the morsels upon his tongue, the delicate popping of corncob kernels between his canines (and McKenna was certain that he didn't; he didn't love these things at all)—he definitely loved what food gave him. It made his body grow.

"I'm too skinny," he said one evening. "A bean pole."

Briefed in cotton tighty-whities, he flexed, shirtless, in front of the bathroom mirror. McKenna brushed her teeth at the sink. Thin but noticeable striations bulged like buried cables along Toby's ribcage, back, and neck. He was two years away from being a teenager, but he had the body of an adult.

"Feel my thigh," he said. He turned from the mirror and propped his left foot on the lidded toilet.

McKenna spat noisily (although if Toby had been listening carefully, he would've noticed that nothing came out of McKenna's mouth) in part to make Toby think she was expelling her toothpaste, but also to show her displeasure. Every other night it was "Grab this," "Measure that," "Check out how hard this is." McKenna was reaching some sort of resolution on the matter of her brother's demands, although it wasn't formulated yet in her mind. The overarching sentiment, though, was this: Toby frightened her.

Talking around the toothpaste, McKenna answered, "I'm sure it's fine." McKenna turned on the water, the hiss. She watched the foamy spittle that Toby had left in the sink being lifted and carried, swirling, down the drain.

What did the toothpaste feel, McKenna wondered, when it was so violently disturbed? What did it feel like to be devoured by the drain? Did it thrill in that moment of surprise? Or did it shudder at the horror of the unknown, the awaiting darkness?

She swallowed her toothpaste. Then she burped it back up, burning her throat.

"See if you can get your fingers around it," Toby said. He squeezed his thigh. "I can, and that sucks. But you got normal little hands. Mine are huge. Come on."

"No, thanks," McKenna said.

"*No, thanks!*" Toby peeped like a songbird. "God, you're so gay."

"Takes one to know one." McKenna pressed the newly regurgitated Aim under her tongue. She could smell the bile on her breath. The taste, though, was pure mint.

Toby stepped off the toilet. From behind, he wrapped his forearm around McKenna's neck. He forced her to the floor.

"What does that even *mean?*" Toby growled. He lay on top of her, squeezing the air out of her. "Why are you such an ass?"

McKenna's cheek was flattened against the cold tiles.

"There's-a-cook-," she rasped. She could see, in the slight gap between the wooden cupboard and the floor, half of a Chips Ahoy. Why was it there? From when? She suspected Audrey. McKenna knew—it was their secret—that Audrey often stashed uneaten food around the house.

Toby released McKenna's neck. He lowered his head until his face was inches from hers, his breath heating her eyes. "You're talking about a goddamn cookie?"

"Half," McKenna said. "Under there."

Toby drew the cookie out, rolled off McKenna's back, and stood. He wiped the Chips Ahoy on his underwear before popping the whole thing into his mouth. He reached down and helped McKenna to her feet.

"Ah wu jush ki'in," he said.

The wedge garbled his words, but McKenna knew what he was saying; she'd heard it before. She nodded, rubbed her throat.

Toby swallowed. "Friends, Kenny?" He was waiting for eye contact. "You know I just mess with you because I can."

McKenna lifted her gaze. Looking Toby in the eyes always felt like a worse defeat than the physical domination itself. He attempted a tender expression, which manifested as strain, as something like constipation.

"It's fine," McKenna said. "Whatever."

Toby punched her shoulder. "See? We're friends. My sista."

McKenna studied the boy in front of her. What had once been a reflection of her own face and body was now a funhouse mirror. Unwashed, scraggly hair that hung over his ears. Fists like massive walnuts at his sides. A bloated face. A body twice as heavy as her own. His chest thrust out like a baboon's, showing the beginnings of hair.

The coming years would see this monster distort, bulge, and ripple in ways McKenna couldn't have even imagined at that moment in the bathroom, at age eleven, standing under a yellow bulb in the increasingly grimy Mapes home on that early August day weeks before starting the sixth grade, weeks before Audrey began first grade at the public school, months before Misty's first real break from reality, and years before McKenna learned the name of the disease that had made her swallow and regurgitate the toothpaste before, during, and after her brother had choked her on the floor.

"Seriously, though," Toby said, as they left the bathroom. "Feel my thigh."

22.

Grandma Pencil had hands like a farmer's. That's what Murray said, and his tone made it clear that he wasn't fond of farmers or their hands. But to McKenna, as a child, Grandma's hands were beautiful.

The backs of them were soft, speckled with brown circles that McKenna called "polka dots." Her fingers were thick like the roots of a plant yanked from the soil. Her palms and fingerpads were so calloused that they clicked on the table, a sound that drove Murray crazy.

There was no explanation for why the backs of Grandma's hands were like fresh cookies and the fronts were like stale ones. She certainly hadn't done any hard labor—not in a long time, if ever. Her husband, while he was alive, "discouraged" her from having a job (Misty's word). Grandma's life after the march had been a long series of formal education, childrearing, mental break-downs, and meddling.

McKenna didn't know any of these things at the time. She liked Grandma's hands because they were warm like Misty's. The hands communicated to her. Her own mother and father barely touched her. Grandma Pencil routinely placed a palm on McKenna's head, stroked McKenna's cheek, and held McKenna's hands when they danced.

Grandma Pencil was a vibrant woman, if slightly off-balance. She was tall—same height as Murray—and lean. Her face looked like a monkey's, with a wide mouth and big, expressive eyes. She wasn't pretty, not like her youngest granddaughter. Wrinkles had carved a frown into her cheeks. Her ungainly arms never could find a comfortable resting position, so they were constantly crossing and uncrossing over her chest. Her thumbs fidgeted with her back pockets. Her fingers tugged at her dry, copper-colored hair.

She was nothing like the grandmothers of McKenna and Toby's schoolmates. Theirs were withered Q-tips—bespectacled, white-haired, storybook grannies with walkers and palsied hands. They teetered into the classroom and stared at the cupboards wearing queer, faraway smiles.

St. Monica's hosted a "Bring Your Grandparents to School Day" when McKenna and Toby were in fourth grade. The nuns, a feisty bunch themselves, took to Grandma Pencil immediately. She behaved more like a thirty-year-old man than a senior citizen: she sat with her legs apart, elbows propped on her thighs; she chewed gum with intensity; she wore Wranglers. Like the other grandparents, Grandma Pencil wore faraway looks, but rather than making you depressed, hers made you want to crack them open and climb inside. That gaze—her eyes (blue and crystalline like Audrey's) twinkled in such a way that you knew she was thinking of something profound, or else recalling some moment so black and mysterious that you wanted to see everything she was seeing, even if it might kill you.

She was also a liar. Her eyes and mouth, without a doubt, lied. She never awarded a single silver train for finishing two hot dogs. She'd never been on a death march. Death marches were for POWs, not for the children and wives of private citizens. Probably her mind and soul lied, too. To herself.

She'd lived in a jungle, all right, which is where she absorbed all the compelling chimpanzee and bat details that she would later use to give nightmares to her gullible grandchildren. The truth was she was born in Kalamazoo, Michigan, in 1935. When she was four years old, her father took a job as a maintenance superintendent for a mining operation in the Philippines. The family relocated and lived happily for two years. Then the Japanese invaded. She and her mother and sisters were placed in a civilian internment camp in Los Baños. Her father was captured as a POW and sent to do forced labor. His family never received communications from him, never knew if he would die on any given day. So okay, her life was no picnic.

I've probably given you the impression that Grandma Pencil was some kind of ogre. If not, I've failed.

However, the truth is she wasn't an ogre—not as a child, anyway, and not while McKenna and Toby were in elementary school. Sure, she lied about the death march, but who doesn't lie now and then?

Visualize a face staring straight ahead, wearing a blank look. Expressionless.

Now position a light directly below the chin, shining upward: that face will appear ghastly, frightening.

Now reposition the light so it shines down from the top of the forehead: the person looks sad.

Same face—the only change is how the face is shown.

That's what Grandma did. She moved the light when she thought it might do some good.

She truly cared about the twins. Her heart was very nearly in the right place; it just happened to be in her stomach.

And this makes sense. The internment camp instilled in Grandma Pencil a deep, debilitating terror of hunger, which lead to a profound understanding of the way our souls and sanities are bound to our appetites. For Grandma Pencil, love, trust, and security were all attached to food. Food represented the potential to fill, in some way, the gaping emptiness of the self.

She was stern and grumpy with Murray, but that attitude wasn't her fault, no more than a cornered raccoon can be faulted for swiping at your eyes. With the twins and with baby Audrey, Grandma was a load of fun. She picked up the considerable slack left by Misty's malaise and Murray's self-centered belief that he could hammer, solder, sand, and jerry-rig a happy life.

Grandma laughed with a whistly "Hoo hoo hoo hoo." The "hoos" were so clearly enunciated that they sounded phony. Her laugh annoyed Misty and Murray. McKenna and Toby loved it. The twins did everything they could to hear that laugh. Toby did pratfalls off the couch. McKenna did impressions (the mailman yelling at Snoodles to "Keep away, Mister Pesky!"; Bob Hope saying, "*This* is what I get for fifty dollars?"). McKenna sang the "A-B-C Song" using all "oo" sounds: "Oo hoo soo doo oo oof joo, ooch oo joo koo ool oom oon oo poo, coo oor oos, too oo voo, doobooyoo oox, woo oond zoo. Noo oo noo moo oo boo soos. Nooxt toom woont yoo soong wooth moo?" The twins danced with Snoodles, lifting him by the front paws and jiggling him until great ropes of drool swung from his mouth. They tickled Audrey. They tackled Audrey. They tackled each other. Grandma laughed. Grandma played records. She showed the twins the cha-cha and the fox trot. She helped them build a fort out of couch cushions. When the air was unbreathable from the stench of burning paper or formaldehyde, Grandma took the kids into the backyard, where McKenna and Toby kicked the basketball, and Audrey crawled in diapers across the grass.

That's where Grandma first saw Audrey eat something that wasn't a food item. Audrey was eighteen months old.

"No, no, no," Grandma said, sticking her finger into Audrey's mouth to dislodge as much soil as she could. "I ate dirt, and no granddaughter of mine will do that again. Not while I breathe."

"She *likes* it," Toby said. He ran up to see the action. "She's crazy. I've seen her eat dirt before. Is she crazy?"

"Never call a girl crazy," Grandma told him. Her tone was sharp.

Later that night, the twins lay in their beds.

"*Don't ever call a girl crazy,*" Toby said for the tenth time, his voice mocking. "*Never, never, never.* Stupid Grandma."

"She's not stupid. She's just old."

"Dad thinks she's stupid."

"But Audrey isn't *crazy*. She's a baby. All babies are crazy."

This is how it went.

Grandma told Murray and Misty about the dirt-eating. Misty took Audrey to the pediatrician. McKenna and Toby tagged along.

"It's not uncommon," Dr. Burger said.

He had checked Audrey—had seen that she was able to make eye contact and that her pupils dilated properly; had poked the otoscope into her ears; had pressed his fingers into her belly and found her organs to be well-situated and unswollen; had found that she could clap and could hold two objects at once; had checked her stumps for proper circulation (this was before the Dr Pepper cans). When the exam was finished, Dr. Burger pronounced his double-negative judgment: "It's not uncommon."

He probably would have left it at that and scuttled his bulky, white-coated body out the door—obliqueness and terseness were his trademarks—if Misty hadn't still looked so worried. Or was it sad? Spaced-out from the pills? Take your pick.

Her expression touched Dr. Burger; it made him uncomfortable. Standing in the center of the examination room, he lifted his glasses, massaged the bridge of his nose, and squinted. Then he took off his glasses, folded them, and pinched them between his fingers at his side. As if hearing a voice no one else could hear, he nodded. Then he sat on his stool and cleared his throat. He put the glasses back onto his face. He sucked in a profound breath in preparation for giving Misty more information.

Dr. Burger hated giving more information. Or else he liked to give the impression that he hated giving more information.

We should assume the best about Dr. Burger. We should assume he was only being codgerly, that deep down he loved every one of his patients. We should assume nice things about dead people. Reserve your scorn for the living, if you please.

"There's nothing harmful about eating dirt," he said, "despite what common sense might tell you." His neck wattle thrummed above his tight collar. McKenna imagined popping it with a safety pin, air whistling through the hole like a leaking balloon. "Like I said, many babies go through this phase. Dirt, sand, soap, paint chips, and so on. Keep an eye on her, make sure she doesn't choke, don't let her eat any cleaning products." He handed Misty a roll of puke-green stickers of round faces drawn to resemble the famous *Have a Nice Day* Happy Face. Except these faces weren't happy. They grimaced, Xs for eyes, and stuck out their tongues. "Slap one of these on every poisonous item in the house."

Dr. Burger made his way to the door. He opened it, broadcasting a pleasant, official smile to Misty. He gave Audrey one last sidelong glance. The door closed.

23.

Audrey grew up separately from her siblings. They attended St. Monica's while Audrey was sent to North Park.

Everyone knows this already. It's been documented in fifteen books and a low-budget CBS miniseries. Audrey's public school education is always mentioned as evidence of her spiritual and moral deficiency. As in, "See! *This* is what made her eat that city! I've found the solution!" The number of ex-schoolmates who've been handed obscene wads of cash by fly-by-night media outlets for a personal recollection of the time Audrey ate licorice in the first grade is now approaching triple digits.

What people don't know, what they haven't yet speculated on, is why Audrey went to a public school in the first place. It's one of *the* basic questions, and it's not even asked. People are so focused—I almost wrote "fuckassed," but that would've cost me a Hail Mary—on describing the lurid image of a young woman swallowing a stop sign that they ignore how she might have gotten to that point.

She grew up alone.

While she snuggled with Misty on the queen-sized mattress, the sunlight beams angling through the blinds and warming her bare infant thigh, Audrey was alone. When she lay prone on the living room carpet while Murray's cold fingers gripped her ankles, testing the softness of her stumps and the sturdiness of her shin-bones, Audrey was alone. When Grandma Pencil stooped to peel crusted snot from Audrey's upper lip, exclaiming, "Dirty, dirty

72

girl. Who is going to love you with a nose goblin face?" Audrey was alone.

Her siblings were five years older, a gap too wide. They treated her like a roadblock, a toy, a petting zoo goat. Through her elementary years, adept as Audrey was at maneuvering with her crutches and padded stump socks, she couldn't keep up with McKenna and Toby. They sprinted across the yard, bicycled through the streets, played baseball at the park. She couldn't keep up with her peers, either. Her footlessness excluded her from sports, cheerleading, and Girl Scouts.

When Audrey was in the fourth grade, Misty urged her to try out for concert band. No Mapes had ever played an instrument. Audrey loved the idea but wanted to play the drums. Misty insisted on the flute. She even bought one for Audrey (made of real silver, with open holes—top-of-the-line).

"Where did the money come from?" "Who picked this thing out?" "Why wasn't I consulted on this decision?" Murray asked these and many other questions, around which Misty's answers danced.

No matter how expensive it was, though, Audrey refused to assemble it. She wouldn't put it to her lips. She wouldn't even look at it.

Horrible fights followed, with Audrey screaming and Misty sitting in front of the TV, knitting a sweater. God love her, the girl wanted to break that flute. Audrey shook with anger. She trashed her room, scattered clothes everywhere, upset lamps, toppled toyboxes.

McKenna talked to Audrey. Night after night, she tried to calm Audrey with distractions in the form of board games or surreptitious snacks (a pair of washed handkerchiefs, a pile of rubber bands) smuggled to Audrey as she lay crying on her bed. Audrey kept up the rage longer than anyone expected, and Misty kept up the nonchalance with equal fervor.

Murray was incapable of mediating. When Audrey knocked

bowls of peanuts and pretzels onto the carpet, he stepped into the living room, frowned, and shook his head in disappointment. "Toby!" he said. "See if your sister wants to take a walk. McKenna, get the vacuum."

He tried, didn't he?

Audrey spent her entire fourth-grade year drumming. She drummed on tables, floors, walls, crutches—every surface within reach. She was determined to prove that, drums or no drums, she was going to play the drums.

Misty was unflappable. Her halcyon grin could not be altered, and so she chewed her Gordon's fish sticks with hardly a blink, hardly a dip into the tartar sauce, hardly a batted eye for the still-frozen middles as Audrey tap-tap-tapped.

The drumming affected everyone else. "I swear, I'm going to make your arms match your legs if you don't cut that noise," Murray barked.

But it was all bark, and Audrey knew it. Murray threatened in this way three times a week. Each time, the kids debated if he even knew he'd spoken aloud.

In the end, Audrey lost. Her tapping faded. Her dream of playing the drums vanished. She ate the flute, but this was only a symbolic victory. Misty had won.

Audrey had grade school friends, to be sure. There was the porker Sally Vance, who had the odd habit of not flushing. There was the pallid Mickey Leach, who sported a two-inch-wide part down the middle of her spaghetti hair. A severe case of psoriasis on her arms made her smell like tar. There was Betsy Frost, a redheaded girl freckled like a blizzard. Even her eyeballs were freckled. Audrey's friends were the class rejects, girls who rarely ventured out of their houses and whose histories meant that they were exquisite at entertaining themselves. They didn't visit often

Mostly, Audrey stayed home and painted with Misty. And ate what Misty painted.

Undoubtedly, Grandma Pencil had saved Audrey's legs from amputation when she'd forced Murray to throw away the Dr Pepper prosthetics. In doing so, however, she also killed Audrey's social life.

A girl with pop cans for feet is a curiosity, perhaps even a source of admiration and envy. As in, "Why can't *I* have Dr Pepper feet?"

But a girl on crutches, if you'll pardon the pun, is pedestrian. There's no sex appeal to those armpit sticks. The only thing crutches say is, "Keep your distance—you might catch it."

24.

It's the same old tragic story: Footless baby spends each day with a depressed mother who is warm to the skin but cold to the soul—a distant, distracted, touched-in-the-head mother. Footless baby's father is either at the factory or in the basement with his hissing, clanging toys.

Then again, maybe it's not all sad: Footless baby reveals to her big sister an appetite for paper, wax, cardboard, soil, and other nonfood items. McKenna, captivated by this footless girl—our dear Audrey—becomes her nervous "supplier," going to great lengths to hide her habit from the family. Afraid of being caught, ashamed of what she feels are abnormally intimate feelings toward footless sister, McKenna maintains a distance, avoids footless sister around the house.

(There are, however, stolen moments: feeding Audrey; telling Audrey the story of "The Three Little Pigs"; brushing Audrey's golden hair; bathing Audrey; watching Audrey sleep.)

Overall, McKenna acts like a gutless dweeb. She follows Toby's every lead even while her gut tells her that the only hope for a real connection in this family is with the footless girl playing alone in the corner.

One afternoon, Grandmother catches an eighteen-month-old Audrey eating dirt in the backyard. Dr. Burger assures them nothing is wrong. A few months later, Grandmother finds Audrey eating a crayon. "Don't have a hairy," Murray tells Grandma. "Do you know more than the doctor?"

When the shoddy "feet" Murray labored over for a year with such devotion are removed under threat of legal action, Grandmother becomes Audrey's primary caregiver. Murray never quite recovers from his profound disappointment. Ignoring his bright-eyed footless toddler becomes one of his favorite weapons.

Grandmother continues to discover evidence of sinister gobblings. She catches Audrey chewing the cover of Murray's notebook, half of it already in her stomach. "She's lucky it wasn't any of the pages," Murray growls. He begins storing his notebooks in a fireproof lockbox. Grandmother catches four-year-old Audrey with a ball of Misty's lipstick in her mouth. "Aww," says Misty. "She wants to look like Momma." Grandmother pries open Audrey's lips to find a family photograph, half-masticated.

Grandmother says enough is enough.

"I will not pay for this girl to go to Saint Monica's," she announces at Sunday dinner.

Murray is *way* into his spaghetti. Sunday dinner is the one meal that he always eats with the family. On other days, he takes a Hungry Man into the basement or grabs a bowl of Fritos from an end table. His face is submerged in the noodle pile when he says, "So what's your point?"

Before Grandma can answer, Misty says, under her breath, "The kids really should go to the same school." Her words are a wet paper towel.

There's no sound. No chewing or clanking. Even the children aren't speaking.

"Exactly," Murray says at last.

Grandma Pencil—why has she waited until this moment to make the announcement?—speaks as if Audrey isn't sitting across the table: "The girl doesn't deserve to be schooled in the ways of

Jesus Christ. I won't have it." She taps the edge of her plate with her knife—*ting!*—for emphasis.

Murray looks at Misty, who wears an amused, abstracted smile. She is watching the fork gripped in her own hand as it stirs, needlessly, her potatoes.

(Spaghetti and mashed potatoes? I told you she was touched in the head.)

Murray clears his throat, fist over mouth. "I don't know if anyone .*deserves* that kind of schooling." He waits, looking around the table for a supportive laugh. Getting none, he adds his own chuckle. "I'm glad you're coming around, Annabelle. The twins can go to North Park. Starting next year."

"Yes!" says McKenna, pumping her fist.

"No way!" says Toby. "That's not fair! Just because Kenny doesn't have any friends. That's bullshit."

"Your mouth," says Misty, still monitoring her fork, the tines throttled by noodles.

Toby's curse word lights up Murray as if someone's tickling his toes. "Lot of good that *moral* education's doing, huh, Annabelle?"

"Enough!" Grandma Pencil shouts. Her face has gone the color of Japan's rising sun. She scoots from the table, tosses her napkin onto the plate like a gauntlet. Her lips are quivering.

Nobody but McKenna sees Audrey reach across to grab the cloth napkin. She stuffs it into her mouth.

Audrey gives McKenna a wink. McKenna returns it.

25.

The sun has shattered.

Late afternoon slips between the leaves, strewing shards of light upon the grass.

The wind combs the treetops.

Grilled meat hangs on the breeze, the last barbecue of the season for Oscar Foster.

Toby is wearing sweat pants that match the autumn sky. A sacred color, the color of the Virgin's mantle. Except there is nothing pure or saintly about this boy. He's ready to crack teenhood like a can of beer. Sweat slickens his arms and neck, gives him an unhealthy shine like he's just emerged from the womb. His red face, breathless, squinched in ferocious determination, adds to the effect. A radio on the picnic table in the southwest corner of the yard blasts Night Ranger's "Sister Christian" so loudly that it almost covers the heavy breathing and intermittent moans and grunts, the carnal noises of Toby's free-weight lifting. These are similar to, but slightly quieter than, the noises of his masturbation, which McKenna hears every night, sometimes three times a night. McKenna hears it all and doesn't move. Not a finger.

It's arms today, and upper body: Toby's pride and joy—his "guns"—as well as his "holsters," which McKenna can only assume means his shoulders.

McKenna and Audrey watch their brother from the second floor window of the twins' bedroom. Audrey is kneeling atop a pine toy trunk no longer filled with toys. Now it holds baseball cards—Topps, mostly, some Fleer. Inside this single-compartment trunk, a plywood board, sawed to fit, has been inserted as a divider, forming two compartments. One side is McKenna's, one Toby's.

Toby's baseball cards aren't visible. They're filed away in narrow, white cardboard boxes, each box labeled with team name and years. Every card he owns has been painstakingly logged onto a yellow legal pad, the details written in crisp, careful (primitive-looking) capital letters—MILT WILCOX, PITCHER, 1982, FLEER, CONDITION PRISTINE.

None of Toby's cards are anything less than "pristine." But still, he writes this word on the notepad.

McKenna's half of the trunk, by contrast, looks like it's filled with vomit. The loose cards are scuffed, bent, and jelly-stained. Their corners are mashed, their statistics faded from merciless hours of sifting, of searching for Pete Rose only to find Johnny Bench instead, which sends her scrambling for Lance Parrish in order to compare how many attempted steals each catcher has thrown out. A few of her misfit toys—My Pretty Pony ("Brown"), three Trolls, Papa Smurf and Smurfette—hide within the pile of cards.

The pine trunk is now closed, and atop it kneels seven-year-old Audrey. Her nose is smooshed against the window. Her breath makes a white circle. She leans back, revealing the outline of two lips on the glass. McKenna stands beside Audrey, studying her. Audrey's profile is delicate, meaning she has soft curves of the chin and forehead, round cheeks, remnants of infancy in a head that is still slightly too large for her wiry frame. This only adds to her doll-like quality. She is utterly perfect. Her hands pressed to the glass have left the smudges of fingers and palms. And now, with the added impression of nose and lips, it appears as if a ghost is pushing through the window toward them.

Audrey smells like a carrot. Or a potato. Some freshly unearthed legume or root. Maybe, McKenna thinks, her insides have finally turned into dirt. Then again, she's way past eating dirt by this point. Audrey glances up at McKenna, and a smile opens on her face, revealing gray teeth. Black ballpoints are her latest kick. With her paper route money, McKenna buys bags of twenty-four at ninety-nine cents apiece. Ten bags a week.

It's no longer a secret from the family, of course. How could such a noise be covered or explained away, even by a resourceful big sister? The popping, grinding, snapping. Sounds that do what the Hand-Held Alarmer Bell was supposed to do—reach around corners, traverse walls, find you where you're hiding, tap you on the shoulder.

"Build her a feedbag," Grandma Pencil likes to snarl.

Murray may be doing just that. He has changed from flesh and blood into sound and motion. Months now with only glimpses, noises, speculation. A series of phlegmy coughs in the kitchen. The crinkling of Stouffer's Salisbury steak tin foil. A blur of blue (his work shirt?) on the staircase. The slamming of a door.

Is he crafting another pair of feet? Designing armor and a broadsword for Toby? Inventing a combination salt and pepper shaker/transistor radio? (Wait, he's already made that one.) How about a robot Dad that will actually spend time with its kids?

How many licks does it take to get to the Tootsie Roll center of a Tootsie Pop?

The world may never know.

Audrey is on her knees atop the closed pine trunk that Murray built. Her dress is gauzy and loose. McKenna can see down the front of it, to her chest, like a boy's except for the smallest hint of tightening skin, of trouble rising from beneath the two dime-sized nipples. McKenna's own breasts have already arrived, without fanfare, unable to fill a training bra.

"Now you do a face," Audrey says.

McKenna leans to the window, exhales. Through the translucent fogging, she can see Toby down there, twisting his skullcap in his hands, fertilizing the lawn with his sweat. He looks up at the window, raises his middle finger. He mouths the word "faggot."

In the circle of misted glass, McKenna draws a smiley face with her fingertip.

"My face is better," Audrey says. "It's creepy."

"Of course it is. Look who made it."

She elbows McKenna in the ribs. "Shut your piehole!"

McKenna wraps her arms around Audrey, drapes her over her shoulder. In the center of the room, she spins until they're dizzy, laughing, sick to their stomachs.

McKenna lies on the carpet, breathing. This small exertion has left her rubbery.

Twenty minutes later, before Toby comes inside, Audrey wants to eat. McKenna opens the pine trunk. One by one, she feeds Audrey the 1978 St. Louis Cardinals. So delicious, so pristine.

26.

The family knew she was a freak. They never said it aloud (okay, Grandma Pencil did) but spoken or not, it was an undeniable fact.

And even if we are politically correct and say she wasn't a freak, her behavior was freakish, and as we all know, freakish people are scary.

When Audrey's secret was first revealed to someone other than McKenna, there was no grand revelation, no "Ah ha!" It was a slow unveiling that McKenna tried her best to keep hidden.

Each mastication noise meant the grim, unsettling task of prying open Audrey's lips to see what was inside. With every discovery—a comb, tape measure, scissors, a handful of quarters that had been set aside for laundry—the family's anxiety increased. Murray was confused, then angry. He couldn't commit to a punishment plan—it stressed him to think about punishment, actual punishment. Grandma advocated a three-strike policy, or, barring that, a five- or six-strike policy. She wanted a policy, any kind of policy. But Murray and Misty could do nothing more than shake their heads and say to Audrey, "Why would you try to eat a Lego? Use your head, sweetie!" and then remind McKenna and Toby not to encourage her.

Grandma Pencil insisted it was Misty's fault. The girl wasn't eating enough at mealtimes. Grandma Pencil, like many others, mistakenly believed that Audrey received physical satiation from her habit. No. Truth is, she had no bottom. She wasn't replacing

real food as much as *seeking* real food. She couldn't find it anywhere.

Still, Misty went along with Grandma's plan. She gave Audrey
incredible portions, but the girl wouldn't eat any more or less than
she'd ever eaten. Meal after meal, Grandma Pencil seethed.

They tried to be diligent and observant. They salvaged what
they could from Audrey's mouth, stuck the remnants in Ziplocs
or Mason jars and brought them to the pediatrician.

As the visits progressed, Dr. Burger's nonchalance was replaced
by bemusement, then professional concern, then amazement, then
doubt, and then disbelief. He flat-out thought they were lying.
The family could sense that each new plastic baggy was a building block to this inevitable response.

He had started out wanting to believe. He trusted people, for
the most part. Maybe not in the area of self-diagnosis, but hey, he
was willing to give the patient the benefit of the doubt in the initial stages, until he'd amassed sufficient evidence that they were
wrong.

Every visit from the Mapeses tested Dr. Burger's medical prow-
ess in ways he never dreamed possible. For starters, there were no
physical signs that Audrey's health was anything but normal. Her
height and weight were average. She bore no wounds, no abra-
sions, no signs of physical trauma. Her breath smelled fine, even
sweet. Despite what Misty claimed her daughter had eaten, the girl
passed every reflex test. Exam after exam, Audrey exhibited each
developmental milestone Dr. Burger had been trained to seek as
evidence of health.

And of course, in Dr. Burger's mind—a mind dependent first
and foremost upon empirical evidence—there was simply no way
a four-year-old's teeth could punch holes in a quarter or pulverize
what appeared to be genuine metal screws.

Using tweezers, he plucked half of a mutilated Barbie doll's
head from an empty Jif peanut butter jar. He made a sour face and
dropped it back inside with a hollow clink.

He rubbed his eyes. This was the eighth visit in three years, and his patience had thinned to transparency. "If I had my druthers," he said, clasping his thick hands in front of his chest, his eyes burning with a peculiar excitement, "I'd ask you to eat my stethoscope, pretty lady."

Audrey stood between her mother's knees. Her fingers played with a loose thread on the seam of Misty's yellow skirt. She wouldn't look up to meet the doctor's persistent stare.

"But if I did that," Dr. Burger continued, turning his back and walking to the counter as he withdrew a pen from his shirt pocket, "I'd be sued into bankruptcy." He glanced over his shoulder at McKenna, Misty, and Audrey. He tried to grin but only managed to bare his teeth. "Not that Momma Mapes would ever sue me. She likes me too much." He winked before facing the counter again. His pen clicked.

Audrey began to drool, a thin string like a spider's web descending, ever so slowly, to her mother's bare knee. Misty didn't seem to notice, even as the saliva made contact.

"If what you have been bringing to me is real—and of course, I'm not doubting you, you know that—then I'll need hard proof before we can proceed." There was the sound of scribbling. "I hope you understand Audrey's outward appearance, her behavior, her mental capacities . . . there's no indication that she has consumed the objects you claim." With a squeak, he spun on his heel and handed Misty a sheet of paper. "The next time Audrey eats an unusual item, call this number. He's a gastroentologist, a personal friend of mine. His name is Doctor Maboob. Funny name, I know. Indian, I believe. India the country. I'll call his office and give them a heads-up. As soon as Audrey gets something like *this* down her throat"—he pointed to the Barbie head in the jar—"you call them and take her to see Doctor Maboob. The address is written there. The sooner you go in after she's consumed the item, the better. They'll be able to analyze the stomach contents, and then we'll know how to proceed."

With some effort, Dr. Burger squatted in front of Misty and Audrey. He placed his index finger under Audrey's chin. "Don't look so sad, pretty lady."

Audrey reached out and yanked the stethoscope from his neck. She crammed it into her mouth, all except the tubing, which hung from her lips like a giant black noodle. She chewed and slurped. Up and in went the tubing and the round, silver chestpiece. In three seconds, the stethoscope was gone.

Dr. Burger tipped over backward as if in slow motion. He lay supine on the floor, his face pale. His chest heaved, and he gasped for breath. His eyes, two giant orbs, stared at the ceiling as cigarettes slid out of the pack in his breast pocket and landed willynilly about his face and neck.

The Mapeses never called Dr. Maboob.

27.

Dr. Burger cannot be called "the first casualty of Audrey Mapes's reign of terror," as the geezers have argued. At sixty-three, Burger was no poster boy for healthy living. He, like most senior citizens of the 1970s, appeared older than his years, with his liver-spotted hands, his anemic crown of white hair combed within an inch of its life, his low-slung, rubbery jowls, his labored breathing. A two-pack-a-day smoker for more than three decades, his lungs were the color of the Grim Reaper's cloak. His arteries were packed with the slough of a sloe gin fizz and Eggs Benedict diet. If Audrey hadn't scared him to death, some opossum in his garbage can on a Sunday morning surely would have.

No, I assert that the first casualty of Audrey's "reign" was not a body, but a soul. Annabelle Pensolotschy's soul, to be precise.

Such a sweet name, *Annabelle*. So pure. So melodious. Two palindromes snuggling a "b" (group hug!). Four doubled letters arranged in perfect symmetry, 1-2-1, 1-2-1, like a line of hills inflamed to coppery gold by the sun's plunge. A name that speaks of constancy, poetry, innocence. My beautiful, my graceful, my Annabelle.

How fitting, then, that the mushmouthed toddler McKenna (Toby later tried to claim credit—he could never give anyone else credit for anything) couldn't pronounce "Grandma Anna" without sounding like a barnyard animal. Grandma's appellation was changed, first to her surname (But who could pronounce Pensolotschy?), and

quickly thereafter to a truncated, easy-on-the-tongue version—
Pencil.

So accurate! So reflective of her personality! A tool that de-
pends upon sharpness and pointedness; a tool that can stab and
poison; a tool that communicates feelings, yes, but impermanent
ones, feelings that change with the rub of an eraser and leave no
evidence of the original. A fickle, untrustworthy—dare I say
cheap—piece of wood that messes your lap with curled shavings
and breaks when you push on it too hard.

Grandma Pencil—or "Cheesepurse," as some of the kids took
to calling her because they could always sneak a slice of Kraft out
of there—became a regular presence at St. Monica's. She was a
"floater," a "helper," an "aide" (all unofficial titles, all off the books)
who appeared in classrooms without warning to assist in admin-
istering tests, buttoning winter coats, or monitoring playground
behavior. And always, always, always Grandma Pencil devoted
precious time to standing in the corner, or at the chalkboard, or in
the hallway . . . with the nuns. A little group time for commiser-
ating, whispering, judging, scheming.

Grandma Pencil first met her surrogate sisters on that fateful
"Bring Your Grandparents to School Day" when McKenna and
Toby were starting fourth grade. This was less than a year after
Dr. Burger's fatal coronary. Who knows what it was, exactly, that
made Grandma's initial St. Monica's visit so meaningful.

Had it reawakened an unfulfilled desire to be a teacher, or perhaps a nun?

Or did the sisters merely seem like an attractive crew? Buddies
that Grandma could envision herself hanging out with? Shoulders
to lean on, cry on, and rub with Ben-Gay? Ears to chew?

Maybe it was simply their age that brought them together, that
unspoken camaraderie of the almost-dead, that sorority of Great
Depression barn photographs and Tommy Dorsey albums.

Or perhaps Grandma was chiseling her way into a clique with

front-row tickets to the concert of Eternal Bliss. If so, who could blame her?

More realistically, though, experiencing Catholic school on "Grandparents Day" had probably revealed a structure that Grandma Pencil's own life had always lacked, one that fate had stolen from her. She'd been uprooted from her birthplace of Kalamazoo and taken to the Philippines, where she spent four of her most formative years (six through nine) in an internment camp.

There, the only dependable things were the murderous sun and the empty stomach she carried every day, the stomach that grew to hate her, the stomach that growled and rebelled when she so much as sipped the tainted tap water. Her stomach was a mangy, beaten dog that she longed to snuggle but that she ended up ignoring out of fear that it would soon die anyway. Ten hours a day, Annabelle stood on bare soles beside her mother and three older sisters, cooked by the 120-degree heat, in a line of ragged people as long and depressing as the Vietnam Memorial, only to receive half a bowl of rice and a tin cup of body-temperature water that tasted like blood.

Her father was gone, a hole in their lives. He'd disappeared from their hut two days after they were captured. The unspoken belief was that he was either a POW or was dead. In either case, they were powerless to bring him back. Each day of not knowing his condition meant a fortifying of Annabelle's psychic defenses. Each day meant that another piece of her father—his deep, sonorous laugh, the softness of his flannel against her cheek, his firm palm on her back, coaxing her to brave the public pool—was excised from Annabelle's mind. To hold onto any part of him was too painful, too dangerous.

Her mother tried to raise their spirits by invoking Daddy, by showing them his picture, by telling about the time he dropped his shoe into the toilet or when he accidentally hammered a hole in the kitchen wall. But Annabelle stared coldly at the photograph and listened to the stories without expression. This man was a stranger. She had already buried him, mourned, and moved on. (And so had his POW barracks-mates, as it turns out. Shot in the head by his captors.)

So St. Monica's Elementary was where Annabelle Pensolotschy finally found her family, her routine, her stability.

Nuns are nothing if not predictable. They commit their lives to the sanctity of routine. After all, remember their husband's M.O.—the sun, the tides, the rotation of the Earth—and maybe you'll get some small sense of a Catholic nun's aspirations.

Sister P.V., Sister Robert Ann, Sister Maximillian, Sister Pat, and Sister Michael lived together in the convent behind the church. They woke at 5:45 a.m., even on weekends. Each Sister, beginning with the eldest, was allotted seven minutes of bathroom time. "Age before beauty!" the younger ones loved to say, with chuckles. They said grace before slurping tea and unsweetened oatmeal at one big table. They strolled to the garden to water vegetables and pull weeds. Yes, it was quite a community. They lashed each other's naked buttocks with rosaries if the laundry didn't get done on time. Fortunately, it always got done on time. You see, the laundry routine, like every other routine, was carved into the stone tablets of their wizened heads.

In addition to sharing bathrooms, the nuns shared delusions. They also shared an unwillingness to perform self-examinations of any kind.

Undoubtedly, these qualities appealed to Grandma Pencil.

Where you would see stubbornness, the nuns saw conviction. Where you would see vindictiveness, the nuns saw the even hand (read: the open backhand) of justice. Where you would see pettiness, the nuns saw the Devil in the details. Where you would see nosiness and invasion of privacy, the nuns saw council.

Where you would see hate, they also saw hate (of the "sin," not the "sinner").

Where you would see sin, they saw the sinner.

28.

The years drifted by, as years do. A more accurate verb has never been applied. Like rafts upon an ocean, or astronauts cut loose from their space walks, the anni float at a languid pace, with no set direction, providing an arbitrary definition of "progress." Always moving, yes, always arriving somewhere and nowhere at the same time.

And of course, by "years," I mean our lives. Our selves. Us. You and me. We drift.

1982, '83, '84, '85. A dazzling era. Arcade games, home video games, Olympic Games, *Trivial Pursuit* games, *War Games*. The Year of the Bible. Swatches. Sally Ride. A bull terrier in shades pitching beer. The first execution by lethal injection. Music Television. Moonboots. Styrofoam. Chinese yo-yos. Happy Meals. The Computer is *The Man of the Year*. Saved whales, bludgeoned seals.

What began as a volunteer stint became a paying gig. St. Monica's named Grandma Pencil the official Classroom Assistant—a position created for her. Five days a week, five hours a day, she went into rooms as needed, lending support, zipping zippers, licking gold stars, pitching in, scolding, making herself useful. Never mind that she had no qualifications, no formal training in education . . . Neither did the nuns! So it worked.

Grandma Pencil was, after all, just under fifty years old. A spring chicken by today's standards, and what's a chicken if it's got nothing to peck?

Like her daughter, she'd never held a job. After the G.I.s freed
her and her family from Los Baños on February 23, 1945, the Pensolotschy clan came back to the U.S., to Kalamazoo, and lived off
the money the government paid out to war widows. Her father
hadn't been a soldier, but all internment camp survivors were
given this status. The money was a pittance. Annabelle's mother
knew what she had to do.

She remarried a year later. As Pencil would describe it,
"Mommy got herself a little leprechaun." By this, she wasn't only
referring to her stepfather's diminutive stature, bright orange
shock of hair, and deep Irish roots. What Grandma Pencil also
meant was that Sean Flannery McCain had a giant pot of gold.
But instead of having to be tricked, this leprechaun shared his
gold recklessly, drunkenly. He foisted it on people in the same
way a shore leave sailor passes gas—sometimes without even realizing he's doing it.

And like it or not, everyone gets a taste.

Annabelle and her sisters ascended eight rungs, give or take, on
the socioeconomic ladder. For a while, they lived the good life in
a 5,000 square-foot home on the shore of Lake Michigan, near St.
Joseph. McCain was an entrepreneur, a self-made man, an im-
porter and dealer of exotic "native artwork." He traveled to New
Guinea, Malaysia, Vietnam, Nepal, Morocco, Madrid, Peru, and
Bolivia, snatching up local treasures for pennies and selling them
in the States at one thousand times the price he'd paid. He bought
an even bigger house, this one in East Grand Rapids.

Annabelle was given a respectable private school education at
St. Alphonsus and then West Catholic high school. After graduat-
ing *summa cum laude*, she shipped off to Aquinas College (a twenty-
minute drive from home; she lived in the dorms all four years).
She immersed herself in philosophical and religious texts and ate
copious amounts of peanuts, crackers, Cheetos, and trail mix. The
instant her stomach growled, all of the horror came rushing back:
that furnace of a hut; that stifling air; those mosquitoes growing

fat on her blood; the dysentery; the bones coming to life on her skin like a secret, buried self, threatening to burst forth and erase the girl she could see in the shard of mirrored glass her mother kept hidden beneath the straw mattress.

After college, Annabelle followed in her mother's footsteps by marrying a nice Irish Catholic gentleman named Raynor Childs. Ray, in fact, was the Junior Regional Distribution Manager—or some such nonsense—for Sean McCain's burgeoning Exotica and Tribal Wonders Emporium. Annabelle bore Ray a daughter, whom they named Misty. Shortly thereafter, Annabelle's plumbing went bad. She underwent an emergency hysterectomy. Once Misty entered grade school, Annabelle made it clear to her husband that she wanted to get a job (her major was in Philosophy, her minor in Sociology), but Ray was firm: no wife of his would work. He insisted that she "take care of the house."

What a smothering life that must have been for young Misty Childs! To have her mother at home every second of every day, scrutinizing her every move!

Wait . . . that's exactly how it was for Audrey, McKenna, and Toby. Never mind.

From the outside, it undoubtedly seemed that Annabelle should be happy with her upper middle class, split-level ranch home in suburban Grand Rapids. Not to mention her healthy (if introverted and passive) daughter and handsome husband with his well-groomed mustache, stable career, and no apparent flaws other than a penchant for hoarding dirty magazines under the bed.

Most people would hear this described and say, "Now *that's* the life!"

In truth, though, too much free time, too many quiet, uninterrupted moments of sitting, staring, and thinking . . . well, that can be the worst sort of slow death. Worse than cancer, because nobody actually believes it's a disease. They'll scoff and tell you to get off your lazy ass and *do something*, "Get a hobby, for Christ's sake!"

And I don't think it's a stretch to say that Annabelle Childs, aka Annabelle Pensolotschy, aka Grandma Pencil, went as mad as a Columbian dwarf during those years as a "kept" woman.

No one but Misty and Annabelle knows exactly what went on in that house, but McKenna and Toby overheard many conversations between Mom and Dad. They pieced together a number of incidents: how Annabelle had gone into a rage while Ray was overseas, had torn apart his magazines and wallpapered the living room with nude women; how Annabelle forced Misty to copy lines out of the telephone book if Misty didn't finish what was on her plate ("One page per pea," they heard Misty say to Murray, with a tired laugh); how Annabelle became convinced that Ray had died during a Thailand jungle expedition; how Annabelle pulled Misty, quite literally, out of school and dragged her to the airport with only the clothes on her back (and a passport, one must presume); how they landed in Bangkok and spent the next two months hopping broken-down buses and third-class trains, searching remote villages for Ray, who had returned three days after they'd left town, and in a panic filed a missing persons report and corralled hundreds of search volunteers.

A short time later, Annabelle was placed in a home. "Mental exhaustion," they labeled it. Annabelle's sisters, at this point, were both married to Filipino men and living, ironically, in Manila, fifty miles from the site of their internment camp. Annabelle's mother had long-since passed away, and there was no one to look after Misty. Rather than cut back his workload or stay home himself, Ray hired a full-time nanny and tutor ("My business doesn't *stop* because your mother decides to have a breakdown!").

After six months, Annabelle returned home. Misty spent the next seven years under the watchful eye of her "recovering" mom. Only the imagination can supply the details of that dark time. Needless to say, Misty bolted as soon as her leash was removed. At eighteen, she got her own apartment in the Heritage Hill district downtown. Shortly thereafter, she invited her new boyfriend Murray, who worked at the caulking glue factory, to move in.

Raynor Childs divorced Annabelle in 1972, the same year Misty gave birth to their grandchildren, McKenna and Toby. An alimony payment was agreed upon and signed into action, and then all that remained of this man—Misty's father, Annabelle's husband, and McKenna, Toby, and Audrey's Grandpa Childs—was a washed-out black-and-white photograph showing him with Misty (age five or so) perched on his shoulders. Both of them are staring down into the rising mist of Victoria Falls.

The day is partly cloudy or partly sunny, depending.

29.

By the time McKenna and Toby were twelve, the nuns were regular dinner guests.

They never came all at once; they never came alone. Like Noah's precious cargo, they arrived in pairs, stepping gingerly up the cracked walkway, arms linked, appearing not so much pious as geriatric and scared outside the bubbles of their sanctimonious classrooms. Once they'd climbed the four concrete steps, their knock rattled the metal door with all the force of a dried sponge tossed by a Farm League reject.

Two or three times a month they descended, always unannounced to the family. Grandma Pencil figured that no one would mind. After all, she was doing 95 percent of the cooking these days.

A couple of Mapeses minded, though. The nuns were McKenna and Toby's teachers, ex-teachers, future teachers. For the twins, the dinners ranged from uncomfortable to mortifying. The only choice they had was to hide in their room until the last possible moment, doing (or in Toby's case, pretending to do) homework.

"Fucking penguins!" Toby said.

He'd seen *The Blues Brothers* on his friend Tommy's HBO (Tommy was *Toby's* friend, not McKenna's, you'll notice). Toby loved to say the f-word in all its provocative and hilarious incarnations. He used it like a claw hammer on unsuspecting victims.

Like the time he told a mentally handicapped kid at school, "Fuck a fencepost, you fucking retard." Grandma Pencil had given up on scolding Toby about his gutter mouth, except when he occasionally let one slip in front of the nuns, at which point she flushed with embarrassment and told him to do fifty push-ups. Toby was happy to oblige, and Grandma and the nuns always cheered him to the finish.

"Dad says they're lousy cooks," McKenna said. "That's why they come over."

"Of course they are," Toby answered. He lay on his bed with a *Fitness* magazine held above his face. "They've been sucking Brophy's thingy so long, everything else tastes like cardboard."

"Why doesn't it surprise me," McKenna said, "that you know what Father Brophy's thingy tastes like?" She was seated at the writing desk.

An empty Coke can hit the back of McKenna's head. It landed on the carpet without a sound. These were the pre-divider days, before a floral-patterned chintz provided each twin an 8'×9' empire to rule.

"AUDREY! SNACK!" Toby yelled, returning to an article about gluteals and quads and the rest of his oily dementia.

"Don't," McKenna said. She tried to concentrate on her English worksheet. Pen poised, no answers came. *Identify the indirect object in the following sentence:*

"SNACK, JAWS!" Toby hollered.

The door creaked open. Audrey, on crutches, entered. Her hair was pulled back into a knot and fastened by a barrette that was braided with red and blue ribbon—her "rainbow barrette." Very trendy, very 1984. McKenna hated to see her sister being sucked into the fashion vortex. The barrette matched Audrey's shirt rainbow, which arched across her chest from three-quarter sleeve to three-quarter sleeve.

Audrey stooped to pick up the Coke can, then opened wide and jammed it in. It popped in her mouth like a Flintstones vitamin.

The can was probably half-digested in her gut before she made it out the door. McKenna could hear her singing on the way to her room, "Our house! Is a very, very, very fine house!"

Toby's eyes were still on his magazine. "You gotta look at this," he said. "This chick is built like you. Oh wait, it's a dude."

"You shouldn't feed Audrey trash," McKenna said. She penciled in the answer to number seven: *me*.

"She shouldn't eat trash."

"But she does. And you should know better than to give it to her. She's only seven."

"So it's *my* fault she's a freak?" He sat up and unsnapped the shoulder buttons of his cham shirt. He yanked off the sleeves and tossed them in the corner by his dresser, thereby revealing the upper arms he'd stopped calling "guns" and was now calling "my babies." Typical Toby, beating his gorilla chest. He thought camouflage pants, Van Halen pins, and biceps would distract attention from the swaths of acne on his cheeks and forehead.

"Audrey's special," McKenna said. "She's got a gift."

"You *believe* that crap? Mom only says that cuz she doesn't know what else to say."

"You believe Grandma's crap."

"All I know is 'we aren't supposed to tell anyone.'" His fingers made careless quotation marks in the air. "That sounds like hiding a freak to me."

"You would know."

"Yep. I share a room with one."

From downstairs, Grandma Pencil called them to dinner.

30.

Sister Maximillian and Sister P.V., along with Misty, Murray, and Grandma Pencil, sit at the dining room table. Bowls are passed, plates are loaded, glasses are filled. The record player in the living room offers Vangelis's *Chariots of Fire* soundtrack at a volume not loud enough to interfere with the subdued conversation. To the untrained eye, the scene appears Rockwellian in its vision of domestic ease. Close scrutiny (and honesty), however, reveals that Misty's complexion is too pale, even a bit on the green side. Her smiles are rote. Murray, too, doesn't look comfortable, the way he gnaws a raw broccoli stalk and won't let his eyes rest from their constant flicking around the room, never seeing the dinner guests.

Down the stairs come the children. Toby bears Audrey in his arms, newlywed-wife-over-the-threshold style. Her stumps are frilly-socked.

McKenna, lagging behind, wearing a tan, knee-length dress, carries the crutches—not by choice, but because she's not strong enough to carry Audrey. She watches Toby reach the bottom of the steps, not so much admiring as marveling at the sculpted bulk of a preteen, the boy who used to be her twin. Toby's brow is jutted, and his nostrils have flared so often they've become formidable holes. Vast disparities between the twins' hands, legs, and thighs—every difference Toby had desired as he obsessively measured during that summer before kindergarten—all and more have come true.

And yet, he's not happy. He's gruff and aggressive toward family, friends, and strangers. This may be a result of his involvement with football and heavy metal. Or, it may be the *reason* for his involvement with football and heavy metal. The point is, the kid is a jerk. Just plain not nice. McKenna has long ago stopped trying to like Toby. And trying to understand Toby hasn't led to any great revelations. As young kids, they shared an affinity for Mommy and an unspoken respect for Daddy. Now, Toby hates both parents. The only love he shows is a love of mocking their every decision, action, or utterance.

So Toby was a miserable teen. So what. Was McKenna happy? If Toby was *too* concerned with his weight, muscle mass, and size, then maybe McKenna wasn't concerned enough. She knew she had a weight problem, a body problem. It didn't make her feel good to be the skinniest girl in the seventh grade. Thinner than the sixth-graders. It didn't make her feel good to hear the boys whisper "Skeletor." It didn't make her feel good to break a bone every six months (ankle, collarbone, forearm, other collarbone). It didn't make her feel good to know that if the house was burning she wouldn't be able to carry Audrey down the steps and out the front door.

McKenna was used to not feeling good, however. She'd not felt good her whole life. Why should now be any different? She only saw her dad twice a month. Her mom was a basket case. Her brother mocked her at every opportunity. Her Grandma appraised her scrawny arms like she wished she'd never been born. And the other day, while wrestling with Audrey, she'd bled into her panties. Her first period. McKenna wondered why it happened when she was wrestling Audrey, right as she pinned Audrey to the floor.

The incident kept her awake. She worried that she might be a pervert like Grandpa Ray.

But really, was life so terrible?

NO, NO, NO! Not with this beef stroganoff in her mouth. Not chewing the soft meat, savoring the tangy sauce. Swishing, swallowing. Feeling the burn at the back of her throat—such raw skin, such an overworked tube.

Upchucking. Chucking up.

Chewing again. Swallowi—

Upchucking. Chucking up.

Chewing. Swallo—

Upchucking. Chucking up.

"McKenna, you don't like your Grandma's cooking?"

Chewing. Swallowing.

"I do. She's a great cook."

"She's a great cook *what?*" Grandma Pencil says, fork pointing.

"She's a great cook, *Sister Maximillian,*" McKenna says.

McKenna takes another bite. Her third bite.

"Maybe she's just slow," Sister PV says, mopping the last trace of gravy with a wedge of bread.

"No maybes about it," Murray answers. He loads his mouth so he doesn't have to say anything else.

31.

As people age, they get better and worse. They improve as they decline. They sink to new depths while they ascend to new heights. They become more beautiful and more grotesque. Smarter and dumber. Bolder and more withdrawn from the world.

The weeks and months become years, the same way boys and girls become men and women.

We walk the same route every day, discovering one afternoon that without realizing it we've memorized the number of sidewalk cracks between bus stop and house. Our friends no longer telephone us, they're so busy. We only had two of them, anyway. The neighborhood children become automobile drivers, zip off to college, get married, die in scuba diving accidents—still nameless.

Favorite television shows get cancelled, replaced by inferior ones. But we watch anyway, to "give them a chance." Magazines guilt us into resubscribing every year. We get turned down for major credit cards. We keep secrets. We attend work-sponsored Christmas parties. We revisit a few choice photographs that remind us how each passing day makes us less and less like ourselves. Dreams of success, of fulfillment—intellectual, spiritual, physical, emotional— fade into bathroom graffiti while the bank teller job that pays the bills becomes our newspaper, our connection to the world. Hair abandons ship. Boobs droop.

We turn cynical: "Sister Janice only wants to come over because I have the satellite and can get the World Cup games." We turn lazy: "I'm not going to see that new Ang Lee movie. So what if Shalit called it 'As important as *Schindler's List*!' I don't care! Leave me alone while I empty my mower bag!" Being demanding is no longer a negative trait: "The menu says coleslaw. This is shredded lettuce and mayo!"

And how nice to finally be smart! How wonderful to have the *time*, at last, to think! To write, to mull, to live through *reliving*.

Sure, children possess admirable illness-recovery skills, excellent athleticism, endurance, and energy. And Lord knows they've got hope—buckets of it, full to the brim, sloshing everywhere as they walk. If you're not careful, you might slip in it and break your neck. Hope is a potent fuel. It'll keep you moving. But doggone if kids aren't stupid as burlap. They can't survive on their own. They can't control their urges. They think like animals, if what animals think can be called thought.

Eat. Run. Kiss. Punch. Cry. Sleep. Betray.

Kids don't even *get* that they're going to die. How dense is that? And this stupidity doesn't only afflict babies and toddlers—it infects grade school, high school, college. Basic skills like taking out the trash, paying rent, getting price quotes for a funeral? Don't count on a kid!

But don't count on adults, either. Just because they "know" things doesn't mean they know what to do with that knowledge. A teaspoon of self-understanding doesn't equal the recipe for happiness. Grown-ups can master the basics, but will they ever live in the bliss of childhood again? Never. Will they ever again know the thrill of possibility? Not likely.

Will they dream of sinning and wake up with smiles on their lips? Will they suck popsicles with abandon? Will they believe in themselves without worrying what the neighbors think? Will they just *stop*? Stop looking at me that way. Stop taking pictures of the house. Stop calling. Stop sending threatening mail. Stop telling me I need to be forgiven. Stop writing about me. Stop peering into my windows. Just *stop* for a minute.

Will we have the opportunity to start over? A second chance where we might *not* hold onto every experience?

To live in the moment. To break all the mirrors in the house. To push a bully into a puddle. To ride a bicycle no-handed down a hill in winter. To descend into the basement and see what all that noise is about. To be wonderful. To be wondrous. To be worthy.

To erase that bewildering girl.

To steal a lungful. To taste her ripe mouth with no fear of damnation.

Part Two

Barking at Phantoms

32.

The Mapeses and Grandma Pencil took an Amtrak to Kalamazoo in the summer of 1988. It was a sixty-eight minute ride for a three-day weekend. Not exactly an ocean liner to Australia, but to the kids, it was like going to the moon. They'd never left Grand Rapids (except for a few of Toby's football games in neighboring Rockford).

Each year, Murray depleted his week of vacation time. But he spent it you-know-where (underground), cranking out you-know-whats (inventions) for you-know-who (nobody). In fact, the Mapeses had only gone out as a family—as in, "Mom, Dad, Toby, and McKenna leave the house together, pile into one car and drive to the same destination"—some two dozen times during the years of 1972–1988.

The Kalamazoo vacation was Grandma Pencil's idea. She insisted. She made all the arrangements. It was her birthplace, the city where she'd lived her happiest days until being taken to the Philippines. Her father was buried in Kalamazoo's largest cemetery, a place called Mountain Home. She hadn't "visited" him in over a decade. Although she admitted to remembering nothing of her time in Kalamazoo, the city occupied a special place in her persistent little heart.

Grandma Pencil was not a driver. She never owned a license. In general, she didn't trust machines, and she especially hated cars. It's reasonable to assume that one of her main automobile memories was of riding behind the hearse that carried her father's corpse.

The Mapeses deboarded the Amtrak train on a muggy, overcast July afternoon. Murray's forehead was beaded with sweat, and his Polo knockoff had black armpits. He carried Audrey down the steps, followed closely by Grandma Pencil, McKenna, Misty, and Toby. An observer—of which there were none (save for the shoeless lunatic reposing beside a newspaper box and staring out of two rheumy eyes, perhaps struggling internally against the realization that he'd slept through yet another opportunity to hurl himself in front of a train)—would have thought the Mapes clan was from another country, if not another planet, the way they tentatively descended the steps and clumsily arranged themselves on the platform, eyes wide with wonder and trepidation.

They found a taxicab idling in front of the station. They piled inside. Grandma Pencil sat shotgun. Murray and Misty bookended the children in the back. Audrey's crutches lay across their laps like the protective bar of a roller coaster. The cabbie didn't comment on the unusual suitcase and suitcase accessory he'd been asked to put in the trunk.

It was a tight squeeze for the Mapeses. They were crammed in not so much like sardines as like teeth in an overcrowded mouth, leaning upon one other in a crooked jumble. Toby expressed irritation in his way, mumbles and growls, and before the cab had even exited the lot, he'd lifted Audrey onto his lap. This seemed to satisfy him, and Audrey did not resist.

The first stop the family made—before food, drink, or toilet—was Mountain Home Cemetery. The taxi climbed the winding, narrow roadway as Grandma Pencil squinted out the passenger window. The cab was air conditioned, but humidity filled the cramped space. Murray's B.O. was not charming to anyone, least of all the driver, who stopped the car abruptly before Grandma had located her father's plot. The cabbie apologized as he opened the trunk, saying he had to hurry back to the station for more passengers. No one argued with him; they took him at his word. Even though they were from a city twice the size of Kalamazoo, they might as well have been country bumpkins. Their immediate surroundings were unfamiliar, and therefore they assumed everything else in this Bizarro World was operating under a mysterious set of rules they had yet to decipher.

The cemetery was immense. Twenty-eight acres rolling to the horizon in all directions, white and gray markers dotting the green hills. Some gravestones were no wider or thicker than a three-subject notebook, stained an ashen hue. Names and dates had faded into ghostly suggestions, as if despite mankind's best efforts, nature was determined to purge the last traces of these people from the Earth. Other markers were monoliths, epic in their construction, a wonder and a horror to behold: Columns looming two stories high; rectangular blocks the size of automobiles; a monstrous sphere of reflective marble ten feet in diameter, balanced atop a pedestal. These two-ton raised middle fingers to Time, Nature, Impermanence, Rot—to Mortality itself—represented dead people who dared God to just *try* to erase them: *HENRY UPJOHN, CHARLES B. HAYS, EPAPHRODITUS RANSOM.*

The band of merry Mapeses puttered among the tombstones, admiring and critiquing in the oppressive heat. They laughed at names like *Constance Noring* and *Paige Turner*. They fell silent at the grave of little *Louis Merchant 1889–1892.*

Toby unceremoniously whipped out his thingy and began hosing the base of *Earl Coleman 1922–1980*'s rather average-sized granite cross.

"Classy," said Murray.

"You gotta go, you gotta go," Toby answered.

"We *all* have to go," Audrey said, and on her crutches she began beating an impressive path up the grassy slope. "Come on!" she hollered, and Misty followed.

McKenna was in "sled dog" mode. She'd lost the paper-scissors-rock competition with Toby and was therefore hitched, via shoulder and torso harness, to the cart on skis that Murray had invented the year before as a way to transport luggage.

At this time, wheeled suitcases were not yet standard. When luggage did have wheels, it was often difficult to pull without tipping. The sled was a cool idea—a rack mounted on two ski blades, upon which a piece (or pieces) of luggage could be strapped. But then some joker invented extendable handles and stuck the wheels on the vertical end of the suitcase. "Roller Boards," they're called now. Everyone's got one. Murray saw another opportunity slip away.

Truthfully, though, he never gave it much thought. He was just happy to have made the SledDogger, an idea that had come to him one year earlier, when Grandma Pencil first mentioned the upcoming anniversary.

"Next summer will be thirty-three years since my father's death," she said. "The family must make a pilgrimage."

"Make a pilgrim *itch?*" Toby asked. "Why?" The family was eating dinner, and Toby was on his second helping.

"I want to be a pilgrim," Audrey chimed in.

"It's *forty-seven* years, Mom," Misty said. She sounded embarrassed.

But Grandma Pencil couldn't be bothered by mathematical trivialities. "Thirty-three was the age of our Lord Jesus when they nailed him to that tree."

Sister P.V. and Sister Robert Ann joined Grandma in crossing themselves.

"More importantly," Grandma continued, "thirty-three was Jesus' age when he rose to join his Heavenly Father at the throne."

Murray, brow furrowed, made calculations. "So," he said, "if Jesus was thirty-three, then God was what, in his early sixties?"

Audrey giggled. The nuns frowned—not at Murray, but at Audrey. No doubt every one of their withered hands itched to give her a thumping. No doubt they were all imagining the perverse joy of laying her over their knees. Grandma muttered under her breath, most of it inaudible. The phrase "devil child," however, was quite clear.

McKenna's face burned with anger, burned as much as her throat. She told Grandma Pencil to shut up. She was sent to her room without finishing supper. Little did anyone know, she would savor her lasagna for the next half-hour.

Misty knocked on the door. McKenna lay on her bed. Misty took a seat in the desk chair and scooted it across the carpet, to the bedside. McKenna closed her eyes as the scent of Misty's perfume filled her nose.

"Grandma Pencil hasn't had a happy life," Misty said.

"So no one else can have one, either?" McKenna's voice came out as a rasp.

"Darling, have you been feeling well?"

"So now it's *my* fault."

"You don't eat. You're very thin."

"I know. I need to be like Toby Dick, the great white whale. He's super cool, and I'm a loser."

Her mother's voice. McKenna wanted to lay here forever with her eyes closed, listening, letting Misty's words brush her, baste her, tenderize her. Arguing with Mom was the last thing McKenna wanted to do, but she needed to hear Mom's voice, so she hurled stones. Misty was a pond; her surface would suffer only the slightest ripple before returning to its smooth, natural state.

"Grandma loves all of us," Misty said. "Even Audrey. I know it's hard to see, but it's true. Sometimes what shows on the outside is the opposite of what's inside. When people act angry, they're usually hurting. Sad and hurting."

"Those are your specialties."

Got her with that stone. Misty stood without a sound and left the room. So she was human after all. And McKenna wished she could take it back.

Nothing is taken back. Nothing is erased. It piles up. Walls us in.

McKenna dragged the SledDogger (Patent no. 40457A) up the hill, trailing fifteen yards behind her father. They arrived at a thicket of trees at the edge of the cemetery. Murray unzipped and began shooting a heavy stream into the dirt. McKenna, embarrassed, unsnapped the harness (it *was* easy, the "push of a button," exactly as Murray had boasted during the demonstration). Where had Misty and Audrey gone to pee? McKenna had to go, too. Her hips ached. Salty sweat flavored her upper lip.

With a determined puff of air, like a dragon, she yanked down her jeans and panties and squatted. The splashing increased, deepened in resonance, as a puddle formed beneath her. She decided she wouldn't be embarrassed. She didn't care that she wasn't with the girls.

"You got your dad's bladder," Murray said. They'd been going for over twenty seconds, neither showing signs of slowing.

"I guess."

"You WHAT?" The hearing loss had begun.

"I GUESS."

"I could've sworn you said, 'I'm blessed.' "

"You guys pee forever," Audrey said.

She'd materialized from behind a marble block marked *ASHTON 1922–1977.*

"What do you think of Kalamazoo so far, honey?" Murray said. He was trickling now, as was McKenna.

"The people aren't very talkative."

Murray laughed. "And their name tags are waaayy oversized."

McKenna, Murray, and Audrey rejoined Misty and Toby, and they fanned out like a search party to track down Grandma Pencil. They found her kneeling on a patch of grass. There was no standing grave marker in front of her—only a rectangular bronze plaque laid into the ground.

Her eyes were closed. Her lips formed words. Following Murray's lead, the family stopped a few yards away. Nobody spoke.

The air was pasty. Above, the clouds hung like clumps of dark berries, ready to burst. Grandma Pencil's lean torso swayed in the breeze. In her dress and velvet millinery hat, she resembled a flower, a black-stemmed flower crying for its daddy.

33.

The Mapeses picnicked in Bronson Park, downtown Kalamazoo. They spread blankets between two poplars near a poop-spattered cannon honoring the local Civil War dead. Afternoon was becoming evening. The ominous clouds had migrated east, making way for clean, cottony ones. A smattering of college kids, families, and senior citizens strolled around the central fountain, which rushed with watery life. Roast beef sandwiches and pickle spears wrapped in wax paper were served by Misty. Cans of Mr. Pibb (Dr Pepper conjured bad memories) were distributed by Murray. Audrey unpacked her own special dinner: a Ziploc bag of buttons; two unopened packs of Topps NHL cards; a ball of twine; a fistful of superballs.

Out of habit, Audrey used her forearm to shield her meal from passersby, bringing her food out into the open only long enough to load it into her mouth. The family members also positioned themselves so that they formed a solid but inconspicuous barrier between Audrey and the sidewalks that traversed the park.

Every move was designed to hide Audrey's eating. They'd been hiding her for years. It was second nature now. Grandma Pencil was disgusted by any public display of sin. At home, the "bad eating" was relegated to Audrey's bedroom. At the dinner table, Audrey was forced (read: shamed) into consuming a token portion of "real food" as a way of keeping Grandma Pencil at bay.

Not that Grandma was a total Scrooge. She worked hard to be

pleasant; this was obvious in the amount and degree that her face contorted. She had cultivated a rigid tolerance toward Audrey's gustatory preferences, although she couldn't help uttering the occasional jab. Such as reminding Audrey that the ultimate consequence of her "unnatural habit" was an eternity of slow-roasting in the pits of Hell.

But Audrey was approaching twelve, approaching teenhood, and Grandma's jabs had begun to bounce off. Audrey was an avid reader of science fiction, mystery, and World War II history. She shunned the Judy Blume books. Her favorite author was Edgar Allan Poe. McKenna was proud of this. She'd read classics to Audrey for years—London, Poe, Kafka, Gilman. If they hadn't been library books, McKenna would have fed them to Audrey one page at a time after they'd been read.

Audrey didn't just read books. She could go almost anywhere, do almost anything, on her crutches. She took walks around the neighborhood, going as far as the Grand River a mile away. She rode the bus to the mall with girlfriends. She inked the names of her crushes in balloon letters on her arms. Mötley Crüe, Ratt, and Poison posters covered the walls of her room. She and her friends toilet-papered houses on Halloween. Her independence was a source of pride but also a source of anxiety for the family. She had cultivated her own tastes, her own personality, her own mind. The years of sneaking, of being called a "devil child" by her own grandmother, had made Audrey numb, even callous, toward other peoples' opinions. If she'd ever possessed a sweet nature, she was now losing it. She'd been ignored with regularity, maligned with impunity. She'd come to know her boundaries. She'd also learned that Grandma Pencil's—or anyone's—judgments couldn't hurt her any more than a bee sting. She might carry the welt for a few days, but in the end, it was little more than a nuisance.

To McKenna's dismay, Audrey was becoming a smaller, girlier version of Toby. A smarter, better-looking Toby, but still—the meanness was blooming inside her.

After Audrey's secret had come out eight years ago, Toby had gradually hijacked the role of her supplier. On grocery day, Toby was in charge of the "Audrey Budget." While Misty shopped for the family food, he and Audrey jetted off to various departments of the Meijer Thrifty Acres to gather her nourishment for the week.

McKenna was wrecked by this development. Toby was more forceful, his personality "bigger" than McKenna's. During the last few years, McKenna had been pushed aside because she didn't know how to assert herself. There was a charm to Toby's brutishness that Audrey latched onto in the same way so many girls at St. Monica's had done.

Girls liked to be pursued. They liked to be bullied into love. This fact made McKenna ashamed to be a girl.

As the family picnicked on two ratty blankets, Audrey popped a superball into her mouth. She sat crossed-legged, gazing into the branches above her head. What was she thinking? Her eyes twinkled, suggesting that a fire blazed behind them. But a fire can be used for good or for evil. The fire itself is neutral. We shouldn't forget this important point. As Audrey's head tilted back, the superball appeared under the skin of her neck, a round protuberance like an Adam's apple. For a split second, she was a boy.

The ball worked its way down her throat at a leisurely pace. It reached the base of her neck and paused between her collar bones. Then it began to rise. At the top of her neck, it stopped. Paused. The ball descended once again, to the same point. Then it climbed her neck a second time, like an elevator.

McKenna had witnessed Audrey's incredible esophageal control many times. She understood the message Audrey was sending to her now: "I know about your eating disorder."

Perhaps it had been apparent all along, to everyone. Perhaps McKenna's throat bulged, too. Presently, in fact, a masticated clump of roast beef was riding her esophageal highway. Perhaps it was obvious. More likely, though, Toby had told her. Whatever the reason, Audrey knew. And she was mocking McKenna.

An elderly man, whom no one had seen approaching from across the grass, pointed. He said in an urgent voice, "That girl is choking!"

"She's okay," Murray answered coolly, reclined on one elbow, picking his teeth with a fork. He didn't even bother detaching his gaze from the *Gazette* article he was reading.

"I don't think so!" the stranger persisted. The man wore a rumpled, oversized brown suit. His mouth showed more gaps than teeth. His white hair was parted in a meticulous, gentlemanly fashion upon his head. He was either a homeless pervert or a wealthy pharmaceuticals baron; flip a coin, you might get it right.

What was undeniable about the man was his concern for Audrey's safety. "I watched her eat buttons from that bag! She ate buttons! Craziest thing I ever saw! Now she's got a rubber ball in her throat!" His finger, trembling—from terror, from drink?—led the way as he approached Audrey.

Toby sprang to his feet. "Mind your own goddamn business," he warned.

"Sit down, Tubby," Murray said. Then, to the man (though without looking up): "You saw it wrong, mister. No one's eating buttons. It's candy. She's fine. We're all fine. Run along. Have a great evening." He made a shoo-ing gesture with his hand.

"When will this family admit that YOU ARE NOT FINE?!"

This lion's roar was Grandma Pencil, who for additional emphasis had hurled her half-full Mr. Pibb at a nearby tree.

"This girl is sick! She needs help, do you hear me?! She cannot live on pencils and Matchbox cars and Barbie dolls! She CANNOT! You laugh, you smirk. What is wrong with all of you? This is trouble! Demonic possession! You cannot deny it any more!"

"Mom. Now's not the time—"

"Now isn't the time! Now isn't the time! The time is NOW!"

Grandma Pencil struggled to stand. She took two mighty steps across the blanket and began walloping Audrey's back and shoulder blades with the heel of her hand.

This old dog had indeed learned some new tricks, courtesy of the penguins: Punishment, retribution.

To the brown-suited observer, however, and to the civilian onlookers who were now crowding the sidewalks, it likely appeared that Grandma Pencil was attempting to save Audrey's life by dislodging the object from her throat. The man stiffened in his tracks and drew in a nervous breath.

Grandma Pencil herself probably believed she was saving Audrey. After all, this is what the nuns did to every child who flirted with damnation.

Audrey wasn't like those children, though. She hadn't been cowed into submission. She wasn't going to grin and bear it. She wasn't in a classroom. Her bravado wasn't being measured by the number of spine-tinglers she could bear. And this lady had no authority over her, no uniform to show God's sanction for this corporal punishment. Grandma Pencil's arm moved so quickly that she managed to land three strikes before Audrey even knew what was happening.

Once Audrey knew, though, she didn't hesitate.

"She's beating me!" she yelled. "Help! Oh God, it hurts!"

"Yelled" is too flimsy to describe it. Audrey shredded her throat. She startled squirrels out of trees; they crashed like writhing fruit onto the grass. She shattered windshields on nearby cars. Flight patterns were disrupted. Planets were knocked out of orbit. Her voice was sonic boom, dog whistle, and exploding dishwasher all in one. And in addition to raw volume, her voice contained genuine panic. Even McKenna, who knew that it was an act, felt a surge of pity as Audrey burst into tears.

But Grandma Pencil was a boulder thundering down a hill. She had momentum. She had gravity. Her hand rose and fell another half-dozen times. The deep, fleshy *thumps* resounded, all witnessed by the gathering crowd.

Their judgment was swift and unanimous.

Boo! Roar! Outrage! Someone's got to help that innocent little fragile gumdrop marshmallow of a girl! She's on crutches, no less! Poor thing!

A take-charge middle-aged man dressed entirely in denim ventured into the shaded area where the Mapeses were picnicking. His ponytail wagged as he gently but insistently gripped Grandma Pencil by the shoulders and pulled her out of reach of Audrey, who cowered with conviction.

At the same moment, Toby lunged forward, either to get the ponytailed man off of Grandma or to get Grandma off of Audrey. He was foiled when his bare foot stepped into McKenna's uneaten roast beef sandwich. He lost his balance and tripped over the cooler.

McKenna sat, frozen, not knowing what to do—laugh silently, or laugh out loud?

Misty and Murray sat, well, frozen.

34.

Audrey began with the building she loved most. That was her way. She would never let emotion stand between her and her mouth. (At age eight, she'd swallowed four of McKenna's favorite *Star Wars* figures.) The normal rules of empathy never applied to Audrey. Not that she was a sociopath, no more than a landslide is a sociopath. She was obeying some primitive, nameless drive that we couldn't understand. An instinct. Or, if you prefer, a law of nature that the rest of us have either evolved past or haven't yet evolved to—it's not clear which, but the difference is purely semantic since it's in the eye of the beholder. And anyway, emotions had nothing to do with it.

Still, Audrey did love. She was capable of love. She did "feel." In her early years, and perhaps even throughout her life, she undoubtedly favored McKenna, and yet she hugged every one of her family members on occasion. She cried a box of Kleenex into paste when Mister T the hamster ate his last pellet (1986, when Audrey was nine). Contrary to some opinions, she wasn't dead inside—not at all. Remember, life appears in all forms on this big blue marble. Even cancer is alive.

Audrey loved a tiny restaurant called The Caboose, a one-room dive on the corner of East Main and Rambling Road, if not a stone's throw then certainly a skilled disk-golfer's throw from the Kalamazoo River. The Caboose was one of those all-night greasy spoons that served swampy coffee and soggy bacon under lights

that made every customer look like a pedophile. It was a favorite
spot for truckers and unsigned bands passing through town on
their way from Detroit to Chicago or vice versa. The bands, who'd
usually just played The Club Soda downtown, propped their
combat-booted feet on the tables. Dressed in leather and long hair
in even the hottest months, they giggled into their hands, stunk
like reefer, and paid with wadded dollar bills. The truckers, meanwhile, chewed toothpicks and stared without expression at the
black and white television mounted in the corner above the orange juice dispenser. There were also the solitary old women,
necks rubbery, eyes like empty napkin holders. They sat at the bar
and craned to sneer at whoever walked through the front door.

(Audrey ate that door fast, I'll bet. Probably ten bites. That TV,
two bites. And the bottles of ketchup—down the throat like
M&Ms. Sometimes, in spite of everything, I'm quite proud of her.)

Audrey, along with her friends—a painter and sculptor gang
from Western Michigan University—had become affectionate
about this dump because spending time at The Caboose gave
them credibility. Most of them were children of 150K-a-year parents from Detroit suburbs, but living alone in a college town on
the opposite side of the state let them pretend to be starving artists. These artists longed to touch the common man in order to
express the dimness of his soul. These artists chain-smoked,
downing pot after pot of coffee while splitting an order of fries
five ways. These artists suffered physically, hunger being a tried-
and-true method of unearthing the worms of their genius. These
artists would impale the wrigglers onto hooks that they would
then use to pierce a nose, a tongue, or, in the case of Audrey, a labia.
A tortured metaphor, to be sure. But lest we forget, these were
"creative types."

None of Audrey's college freshmen pals knew about her secret
diet—the heaping helpings of Corningware, the bowls of hair-
clips, the twelve-packs of ankle socks, and the doughy slabs of poster
putty that got her through each day. Perhaps these bohemians

wouldn't have minded at all. They might have even urged Audrey into performance art or into a Battle Royale against Herr Essenalles.

Or maybe they would've done what her family did. Sought help. And when that failed, maybe they would have hidden her secret, would have internalized the shame Audrey should have felt for her unnerving, freakish tendencies. The burden of this secret, and Audrey's unwillingness to feel guilt for it, might have led them to resent her. Maybe each of her friends, then, in their most private moments, would have given serious thought to what it was, exactly, that had made them like her in the first place.

35.

The news footage is quite famous now. If one is to believe what bank tellers say in breakrooms, it has become a ubiquitous presence in Psychology, English, Sociology, Media Studies, and Communication courses in universities across the country. An amazing phenomenon when you consider that neither Audrey, nor her feat, actually appear on screen. Still, it's worth recounting here. For grins. I know it makes me grin.

WKZO Channel Three, the local CBS affiliate, broke the story on October 19, 1995. The medium shot is of Judy Holland, a woman heavy with mascara and rouge and crowned by an impressive dome of blond hair. She stands in front of The Caboose at approximately twenty yards' distance. The sky is grayish-white, showing no sign of the sun. The day is blustery, evidenced by Judy's occasional wince as the wind assaults her face. Judy holds a slender (the girth of a hot dog) microphone in her right hand, positioned so its tip is just below her chin. Her left hand is pressed against the side of her head, presumably to put a finger into her ear. She is broadcasting a live feed to desk anchor James Riley. James is a round-faced man in his early fifties, with square, rimless glasses and thinning hair. He looks relaxed and moderately handsome in his conservative blue suit and yellow tie. His right forearm rests on the desk. A confident, almost cocky gleam lights his turquoise eyes. The screen is split—left half James, right half Judy.

"What's going on there, Judy?"

"James, I'm here at The Caboose, a diner that has been a fixture in Kalamazoo for over twenty years. As you can see, there's a crowd gathered behind me. According to the owners, these folks were in the middle of eating their breakfasts about four hours ago when a young woman walked inside the restaurant, and without even waiting to be seated, started to eat one of the chairs."

"Judy, I need to check my earpiece. Did you say *eat* one of the chairs?"

"Yes, Jim. I talked to one gentleman who was enjoying a pancake stack with no butter at a nearby table, and he described hearing a loud breaking sound. He looked to his right to see this young woman with the wooden chair leg *protruding from her mouth*. He said it took *less than five seconds* for her to swallow it. 'Like she was eating a carrot,' he said. Jim, I've talked with a few other people who confirm that the woman consumed the entire chair."

"What kind of chair are we talking about, Judy? A toy chair, like a dollhouse thing?"

"No, James. A regulation-sized chair, like you have at your dinner table. Solid wood, most likely some kind of tree-based wood. Put it this way, The Caboose has never replaced their original chairs, so we're talking about an actual adult table chair. The young woman went on to eat the napkin holders, the carafes, the upholstered booths . . ."

"Judy, is this some kind of college prank? Fake props, that sort of thing?"

"Jim, that's what the owners originally thought, but to hear the eyewitness testimony, this would've had to be a very professional, very well-funded hoax. People we talked to described 'ferocious teeth,' 'mouthfuls of glass and metal,' and a 'blankness in her eyes that chilled the blood.' Until proven otherwise, the authorities are operating under the assumption that the woman is literally *eating* The Caboose. As a precaution, the building has been evacuated, and police have cordoned off the perimeter to keep new patrons away. Now, we can't tell you exactly what is going on inside, but if you listen—I don't know if you can hear this—there is a definite sound that I would describe as gnawing or chewing. If you can imagine someone munching a bowl of Grape Nuts or stale potato chips right beside your ear. It's sort of like that. I don't know if that's coming through or not . . ."

"There *is* a grinding in the background, Judy . . ."

"We can definitely hear it out here in the parking lot. It's been a constant background noise since our crew arrived. So again, without visual confirmation, police are operating under the assumption that the woman is still inside and is genuinely eating the restaurant."

"Well, at least she's being genuine."

"What's that, Jim?"

"Judy, what are the police doing? Do they have a plan?"

"Jim, they've decided to wait it out. I spoke with their captain, and his rationale is that the woman isn't hurting anyone, except possibly herself by ingesting some sharp or corroded metals, but that if she is bound and determined to eat a few chairs and salt shakers, then they'll go ahead and let her do what she needs to do until she gets full and incapacitated, at which time they will arrest her for destruction of private property."

"Judy, are the owners okay with that strategy? They can't be happy that their restaurant is being eaten, can they?"

"Surprisingly, Jim, they're fine with it. I spoke with Claire and Bart Cooper, and they told me that this was the most attention their restaurant has gotten in twenty-three years. Bart told me, in fact, that they were already considering using this incident in future promotions—something along the lines of 'The restaurant so good, you'll want to eat the furniture.'"

36.

Audrey was arrested, but not until the The Caboose was gone—flooring, windows, booths, chairs, tables, toilets, sinks, meat slicer, conventional oven, cash register, walk-in freezer, microwave oven, orange juice dispenser, gumball machine, newspaper dispenser, walls, ceiling—even the fiberglass sign above the front door. It took thirty-two hours. In your face, Essenalles! She was taken away in handcuffs. She didn't resist.

The cops had counted on Audrey getting full, exhausted, or dead before she ate the whole thing. Containment was their plan, which, if you think about it, isn't really a plan (unless you count "not dying" as a plan for living; if so, good luck to you).

Twelve officers had waited. Eagerly at first. Then patiently. Then irritatedly. Then apathetically. And finally, exhaustedly.

All the while, nothing happened. Birds chirped. Traffic rolled past. The wind carried the stink of the peppermint plant from upriver. The cops kept listening to that chewing noise emanating from the building. The unrelenting drone. It lulled them. It hypnotized them. Whenever one of them peeked into a window, they thought they saw a figure, indistinct, squatting on the floor, hunched, hands pressed to mouth, jaw working. Or maybe it was only a pile of boxes. They'd been up all night. The lighting was bad. The cops knew—had been told, anyway—that the woman was unarmed, so they just hung back and made sure she didn't do anything like cause a fire or flip them the bird.

Most of the curious civilians (whose number peaked at forty-eight near dusk on the first day) only lasted a few hours. A few diehards hung on, camping out in sleeping bags in the parking lot. But with nothing to see, with only a grinding sound and some hearsay and speculation to fuel their curiosity, these folks went home to feed their cats before the second evening fell.

Only two uniformed KPD officers were on hand at 3:30 a.m. when Audrey Mapes finished.

Afterward, the *Kalamazoo Gazette* and local television news were abuzz with "The Incredible Eating Girl" for about two weeks, while she was detained for her hearing. But other than a handful of eyewitness testimonies, there was no documentation of the event, so people soon chalked it up to a stunt. Theories ranged from an ingenious Caboose promotional strategy to a performance piece for a university art class—a protest of animal slaughter, or perhaps some kind of elaborate statement for workers' rights. The common denominator among the theories was the firm belief that this girl had not acted alone and that she certainly hadn't eaten what they said she'd eaten. To quote twenty-year-old J. D. Poke, editorial writer for the *Western Herald* (Western Michigan University's newspaper)—this part of the story was "a load of ca-ca."

"I'm going to shut down the folks who believe the myth. There's no way a human tooth can penetrate steel," Poke continues, feeding the reader a logic sandwich with sarcasm spread. "Simple as that. Try it sometime and let me know how it goes!"

How could any Kalamazooan resist such pithy wisdom? The issue was solved. The girl and her fraud were forgotten.

37.

After the incident, Audrey is detained in jail. Her father is called, collect. Jab to the old guy. An attorney is appointed by the courts because Audrey can't afford one. Bond is set at only $5,000 but is not posted. Jab to Audrey.

She spends two weeks in a holding cell while waiting to enter a guilty plea for reckless destruction of property and creating a public disturbance. During Audrey's confinement, McKenna takes a Greyhound to Kalamazoo every other day. Sometimes Audrey comes out to talk to her. Usually, she doesn't.

One day, she does. Tapping her sandal nervously on the concrete floor in the visitation room, McKenna asks Audrey why she doesn't chew her way out and come home. "I've got the getaway bus and everything," she says.

Audrey flashes a crooked smile. Her smiles are maps of Tunisia— jagged, desolate. "I eat myself *into* situations," she says. "Not out of them. Situations are more fun."

"Yes," McKenna says, nodding like she always does for Audrey, eager to please. "Because what's the alternative, right?"

"I'm looking at it," Audrey answers. The gum in her mouth is being murdered.

McKenna blurts it out: "You shouldn't have eaten that restaurant." She feels the ground buzzing beneath her feet. It's what she's wanted to say every time she's visited. It's what she has rehearsed a hundred times. Still, her voice shakes. "Now people *know*, Audrey. What are we going to do?"

Audrey stares. Her eyes strip McKenna naked. This isn't love. There's risk in love. Audrey's malignance risks nothing, puts nothing at stake, exposes none of her own vulnerabilities. Her stare is pure and purposeless, like the desert sun, like cappuccino foam. Hot, frothy disdain. No room for salvation.

McKenna is unable to move. In the windowless room, the air is tropical. McKenna feels comforted that the security guard, an arm's length away, could withdraw his nightstick and swat Audrey if she decides to lunge across the table and bite off McKenna's head.

But Audrey wouldn't do that to her own sister, would she?

Would she?

The cop gnaws his thumbnail. Looks at it. Bites it in the same spot. Looks at it. Bites it again. The idle smirk under his moustache says he's damn amused to be the guy—*the guy!*—who gets to stand guard over Kalamazoo's biggest, dishiest news story in decades. Tonight, his buddies and their wives will gather around the electronic dartboard, stuffing their faces with jalapeno poppers, and ask him: What's it *like*, man, what the hell is *she* like? Do you think she really *did it*? What's her problem, man, is she a psycho? How did she fake it, cuz she couldn't have actually *done* that, could she? And is it true she doesn't have any feet? That's fucking weird, but who gives a shit, right? She doesn't need feet does she, she sure is *hot*, man, she can eat me *anytime*!

At Audrey's arraignment, the bombshell:

The Caboose owners drop all charges. They've gotten so much free publicity! They were even mentioned in Jay Leno's opening monologue on *The Tonight Show*! And besides, the insurance is covering all the damages and then some, with enough to install a modern kitchen and hands-free faucets in the bathrooms.

"Your Honor," Bart Cooper tells the judge, "We can't in good conscience punish the girl who brought us this bounty. She is like a forest fire whose hellish destruction is an ugly but necessary purification to allow precious new fauna to spring forth from the earth."

His Honor accepts their wishes but wants to know one thing before Audrey is dismissed: "How, my dear, did you do it?"

She doesn't react to the demeaning "my dear," except for a barely perceptible clenching of her jaw. (Brave girl, spineless girl—you decide.)

Audrey's response, channeling the soothing, emotionless tone of KITT, the *Knight Rider* car: "I chewed and swallowed, Your Honor."

The judge gazes onto the sea—nay, the ocean—of chuckling faces in the courtroom. Out there, adrift, suffering from seasickness, sit Murray, Toby, and McKenna. The color of snow, all of them. They don't understand the outside world. They want to be safe at home, far away, behind closed doors.

The judge turns to Audrey: "If you won't divulge *how* you did it, will you please tell the court *why* you did it?"

Audrey: "I heard it was a good place to eat."

Amid the uproarious laughter, a psychiatric evaluation is ordered.

38.

Audrey doesn't pass. But she doesn't fail, either. Psychiatric tests, it turns out, have something in common with our great American pastime: A tie goes to the runner. This means . . . she passes!

Audrey is unbound, unmuzzled, uncaged again. She returns to Grand Rapids, to The Cave (as she calls the house on Moriarty Street), to her family.

Things are different now, though. It's not her choice to return. She has compromised her college career, has killed the flower of higher education before even a bud broke through the soil. Murray "won't waste another goddamn dime" on her tuition. He yanks her from her classes.

Trust is a vase. It slips through the fingers. You regret it the moment it leaves your grip, in that breath of time before it explodes on the linoleum. Careful where you step. Use a broom. Wear shoes.

Toby and McKenna are twenty-three years old. Toby is a humorless, thick-armed, thick-necked stallion who works full time for Fast Way Moving and Storage. Each morning, he drags his hungover slab of a self out of bed, performs seventy-five pushups and one-hundred sit-ups on the carpet, then drives to McDonald's and inhales three Egg McMuffins, one order of McGriddles and Sausage, and two orders of hash browns. Washes it down with a Supersized Coke.

He and Murray have teamed up to construct a wooden privacy

fence in the backyard. Other than that, Toby has accomplished nothing in his life. Oh, yes, more body density. Bigger arms. A membership to Gold's Gym. A steady stream of girlfriends who believe strongly in halter tops and are skilled at popping back pimples and waxing body hair.

McKenna is a full-time student at Aquinas College, in her fifth year, studying English and Religion. Her sense of humor, she tries to convince herself, remains intact, although now it's like the world's largest spider—the wolf spider, which peeks out of its cozy hole only when provoked, and then, bites. She has a 3.8 GPA and is trying to believe in God. One night a week, she attends catechism class. Her conversion has begun. If only her breath didn't stink so badly, she might have friends. Or a date. But she doesn't socialize much with other students. Sometimes a study group or a passing chat before class. That's all. She reads novels. The characters are a form of company.

Misty wears her yellow spring dress every day. Her eyelids are sewn closed, the long sleep she always wanted. Her hands are folded atop her breast. Her cheeks are packed with sawdust. For five years, she has lived in a wooden box in the earth. McKenna thinks of her every day.

"She's at peace," says Grandma Pencil, licking an envelope and passing it across the table. "At rest."

McKenna inkstamps St. Monica's address onto the top left corner of the envelope. She gasps in surprise: "You mean my mom?"

Grandma clucks her fat tongue before thrusting it out of her mouth and lubricating another gummy strip. "There's that cynicism again," she says, sealing the envelope. "That was not a feature of my generation."

She calls it cynicism. McKenna knows it's the wolf spider. "I'm just giving you a hard time, Grams," she says. She stamps another envelope, another invitation to Sister Maximillian's "heavenly reception."

Sister Max passed away in her sleep ten days ago, and now, according to Grandma, she is "at peace." It never fails to impress McKenna that Grandma knows such things. She really does *know*. Somehow. After all, that's how faith works: Somehow.

But even considering Grandma's admirable belief, there are questions.

To be "at rest"—is this really our ultimate goal?

Congrats, Sister Max! You DID IT! You're RESTING!

And by the way, Misty? You failed.

McKenna has asked Grandma Pencil many questions. These days, she enjoys a surfeit of opportunities to push Grandma's buttons, all ostensibly in service of McKenna's curiosity about Catholicism. She loves to watch Grandma squirm, loves to make her squinch her lips in rage, sip her tea before it's cooled. After all, McKenna lives in Grandma Pencil's thoroughly unmodern two-bedroom house. It's a 1,200-square-foot two-story just down the hill from Murray and Toby.

McKenna moved in five years ago, soon after Misty OD'd on a combination of antidepressants and gin.

Misty's death. Imagine a woman walking down the street. Now imagine the skeleton vanishing from her body. The remaining skin, muscle, fat, cartilage, and arteries—once bound together and given direction and purpose by the bones—plunge to the concrete in a thunderous *sploop*, leaving a dense blob that can twitch but not really move. That's what McKenna's life turned into when her mother died.

McKenna couldn't have seen this coming, this squishy dead weight of daily existence. In her heart, in fact, she thought her life had been like this all along. Spongy. Flat.

She didn't realize she had a mother until she didn't have a mother.

It's a common mistake. It's why we want to see ghosts. It's why we dream.

Now imagine that woman again, walking down the street, skeleton intact. Imagine her flesh and muscle disappearing, leaving only the bones. That's McKenna. She's a sight. Ninety-four pounds. Sunken eyes that bob in her skull. Veins in her temples that love the daylight. She wears baggy clothes to hide her body, although honestly, if she wanted to wear non-baggy clothes, she'd have to shop for an eleven-year-old. She's twenty-three. She's not anorexic. She knows she looks awful, but she can't stop. She has tried stealing Toby's high-calorie shakes. But liquid doesn't do it. She needs to chew. Can't chewing be enough?

Murray's hair has gone white. A full beard, also white, touches the top button of his work shirt. The hearing in his right ear is effectively gone; he wears an aid. His hands are still strong, but they're stony and cold to the touch. He's forty-three.

He has given up inventing. There was no grand proclamation. One day, he simply cleared out the basement, hauling armfuls of scrap metal and wood, assorted scales, tubes, and sawhorses, stacks of *Popular Mechanics* and *Inventors Digest*, to the curb. He even set the inventions themselves out there, for anyone to take. All of his tools, except what fit inside one small toolbox, were sold through the classifieds for a total of $1,100.

To Murray's credit, he has tried to connect with his children since Misty's death. The living room television, upgraded to a 16" color set, glows around the clock. He ponied up for basic cable. This gives him football, basketball, hockey, bowling—anything that might provide a bonding moment (with Toby). Not that Toby has much time to hang. He's got a life. Murray has learned to cook asparagus and spaghetti, although he still relies mostly on Burger King and frozen dinners, and he mostly eats alone. You see, the twins aren't children anymore. An old tree can't reattach the apple that's been dropped, bagged, cored, and baked into a pie.

And his baby girl isn't a baby girl anymore. Audrey is a 5'6", 132-pound adult woman who wears a C-cup, menstruates heavily for three days a month (spotting for two more), has had sex with three different young men, is getting ready to leave for college, and can't wait until next year, 1996, so she can vote for Bill Clinton.

Audrey knows she was never really a baby girl to Murray anyway, never a daughter. To him, Audrey was only two stumps on the end of a tulip. Her deformity, the mechanical conundrum, was all he saw. She stood as a living question mark to the quality of his genetic material. She was The Horrific, The Real, The Heartbeat of the Beast. She terrified him.

McKenna has mentioned these ideas to Audrey on a few occasions. McKenna provided evidence: For all of Audrey's life, Murray scampered down to his dungeon whenever his nose detected strawberry shampoo in the air.

"Saintly in his patience . . . Murray's passion and love provided more than soda pop cans to stand upon. He gave spiritual footing to the footless girl of his dreams."

"A genteel blue-collar man—a truly Thoreauvian figure who only longed to fulfill the American Dream but whose demanding family choked each of his aspirations until they died."

Let's not give the authors of these quotes any free publicity by mentioning any names, nor the titles of their books.

Let's just say that what most imbeciles have written about Murray Mapes isn't true.

Even the non-imbeciles could never get it right.

Makes you wonder why people write anything at all.

39.

Audrey's homecoming from the Kalamazoo detention center, the return from her aborted first year of university education, was not joyous. Even with Grandma Pencil officially banished, the Moriarty house was repellent to her.

So after six months in her unhappy home, Audrey did what any nineteen-year-old would have done in her situation: She joined the most famous traveling freak show in the country.

Lollapalooza. The alternative music festival had exploded onto the national scene four years earlier and had become a well-oiled (and well-greased) machine—the nation's most popular touring rock, rap, and punk-vaganza. A blowout of tunes for goons coming soon to a town near you. Slop-happy dirters like Dinosaur Jr., Babes in Toyland, and the Butthole Surfers rocking their wormy psychedelic chili. Fishbone, Primus, and the Red Hot Chili Peppers spewing funk onto the mud-coiffed masses. Ice Cube, Ice-T with Body Count, and Arrested Development kicking it with their verbologic mythic. Massive crowds of nineteen-year-olds dropping acid, smoking reefer, and looking for someone to sweat on. Side stages with the likes of Vulgar Boatmen and Moister Nipples. There were other attractions: jungle gyms; open-mike poetry readings; shallow pits where for five dollars you could whack a television with a sledgehammer; booths where a bald meathead tattooed a Celtic design around your bicep while you breathed pure oxygen for a dollar a minute before getting your

eyebrow pierced. Sucks to your commercial sponsors and manu-
factured boy bands! Lollapalooza was the youth culture of *now*,
where the kids could rock to non-radio bands!

It also had the Jim Rose Circus Sideshow.

Jim Rose telephoned Audrey personally. Before she even hung
up the phone, she was mentally packed and heading out the door.

The audience didn't know what to expect when Audrey took
the stage. Dressed in non-ripped jeans and a comfortable sweater,
she looked like a pretty co-ed. A trim, shapely figure. Someone a
guy might turn his head for, but no more than that. Mostly, she
looked too *nice* to be there. Not *this* show. This girl couldn't follow
Matt "The Tube" Crowley or Bebe the Circus Queen. This girl's
arms weren't black with tattoos. This girl's ears, lips, nose, and
eyebrows weren't disfigured by hoops and studs. (Alas, only her
labia.)

Visually, the only thing that made her a freak was her under-
arm crutches. And then, upon careful inspection, her lack of feet.
Most people, though, didn't examine her so closely. When Audrey
maneuvered onto that 10'×10' stage under the daylight glow of
that bright yellow tent, no one felt a sense of danger. Not a single
dreadlock-sporting slacker thought he might upchuck from this
act—not like when The Amazing Mister Lifto hoisted a beer keg
with his nipples!

This becrutched girl was an Alpha Delta Pi, for crap's sake.
Pre-faded Gap jeans? Conditioned, wavy blond hair? Lipstick?
Blush? Tasteful eyeliner? A friendly smile? Who *was* this impos-
ter? Was this some kind of *joke*? Murmurs arose from the audience.

At center stage, Audrey mounted the stool. She squeezed her
crutches between her knees.

From the crowd came snickers. Whistles and catcalls. A lone
request to "Take off your shirt!"

At this point, Audrey would lift one of her crutches—titanium-
aluminum alloy—and devour it.

It's easy to write, "She ate her crutch." But witnessing this act, live, was another story.

Her eyes were stones. With two hands, she positioned the crutch like a giant hoagie, the narrow end pointed toward her mouth. She bit. Then came the backfire of snapping metal, loud as a rifle. Two or three rapid chews and swallows, and she was onto the next bite. Again the violent report, followed by emotionless, machine-like crunching.

A little-known fact: Metal sings when it's pulverized by teeth. The stress—the bending, the flattening, the tearing—emanates an eerie, sonorous wave. High-pitched and steady, like the ringing of a triangle. But this tone isn't warm. It's an atonal mish-mash, a sickening blend, like an entire scale struck simultaneously on a piano. The varying lengths and densities of the metal fragments create this otherworldly groan while Audrey's mouth attacks. She looks like a starving rodent—a rat or a beaver—gnawing for its life. Her spittle, like holy water, showers the crowd. Her chest heaves. She pants. Her throat swells until the skin is taut as a balloon—tension, oh man, is it going to pop?—and then it shrinks. Again, it swells. And shrinks. Low grunts and arrhythmic nasal breathing. This savage, strangely erotic scene lasts eight seconds. Then she is finished.

Mayhem. Gasps. Vomiting. Fainting spells. Ecstatic howls. Primal thunder shakes the tent.

Within a month, Audrey's carefully planned fifteen-minute act, during which she consumes two crutches, four saxophones, five effects pedals, an electric guitar, and, as a finale, a drum set, turns into an unscripted challenge: Bring something The Amazing Audrey *can't* eat, and you'll be jamming with Sonic Youth on the main stage tonight!

It was an all-request free-for-all. Audience members offered patio bricks, baseball bats, hypodermic needles, the leather jackets off their backs, full bottles of Bordeaux or Jack Daniels (for reasons unknown to this day, the alcohol didn't affect her), crowbars, tubes of wasabi, radial tires, fish tanks, thermometers, razor blades, oak end tables, and so on.

She never hesitated, not even for dramatic effect, as Jim Rose often counseled her to do. She didn't pretend that an object frightened her, didn't feign worry that it would never fit in her stomach, that it might—no, no, NO—kill her! Audrey was no showman. She was a hungry, violent, pissed-off young lady who mutilated everything in her path with her gorgeous chompers. Without flair, without flourish, without sentiment.

Day after day, show after show, the crowds went berserk. These were disenfranchised youth of America—bored suburbanites with no war to protest and no repressive economy to repress them. Freedom had become the oppressive force. Freedom meant skateboarding headfirst into trashcans. Drinking forties and watching syndicated episodes of *Small Wonder* as the sun came up. Stealing hubcaps off police cars. Sucking down balloons of nitrous oxide. Freedom was excess, and these kids turned their hatred of freedom toward anything with flourish—extended guitar solos, hairsprayed bangs, sports cars. They flushed wads of flair down the toilet and giggled when it backed up the sewage lines. Their hearts were full of anarchy, and their bank accounts were full of cash.

But their nihilism was cautious. They wanted, above anything else, to see how fucked up *you* could get, so *they* could seem fucked up by proxy. When they described to their pals, over a bong of chronic, how they'd actually *been there*, how they'd stood ten feet from the stage and watched it all without flinching, how they'd even *cracked up* because this one dude was white as a sheet, how they couldn't believe how crazy it all was, *that shit was out of hand*—when they narrated this scene in all its gory detail, *they* became kings for a day.

This isn't news, though.

Nothing this generation did, thought about, laughed at, loved, hated, or rented was worthwhile or original.

Being messed-up to impress people is a primal urge. Think elementary school. Picking up the worm to gross out the girl. Eating it to win her heart. Plenty of schoolboys ate worms for Audrey.

Nobody ate a worm for McKenna.

But the worm-eaters made Audrey a small fortune.

40.

Back to 1988. We last left our motley crew in Bronson Park during a heavily-trafficked dinner hour. Eleven-year-old Audrey was enduring a spirited beating from Grandma Pencil while a gaggle of outraged Kalamazooans looked on. A ponytailed white man with a paunch like a sack of kitty litter earned himself a few hundred Good Samaritan points and a round of ravenous applause by stepping in to stop the abuse.

Then it was up to the Mapes family to regroup and collect what dignity they still possessed. Gradually the crowd dispersed, shaming Grandma with sidelong glares. The picnic was over. Misty repacked the basket, and the family headed toward the walking mall. Audrey and Toby trailed fifty feet behind, Audrey crutching herself and Toby leaning down every thirty seconds to whisper into her ear. They laughed conspiratorially. When the rest of the family stopped for a traffic light, Audrey and Toby hung back until the signal said *WALK*.

Grandma Pencil hadn't spoken a word since she'd been pulled off of Audrey by a stranger. Her nostrils flared. One side of her hair looked like a snowdrift, while the other would've made a nice home for a family of robins. The sour pleasure in her eyes suggested she was running through a detailed scenario of torturing Audrey, or the ponytailed man, or both.

Murray scuffled along the sidewalk in his sandals, pointing at every building, giving a running commentary: "The library? Yep.

Looks like a lot of books in there. Pastries and baked goods? Makes more sense than baked bads, I guess. Wonder how much they charge for a muffin. Is it me, or does this town have a ton of crazy people? One, two, three . . . maybe not that guy. Hi, how you doing? No, he's drunk. Hey, look. That's where they print the newspaper." And so on.

Why, Misty? Why wouldn't you talk to your mom? Why were you incapable of confronting her? Why couldn't you defend your youngest daughter?

Instead, Misty grabbed Murray's hand. She rested her head on his shoulder. McKenna sled-dogged luggage behind them. The one thing that made sense to McKenna was her parents' love for one another. They were best friends. They respected each other. They rarely had a disagreement, and when they did, they worked it out.

In other words, parents who modeled a healthy relationship and provided a modest but stable income—all the basic necessities. So why did day-to-day Mapeshood feel so frayed, so tenuous? Sure, Murray's hobby stole him away for long periods. And sure, he never tried to include them in his inventions. And sure, Misty was prone to bouts of emotional paralysis and sullen daydreaming. But who isn't?

As the Mapeses meandered up South Street, McKenna knew, quite suddenly, the reason for the family's unhappiness.

And as soon as she envisioned it in her mind, there it was in the flesh, ambling up beside her on the sidewalk. The odd person out. Grandma Pencil.

It seemed so obvious now. Grandma hadn't been bad when they were kids, but since she'd gotten close with the nuns, she had changed. Along with her strengthened faith had come a sense of entitlement. Grandma simply couldn't let Audrey be—she was determined to make the poor girl suffer for what she perceived as the "sin" of her diet. Never mind that Audrey had no choice.

Never mind that it did no harm to Grandma if Audrey lunched on a bag of charcoal.

These things didn't matter because Grandma knew the "rules." The body was a temple, and to befoul this temple was to spit in God's face.

Which made sense, really. Deep down, McKenna agreed that there was something unseemly, something so unnatural as to approach deviance, in Audrey's appetite. Sometimes at night, when McKenna was sinking into sleep, she swore she could feel the soft weight of baby Audrey upon her breast, could sense that abyssal mouth yawning toward her.

McKenna had stood there, motionless, while Grandma's hand fell, again and again, upon Audrey's spine. She hadn't rushed in to knock Grandma away. She hadn't screamed at Grandma to leave her sister alone.

In that moment, mixed with embarrassment and anger there had been giddiness and satisfaction.

In that moment, she'd felt joy rushing to the surface like a black-eyed Great White.

A voice whispered amid the spray of water and blood, "Give it to her. Give it to her. Take that. Take that."

41.

Remember what Henri Rousseau said about beauty?

"To see something as beautiful is to see in it the promise of happiness."

Very few people saw Kalamazoo as a beautiful place.

Statistics tell part of the story. In 1997, at the time its devouring began, the city itself, located along Interstate 94 in southwest. Michigan, midway between Chicago and Detroit, boasted an estimated population of seventy-five to eighty thousand. This number had remained relatively unchanged for forty years. The metro area took up twenty-five square miles. Some 31,000 housing units existed within city limits. Racially, 70 percent of the citizens were white, 20 percent black, 4 percent Hispanic or Latino; 3 percent were of mixed racial backgrounds, 2 percent Asian, 2 percent "other," and less than 1 percent Native American. The median income was thirty thousand dollars a year. For every ten females, there were nine males. The average household held 2.3 members; the average family consisted of three.

This information tells one kind of story. There are other stories.

The inside of a clam would be an apt way to describe Kalamazoo in 1997. Damp, raw, cold. Contact leaves a sticky residue on the skin. Entering this rumpled burg from either I-94 or US 131, visitors were overcome by bafflement: Where's the city?

The sky was a gray blanket on most days. On other days, gangs of muscular clouds taunted the residents who scurried, insect-like, below. In autumn and winter, trees stood naked, as they do in all northern climes, but here, the maples and cedars actually shivered. Black shadows stretched like bony fingers across the snow. Soon, the winter whiteness became slush. Cars sizzled along streets, their undercarriages rotting from salt. Goop the color of an unwashed nickel clung to the soles of office women who scurried from the parking ramp to the City Hall. Once inside the foyer, they stomped their boots on the rolled-out red carpet, which was already as saturated as a burst artery. They chain-smoked Benson and Hedges Ultra Lights and discussed accumulation, lake effect, and Doppler radar. In thick, morning voices, they bemoaned the fact that City Hall never closed, not even when Kalamazoo Public Schools declared a snow day.

All of these women, and in fact nearly everyone who worked downtown, was born and raised here—here, or in one of the outlying towns and villages: Portage; Paw Paw (the town so nice they named it twice); Lawton; Parchment; Comstock; Galesburg.

None of these lifers loved Kalamazoo. Unless you count the kind of love we feel toward the moon—a dependable, steady presence that smiles upon us when we fall asleep. Sometimes it's merely a sliver, but it's always there. Not necessarily something we *think* about, but it's not going anywhere. Yes, they loved Kalamazoo in this way. And when uninformed out-of-towners cast aspersions, they defended it like wolves.

While no romantic love was felt toward the city, its citizens were a sturdy brood, and down to the last, each credited Kalamazoo for making them this way. When temperatures plunged below zero, when cheeks were cut by the wind, they bore it with grim dignity. Their unsentimentality was born of cheerless, six-month winters with less than a week of sunshine. The city maintained a handful of rich folks, but wealthy ones were scarce. And that's the way the Kalamazooans wanted it. Sure, they played the Lotto every week, dreamed of owning four or five pickups, of being high-rollers in Vegas, but in day-to-day life, they happily joined softball leagues and bowling teams. They grilled brats and burgers in public parks. Coached third-grade soccer. Enjoyed a nice fritter with their morning coffee. Thought "Why the hell not?" when someone built another sprawling apartment complex on a wooded lot. These folks had a sense of humor that shattered windows. Their peculiar brand of ossification spoke of flooded basements, chemical inhalants, and dead batteries.

And all of this was mixed with a degree of cultural sophistication. There was a strong love of the theater. Local productions were well-attended and enthusiastically applauded. Twice a year, a modern dance troupe squatted and bent its way into peoples' hearts. Bell's Brewery and Restaurant offered heady ales and syncopatic jazz quartets. There was Western Michigan University, a four-year public research institution. Kalamazoo College, the liberal arts school, was perpetually listed on America's "Top 100 Little Colleges You've Never Heard Of (Unless You're Looking for Colleges You've Never Heard Of, In Which Case You've Definitely Heard of It, Which Is Saying a Lot)." A few downtown breakfast joints tucked feta cheese and gyro meat into their omelets.

Kalamazoo had a storied history. Gibson Guitars began there. Then it moved away. Checker Motors, makers of the Checker Cab, originated there. Long gone. Kalamazoo Stoves produced high-quality stoves. The Shakespeare Company provided fishing rods and reels. Parchment got its name because parchment was made there. Was.

Nicknames, too, came and went with the industries. Once-flourishing paper mills and cardboard mills earned Kalamazoo the title, "Paper City." Juicy stalks growing abundantly on outlying farms: "Celery City." The nation's first pedestrian walking mall, in 1959: "Mall City."

In this sense, Kalamazoo was, in the best possible way, like a used tea bag. It had become a soggy, leaden thing. A few squeezes might produce a final spurt or two of usefulness, but really, who was going to bother?

And yet, you could tell that it had once served a purpose. It had once been meaningful and therefore continued to have meaning. It had once been beautiful and therefore continued to be beautiful. It had once been loved and therefore continued to be loved. Kalamazooans loved their beautiful, meaningful tea bag, and what, exactly, is wrong with that?

42.

Audrey's public thrashing was the first strike in a long, ugly war.

Grandma Pencil probably didn't anticipate any retaliation from Audrey, but McKenna did. She knew her sister. After Bronson Park, everything changed.

A feeling of dread moved into McKenna's gut, bringing all of its clothing, trinkets, bedding, and toiletries. Dread had settled in to stay.

On that fading day in 1988, the family wandered the downtown as three separate groups: Misty and Murray; McKenna and Grandma Pencil; Toby and Audrey. The arrangement fell into place without discussion or planning. It felt natural.

Grandma Pencil linked arms with McKenna. She pointed at the Walgreen's pharmacy that had been on the mall since 1942. "Momma worked there for a few months, believe it or not, after the war." She ooh-ed and ahh-ed at the State Theater's "exciting new marquee" but expressed disappointment that Sinbad was a comedian and not a stage production about a swashbuckler. Grandma grabbed McKenna's arm as they crossed the street. She let out a gasp. "You need to take vitamins," she said. "A teenager needs meat on her bones. How can you even drag that suitcase?"

It was an old story. It was the eight-hundredth time she'd commented on McKenna's weight. But on this day, her voice sounded sweet rather than scolding. She seemed concerned. She touched McKenna's cheek, brushed off a piece of dirt.

"Muscles are overrated," McKenna answered quietly. "There are other ways to get things done."

Grandma Pencil considered this, her eyes flashing with admiration. She appraised McKenna with a long, significant stare, as if daring her to look away. "You're more right than you know." Her body was warm and alive against McKenna's shoulder.

At that moment, McKenna knew that Grandma would never let her go.

The war didn't start right away. Back in Grand Rapids, the routines returned. On the surface, life went back to normal. Murray sank into the basement like a donkey into quicksand. Misty reaffixed her sad smile and boned up on her solitaire skills at the dining room table. Because it was summer vacation, Grandma Pencil was unable to put the "hel" into "helping" at St. Monica's and had taken to assisting the nuns at the convent: plucking weeds; mowing grass; sipping tea; chatting. Domestic duties. She invited Sister P.V. and Sister Maximillian for beef tongue and scalloped potatoes on Sunday afternoons. Toby had been hired for part-time bagging work at nearby Vogel's Grocery, while McKenna continued the paper route she'd started when she was eleven. She was sixteen now.

"You're the oldest paperboy in Michigan," Audrey laughed. "What do you win for that?"

Her tone was an uncanny echo of Toby's, but Audrey's were far more cerebral jabs.

She lay lengthwise on the couch with a throw pillow beneath her head, sipping WD-40 through a straw and watching TV. Her leg stumps were crossed at the calves atop the sofa arm. Ringlets of yellow hair spilled over the edge of the couch, almost touching the carpet. Her teeth and gums were black—a bottomless pit in the center of a glacier-white face. Her rabbit eyes appraised a *Pee-Wee's Playhouse* episode without emotion. Above her right eyebrow, a painful-looking pimple marred an otherwise spotless face. Poor girl.

McKenna kicked her sneakers into the corner. She was sweaty, and her legs ached from walking. The Kalamazoo vacation had forced her to take three days off, and her substitute had done a lousy job. She'd had to listen to eight different customer complaints this afternoon. She ducked out of the press carrier bag and shed it like a pile of skin. "Grandma will kill you if she sees you with that," she said, nodding at the can of motor oil.

"Yep," Audrey answered. "And while she kills me, you'll stand there with your finger up your butt."

Her jabs weren't always cerebral.

The Kalamazoo beating was still a fresh wound. Since they'd returned home, McKenna had been mulling over and practicing the phrases she intended to say in her defense. Now, she could remember none of them. She blurted, "What was I supposed to do? Knock Grandma down?"

"Of course not. You weren't *supposed* to do anything. No one in this family is ever *supposed* to do anything."

"I'm the one who mows the lawn, takes out the trash, does the dishes. I don't see you helping. Except when Toby's dirt bike needs to be washed. Wow. Tough job."

"You're retarded. You don't understand anything anybody tells you."

McKenna lost control. Her hands tremored. Muscle spasms danced across her arms. She'd never fought with Audrey, never wanted to fight, but biology took over. The loudest part of McKenna's brain told her to stop, to rush to Audrey, hug her, and say, "I'm an idiot, let's be friends again; please let me feed you and be your friend."

But rage had seized her.

She won't even *look* over here? Won't take her perfect eyes off the TV to *look* at her own sister? This was Audrey's way, her small, petty way.

She needed to exert power over McKenna because she *had* no power. She was a gimp and a cripple and everyone hated her.

Everyone except me. Oh, you don't remember how I protected you? How I was the only one who thought your disgusting appetite was okay?

Audrey lay on the couch, sipping oil. Black-lipped and smug. McKenna dumped the contents of her carrier sack onto the floor and picked up a *Grand Rapids Press*. She walked to Audrey, mounted Audrey, and pinned her.

"Eat it," she growled. She forced the end of the rolled newspaper against Audrey's lips.

Audrey's mouth tightened. The newspaper bent. Ink blackened Audrey's upper lip and chin.

"Open it! Eat it!" I pinched her face. I wanted to make her scream and bleed.

She whimpered. She struggled and squirmed. Her knees thumped my back and kicked out my air. The oil can fell on the carpet. She slapped my head. She stared at me, horrified, as the newspaper shaft slid inside.

"Play nice, girls," a voice said.

Misty was there, like an angel. So pretty in her nightgown, filling the entryway. Her face sagging like a loose mask. Hair flattened on one side. Barefoot.

She padded into the dining room.

McKenna and Audrey had stopped struggling at the sound of their mother's voice. Once Misty was gone, they looked at each other, panting heavily.

Audrey's eyes in the sunlight are a fairy tale, the color of our daily umbrella. McKenna is overcome by dizziness. Audrey, on the cusp of womanhood, tries to smile with the rolled newspaper jammed in her mouth. (Is it really a smile?) A thin line of motor oil escapes her lips. Black blood.

She begins to eat the newspaper . . . gulp . . . gulp . . . down it goes.

McKenna feels the suction. A vacuum, a machine, a paper shredder drawing her in.

Audrey doesn't blink, blue lights fixed upon McKenna. Telling her.

Lips working.

The paper is gone.

The mouth is closed around McKenna's hand. Wet, warm.

"Audrey, don't."

She feels herself being pulled inside.

She screams for Mommy.

43.

Six bones were fractured, and her wrist was dislocated. Her right hand was cast-bound, so Grandma dropped by every day to do McKenna's chores. Grandma even did the paper route for two weeks—not one customer complaint.

One afternoon, Grandma reached into her purse for a slice of cheese. She searched and searched. She dumped the contents of the purse onto the living room carpet. No cheese.

Not a problem, she insisted to Misty. She calmed herself with pretzels from the end table. "Odd, though," she said, munching. "I put five slices in there this morning,"

The next day, Misty was roused from a nap to help in the housewide search for Grandma's checkbook. Toby and McKenna were also recruited. Audrey watched from the top of the stairs, peering through the rails. The checkbook was never found.

A week later, Grandma's purse vanished. "I set it where I always set it," she insisted. Sweat drops gathered like shimmering paratroopers along her hairline.

"Mom, you need to eat something," Misty said. She led Grandma by the hand into the kitchen.

On the couch, Toby and Audrey giggled.

Ten days later, it was Grandma's shoes.

Early the next morning, seven nuns appeared on the front patch of grass. They sang "On Eagles' Wings" beneath Audrey's window. Sister Juliet strummed a guitar. They recited an Our

Father, a Hail Mary, and an Apostles' Creed. Their stockings got wet from the dew-dampened grass. Then they sang, "They'll Know We Are Christians (By Our Love)."

When they finished, they received hoots and hearty applause from three open bedroom windows—Murray, Audrey, and Toby.

Maybe it was the visual effect of seven nuns standing in a row on the grass below her window. Or maybe Murray had a talk with Audrey after the nuns stopped by. Maybe he said, "Cool it for a while, huh? Stop eating Grandma's things." Unlikely, but a girl can dream. Or maybe Toby told Audrey to cut it out, told her Grandma wasn't a bad person and that she'd learned her lesson. Yes, and maybe a cat can learn to quilt.

Maybe Audrey plum forgot she was at war. Coddling'll do that to a girl.

Whatever the reason, Audrey didn't eat another of Grandma Pencil's possessions until 1990.

After Misty died.

44.

Toby's half of the bedroom:

Posters of bikini-clad girls, muscle cars, muscle men, and Budweiser. A bed. A stereo. A weight bench.

Always grunting, the *tink*! and *clank*! of the barbells, the musky sweat, the wet flatulence, the phone calls to his meathead friends (the hookup is mercifully on his side).

She saw him naked sometimes. She tried not to look at the bobbing piece of flesh between his legs. It was out of place, a transplant. It didn't belong.

He was a beast behind that curtain, all growls and breathing, his laughs like mouthfuls of mud, caveman-ing to his buddies, *Huh huh huh, Uh-uh, Yup, Fuck, Nutsack, Rrrraaa, Feel the burn, Shit.* He raged, slapped his skin with aftershave, slathered his hair with gel, made a swamp of the room. Strutted around in muscle shirts that read, *Your birthday suit would look great on me.*

McKenna's half of the bedroom:

As sparse as a prison cell, exactly the way she liked it. Bare walls. A low bookshelf at the foot of the bed. A dresser, a portable radio, a dozen neatly arranged cassettes. She never competed with Toby's stereo. She preferred her own thoughts. She had a window where she could sit and read with her feet propped on the same sill where she and Audrey, years ago, had made breath-faces on the glass. There was a desk with a typewriter, a digital clock, a basket for papers, and a reading lamp.

"Don't you want some color in here?" Misty used to say. "You'll go blind with blandness." She giggled an actual giggle. Unreal coming out of her mouth, like if Snoodles giggled. "Don't you have any interests, Mac? Decorations can show the world who you are."

"I don't need to hang my personality on a wall."

"Certainly not."

"Or hide it in the basement."

"No!"

"Or wear it on my body. Big, disgusting bulges."

"That's not you."

"Or in my pretty, pretty hair and eyeliner and pink dresses."

"You're absolutely right," Misty nodded encouragingly. "But sweetheart, where *do* you keep it?"

McKenna scratched at a broken vein of wood on the underside of her desk.

"Mac?" Misty asked. "Inquiring minds want to know."

Early 1990.

45.

Mid-1990. She isn't breathing. Her face is chalky. She lies on the queen-sized bed, atop the ratty green quilt. Just like thirteen years ago, when Audrey was expelled into the world.

Her right hand rests on her belly. The left hand dangles over the mattress edge. She went for a nap. The nap has taken her away. Naps always take her away . . . is this different?

Morning light saturates the gauzy drapes, provides fine detail. McKenna, from the doorway, absorbs. Misty's lips show striations of dryness. Chapstick would help. McKenna checks her pockets. No luck. McKenna steps close, leans in. Misty's nostrils are different sizes. The nostrum is bent to the left. Her eyebrows—not arched. Rainbows. Thin. Expressive. McKenna never noticed those eyebrows before. Did she? She never, not once, actually *saw* Mom's eyebrows.

A brown mole on her jaw line. Bare feet, the toenails untrimmed, uncolored. Eyes closed. A doll.

Will she wake when her arm is touched? McKenna reaches in. . . .

Two paramedics arrive. Later, two men from the funeral home.

Murray stands in the corner, smoking and smoking and smoking. The left side of his Hanson Mold collar is popped. Again and again he touches his face, as if to confirm that it's there. But his fingers, once they arrive, are unsure. They pull at his cheeks, scratch his nose, squeeze a lip, tap a forehead. In a soft voice, he answers the paramedics' questions. He looks small and inconsequential beside other uniformed men.

The men act as if they're afraid to disturb the dead. There's no sound but Audrey's wails from her room next door. Toby is with her. In a few hours, inconsolable, Audrey will eat her bed.

McKenna leans against a wall, sinks into it. The wall is a throat, the soft red inside of a throat. The air is soft. The light is soft. Life is hazy and not unpleasant.

As the two men from the funeral home unzip the black canvas bag and place Misty inside it, she opens her eyes. Blinks twice. Stretches her arms, yawns deeply, casts a sleepy gaze around the room. Finds McKenna and waves.

"Bye-bye, sweetie," she says.

At nine the next morning, Murray finds Audrey asleep on the bare wooden floor of her room. She's surrounded by empty boxes that had been gathering dust beneath her bed for five years— Barbie Dream Home; Draw'rific Easel and Paint Set; Mister Microphone.

"Where . . ." Murray begins, scanning.

"No fucking way," Toby says, muscling his way into the room.

McKenna peers from the hallway.

Audrey has never eaten anything of this size before.

"Are you okay?" Murray says. He lowers to one knee. His eyes flit and shimmer. He touches Audrey's shoulder, his fingers live wires. "Sweetie, what happened to your bed?"

Audrey blinks, sits up. "I got rid of it. I needed a new one."

"I guess you won't be having breakfast," Toby laughs.

Audrey, thirteen years old, doesn't mourn. Not conventionally. Certain touchy-feely counselors would probably argue that she was behaving like a "normal" teenager. In the days following the funeral, she is brusque. She doesn't smile; she doesn't frown. Either of these would show weakness. She crutches herself around the house in full-scowl-mode. She hates, actively. Hates the furniture, the trinkets, the appliances, the weather, the clocks, her family, the air. Perhaps she has always despised these things. Perhaps the only person she ever loved is now buried in a cemetery near the Grand River. Perhaps with Misty gone, Audrey is now free to make her feelings known.

Murray does his best "Dad" impersonation. He implements "daily meetings." These are after-dinner discussions designed to help everyone get their feelings out, to talk about the loss, to remember Misty, to "re-inject joy into this household."

Even Grandma Pencil is encouraged to come, encouraged to pray for Misty's soul. "Because that's what you do, Annabelle," Murray says.

He's being so polite, so diplomatic, so accommodating. And it's the worst mistake he'll ever make.

At Grandma's urging, McKenna gets a referral and goes to see a specialist, a dietician.

"A girl your age should weigh one-thirty, on average," the doctor says. "You're ninety-four pounds. Your throat looks like a lobster. It's a darn good thing you came in."

McKenna doesn't tell the doctor about the chew-swallow-upchuck, chew-swallow-upchuck. After all, it's not any of the eating disorders they've warned her about.

"Lots of stress lately," she explains. She recites the list she's rehearsed: Mom passed away; recently graduated high school; boy troubles; social awkwardness; trouble sleeping. "I get nervous. I feel nauseous. I have reflux."

"Do you ever make yourself throw up?" the doctor asks. "For any reason?"

"Nothing I eat ever leaves my mouth," McKenna assures him.

A multi-vitamin is prescribed, as well as a high-protein shake and some pills "to ease your anxiety." Also a referral to see a woman who specializes in eating disorders. "I'm not saying that's what's going on, but there's no shame in making an appointment to talk."

McKenna thanks the doctor, goes home, and stands in front of the bathroom mirror. She resolves to eat like a normal person.

No more of this sickness. Mom can see everything now. Even inside my mouth.

Well, she tried.

Grandma Pencil invites her friends to the daily meetings.

"They're designed for the *family*, Annabelle," Murray is overheard whispering when she shows up with nuns in tow.

"I understand," Grandma replies. "Would anyone like veggies and dip?"

The living room is dim and cool. The nuns and Grandma occupy the sofa. Audrey lies on the floor, her stumps raised in the air, bicycling. Toby reclines in the mustard recliner. McKenna sits cross-legged on the carpet. Murray stands at the far end of the room. He distributes photo albums unearthed from the attic.

"This was Misty," he says. "The mother we loved. The daughter. The wife."

"I have homework," Audrey yawns.

Toby flips pages. "Woah! Look how heavy you used to be, Kenny."

The nuns, Sister Maximillian and Sister Pauline (a new one), politely peruse an album without comment.

Grandma Pencil forces a fistful of pretzels into her mouth.

"I think it's important that we remember the Misty in these pictures," Murray says, tapping his palm for emphasis.

"You apparently *want* me to fail my English test," Audrey mumbles.

"She would've sacrificed anything for you kids."

McKenna pretends to look at the pictures in front of her. In reality, she scrutinizes Audrey. She sees the disgust Audrey flashes at the ceiling, and, occasionally, at Murray.

"Is that *you*, Dad?" Toby exclaims. "God, you look like you're twelve."

"That's our wedding day."

"No shit. I thought the tux was for a rodeo."

"Mind your mouth," Grandma Pencil says.

"I always do, Grandma. I mind Tracy Howerton's mouth, too. And Jessica Bly's."

Audrey snickers. So worldly, so mature. Does she even understand his comment? How could she? She's never dated, never had friends who dated. Right? Not yet, not yet.

The nuns are miming rigor mortis, lips drawn tight. Their nostrils exhale musty lung into the close room. The bowl of dill dip on the coffee table glistens. On the mantle, the Sears-Roebuck faux-wood clock ticks. Audrey pops a gum bubble.

It's time.

"Mom's in Heaven, isn't she, Dad?" McKenna asks.

Murray swigs at his can of Pabst. Licks his lips. He studies McKenna, assessing the tone and sincerity of her question. He seems to decide that it's above-board. She's always above-board. In fact, she *is* the board. That's what they always said at school. Carpenter's dream and all.

"You know I've never been a person of faith," Murray says. He nods, agreeing with himself. "But yes, I believe Misty's there. Don't know why." Manages a tired smile. Eyes are rimmed red.

(Poor Dad. He was collateral damage. But why didn't you ever confess this to him?)

The nuns fidget as if the cushions are getting hot. Grandma's eyes shift in her head. She glances at the penguins. They read her glance, and then make with some holy thumb-twiddling. Audrey, smelling controversy, props herself onto her elbows.

"Why *wouldn't* Mom be in Heaven, genius?" Toby asks McKenna.

(From this vantage point, Toby is one enormous socked foot. Two gaping holes at the ball, flesh eyes.)

"Because there *isn't* a Heaven!" Audrey says, cheerfully. "Right, Dad?"

Murray frowns. Says nothing. Push has come to shove, and he seems toppled.

"The Catholic teachings," Grandma Pencil ventures, "are clear as glass."

Sister Pauline, new blood at St. Monica's, makes a noise in her throat. A winch being turned. "Perhaps," she says, "this is a discussion best left for the adults."

"Nonsense," Murray says, his eyes finally showing recognition. He's like Audrey but with a less keen sense of smell. After a momentary lapse, he's back on his game. He has caught the whiff of controversy, and it smells religious. Even Misty's tragic death isn't enough to shut off this primal instinct. "Misty and I always treated the kids like grown-ups."

There's blood dripping from Grandma's mouth, she's biting her tongue so hard.

"And now they practically *are* grown-ups," Murray continues. Gazes lovingly at his kids, the poor dolt. "Anything I can hear, they can hear, too."

46.

To a Catholic, some issues have no *if.* There simply *is.* Things *are.* A certain way. The way they are. Beyond debate.

One doesn't need proof of fingernails. Or gravity. Or death.

"My daughter Misty was a loving person," Grandma said. She stood from the sofa, like an alcoholic proclaiming her disease. She nodded at Murray: "Misty loved you. Deeply." Her eyes revealed a level of sorrow, and of hesitation, that McKenna had never seen.

The children watched and listened.

McKenna's throat constricted. Lunch was long gone, dammit, nothing there.

"She loved each of you children," Grandma said. One by one, she fastened the kids with a wistful stare. McKenna. Tears lustrous in Grandma's eyes. Toby. Big, simple Toby. She dabbed snot with her hanky. With Audrey, her expression changed. Disapproval. That's because Audrey refused to look up; she pulled at a loose thread in the carpet.

The nuns made a mental note of Audrey's latest infraction.

Grandma Pencil cleared her throat. Turned to face Murray.

After the torturous foreplay, Grandma Pencil finally uttered what McKenna already knew she was going to utter: That Misty was now being broiled on the hottest griddles in the cosmos.

Grandma Pencil used the word "convinced." As in, "I am convinced she is in Hell." Clearly, it was the wrong word. "Convinced" implies that doubt was, at some point, a possibility. "Convinced" suggests that she'd been swayed by a body of compelling evidence before arriving at this view. "Convinced" leaves open the idea that she might have resisted, or questioned, or, God forbid, even *wanted* it to be untrue.

Her utterance spread through the room like poisonous gas. Everyone sucked it in.

Murray and Audrey had no real reference point. *Hell?* It was disrespectful to suggest this about anybody who had died—they knew this much—but really, what the hell was Hell? Something you made jokes about. A red guy with horns and a pitchfork.

Murray's first response was a hammer-and-chisel laugh. It whacked at the air. His hands shot into his jean pockets. He rocked on his heels while his bottom teeth scratched his upper lip.

Grandma Pencil wouldn't wait for him to speak. Her words spilled feverishly. This woman had never doubted herself, yet now she seemed afraid to leave even the smallest gap into which someone might insert a response. She quoted Corinthians: "Don't you know that you yourselves are God's temple and that God's Spirit lives in you? If anyone destroys God's temple, God will destroy him; for God's temple is sacred, and you are that temple." She cited the Fifth Commandment, adding that suicide, by the way, is self-murder. "It is God's decision alone when life should be taken. To do it ourselves is to say we know better than God. Most importantly," she said, "my daughter was not a believer. An unbeliever who kills herself only hastens her trip to the lake of fire."

Spent, Grandma dropped onto the sofa beside the nuns. The Sears clock ticked. Outside, Snoodles barked at phantoms.

Toby broke the spell. His thick neck twisted so he could face Murray: "I don't get it, Dad." He frowned.

Nobody wanted to look at anyone.

"Mom didn't commit suicide," Toby continued. Like a boy, those eyes. Confused, hurt. *But I thought you were going to measure my feet.*

"The death certificate," Murray answered, "is unambiguous." His voice was scarcely a whisper. He'd never gotten angry in front of the children before. Not in eighteen years. He'd always worked things out in the basement. Maybe he wanted to run to the basement now. A vein throbbed on his temple. "*Accidental overdose* is the exact wording. I'm with Toby on this." He turned to Grandma, his face the color of rug burn. "*I don't get what you're saying.*"

Before the nuns had another chance to squirm, and before Grandma Pencil could reply, the noise began.

It was Audrey. She lay on the carpet halfway between Toby's recliner and the geezers' sofa. Hair spread like spilled paint beneath her head. Her mouth, that raven hole, opened wide and belted out a preposterous, shocking laugh.

The nuns plugged their ears. They were frightened.

A liquefied honey bun climbed out of McKenna's throat. *Forgot about you!*

It was ugly, Audrey's laugh. An automatic rifle: hateful, hollow. She added to the noise with her fists, which pounded the floor. "Ha ha ha ha!" Boomboomboomboom.

Murray retreated a couple of steps, eyeing her as if she might explode.

Audrey's face contorted. She gasped, the laughter firing and firing. The noise was so loud that no one could hear Toby imploring her to stop.

"*I* get it!" she yelled, breathlessly, between bursts. "*I* get it! *Good* one, Grandma! Ha ha ha! *I* get it!"

Toby lifted Audrey and carried her upstairs.

The nuns excused themselves, each one touching Murray on the arm as they passed. They vanished out the front door.

Murray and Grandma studied different spots on the carpet.

McKenna chewed.

47.

Grandma Pencil was banished. No dramatics. No tears. No protestations.

After fully processing the thrust of her argument—that Misty had offed herself with her prescription pills—Murray simply said, "You aren't welcome here."

Very politely, he escorted Grandma out the front door. She didn't resist. As she hobbled onto the screened-in porch, Murray added, "And not just tonight, Annabelle. I mean never. You're not welcome again."

She didn't say a word.

Toby and Audrey applauded from the top of the stairs. They sang, "Ding-dong, the witch is dead! Which old witch? The wicked witch!" And so on.

Murray didn't celebrate. There was no happiness in exiling his mother-in-law. He didn't hate her. He pitied her. In his mind, there was scant difference between her and the poor suckers who'd sipped from the Guyana punch bowl. It must have gnawed at him that he'd allowed his own children to be brought into that fold.

However, Toby wasn't a problem. He was a "dim bulb," in Murray's words. Toby never memorized the prayers, never understood what he was singing. "That's a lot of lyrics!" he exclaimed. On Sunday mornings he could always think of something better to do than cramming into a pew and chanting along with a pipe organ: work the bag at Tony's; wrestle a homeless guy; do one-handed pushups in front of the new cheerleader. Besides, that whole kneel-stand-kneel-stand routine? Such a tease! So close to exercise without actually *being* exercise.

Toby's post-high-school plan was to abandon college in favor of a full-time job where he could "act like a man and lift some things."

Yes, as far as religion was concerned, Murray didn't have to fret about his first-born. Toby was a Mapes, through and through.

But then there was McKenna. McKenna the boyish. "Kenny" the virgin, the recluse. McKenna who'd kissed only two boys and had only "made out" with one of them. McKenna who'd never worn makeup, never gone to a prom, never understood why dresses and high heels were "womanly" but reading philosophy was not.

McKenna who'd graduated from St. Monica's in eighth grade and then accepted, against Murray and Misty's wishes, Grandma's offer to pay for her Catholic Central High tuition. (Toby had said "Thanks, but no thanks" and gone to Creston Public.)

McKenna who in her senior year had begun a formal conversion to Catholicism. Catechism classes. Bible study. McKenna who was now enrolled for the fall semester at Aquinas College.

Grandma Pencil vanished from the Mapeses' lives. Truth told, Grandma Pencil was happy to leave. Her possessions—four pairs of shoes, two purses, a set of dentures, her house keys, credit cards, lipstick, pocket mirror—had begun disappearing again. Grandma knew perfectly well where these items had gone, but she could never prove it. *Good riddance to evil* was Grandma's attitude. *More time to spend with my geezers.*

Audrey was ecstatic. She'd slain the dragon. She'd avenged her mother's death. That pruny bitch couldn't piss on Mom's memories so easily. Suicide, indeed! The very thought!

Audrey refused to believe it. So did Toby. But still, the idea had been spoken. And from Misty's own mother, no less. The utterance alone made it a possibility. So the notion remained, nestled in the corners of the children's thoughts. While showering, while dressing for work, while pumping triceps, while playing Atari 5200, while sitting quietly at the front window to watch the storm thrash the trees—at any given moment the idea was whispered by the wretched little goblin in their heads: *Your mommy killed herself. Your mommy killed herself.*

Questions crept in: If she *had* done it . . . then what? What would this mean? Pondering the implications, even hypothetically, was unbearable. Still, the voice whispered:

She wanted to leave. She was miserable. She didn't love you. You made her die.

Individually, McKenna, Toby, and Audrey all revisited moments with their mother. The smallest memory was scrutinized.

A day at the dentist. She pats your hand in the waiting room, says, "You'll be fine." You pull your hand away and pretend to read *Cosmopolitan.*

A Saturday, helping her fold socks on her bed. You get called away by the telephone. It's Ronald Urbane, the boy who will, days later, sweet talk you into kissing him behind the school. When you return, Mom is gone and the laundry basket is empty.

A Christmas morning, her somnolent smile as she unwraps the cheesy fake gold necklace you bought at the mall for $8.95. "Thank you, sweetheart," she says. She brushes a strand of hair from her mouth. Takes a sip of her hot cocoa. No hug? She gave Toby a hug when she opened *his* present.

Where was it? Where was the clue, the moment she crossed from happiness to *other?*

Shouldn't we have seen it? What did we do to make our mom hate life so much? Can't we take it back?

I take it back.

48.

Three months after Grandma Pencil was exiled, McKenna moved in with her.

But why? Was she such a devoted granddaughter? Did she really adore Annabelle, even to the point of worship, as some have speculated?

Not to burst any balloons, but it was a space issue. The Mapes house had three bedrooms. Toby and McKenna were almost nineteen and still sharing a 16' × 18' box. Do the math.

"Cripes, I had my own *apartment* when I was seventeen," Murray said. "Don't you at least want your own room?"

It was a practical matter. A matter of convenience. A win-win situation. A no-brainer.

Left unspoken were a few additional factors that may have prompted Murray's "impromptu" dinner table discussion with McKenna while Toby "happened" to be at the gym and Audrey "happened" to be upstairs wearing headphones, cramming for a history test on her new bed. It was 7 p.m. Murray sipped at his can of Pabst. Every few seconds, he fiddled with his new hearing aid and cocked his head as if trying to pour his brains out onto the table. He looked powdery and lost.

McKenna couldn't concentrate. She kept expecting her mother to appear at the saloon-style kitchen doors. Her voice sounded as real as the wood grain under McKenna's fingertips: "Will you be dining with us, Murr, or should I pop in a Hungry Man?"

"Well?"

This was Murray, asking McKenna a question.

"I don't need my own room," McKenna shrugged. "I don't hang out in there very much."

"I don't hang out in the burn ward," he said, "but you won't find me sleeping there." He frowned, and then alternated snapping his fingers on each side of his head. "Everything sounds like a tin can."

"Does Toby want me to go?" McKenna said.

"He didn't say that." Murray moistened his lips with his tongue. "But yes, he does. He needs space. You need space. You're adults now. Those drapes ain't a wall."

When Toby and McKenna turned thirteen, Murray had installed a rod and curtain in the middle of their ceiling. The curtain provided privacy for dressing and sleeping, and it could be pushed out of the way when not in use. However, it had the unforeseen effect of making the room feel like a hospital. Still, McKenna had never slept anywhere else.

"Why doesn't Toby get his own place?" McKenna said. "He's got a job."

Murray bounced a cigarette from the pack in his shirt pocket. "The thing is, Grandma Pencil could use the company," he said. He struck a match, puffed, then shook the match and dropped it on the table. He would have never done this when Misty was alive. The smoldering match reminded McKenna of her mother's corpse.

"You've always been the closest to Grandma," Murray continued. He blew out a cloud, then tipped his head back and touched the glands in his neck. He was always "coming down with something" these days. "You two are sort of alike, I think. You might enjoy yourself. You probably have a lot to talk about."

McKenna felt herself flush. She tugged at one of her braids. Pippy Longstocking. That's what they'd called her at St. Monica's. Half a decade later, she still wore her hair like this. What was the point of changing?

"Listen, Mac," Murray said. He fixed her with a stare. Jarring to meet those eyes. His face was in the midst of a quiet collapse, the erosion of aging, but his eyes still gleamed like precious stones. "I always thought you were the most like me. Out of all you kids, I saw myself in you." He snapped his fingers at his ear. "You keep to yourself. You're a thinker. Toby . . . Christ, who knows where that kid came from. He scares me, frankly. He's my son, but what the hell? Protein shakes, flaxseed oil, bandannas? Kid's a tree." He knocked on the table for emphasis. "But that's how we raised you kids. We wanted you to find your own direction. That's what you did. And your mom and I were always proud of you. You, Mac. We probably didn't say it enough, but I'm saying it now. We didn't mind that you weren't dating, proms, mall, who cares about that stuff? That'll definitely be Audrey's thing, doesn't have to be your thing. Dating's overrated, frankly." He rang the Pabst can gently, a liquid bell, before draining the remainder into his gullet. "I mean, I wish you'd eat better. That's not a criticism. It's just . . . what it is. Take it or leave it." He looked around the dining room. He sniffed. "It's weird, isn't it, without all the bowls?"

McKenna nodded. "Very."

"Be right back." Murray scooted his chair and went into the kitchen. McKenna heard the basement door open and his footsteps descending.

A minute later, he returned with a shoebox and a fresh beer. He slid the box across the table and sat down. "You probably haven't heard much noise from the basement in a while," he said. He didn't wait for McKenna to answer. "I've slowed down over the years. But I haven't been picking my butt down there." He smiled and winked, "Well, maybe a little picking." He nodded at the box. "I figure that's my last invention. I made it for you, kiddo."

The box was so light it felt empty. Was this some kind of perverse commentary on her weight? Was he saying she was empty inside? He'd always been absent, but he'd never been cruel. Audrey had put him up to this. Audrey and Toby. McKenna worked her stomach and throat, but there was nothing to bring up.

"Go on, open it," Murray said.

Inside was a black plastic contraption, perhaps seven inches wide, which resembled a miniature clothes hanger with two clips on the bottom. Instead of a hook on the top, there was a one-inch plastic arm with a tiny, hooded light bulb on its end.

"Pull that light," Murray said.

When McKenna pulled, the plastic arm extended to five inches. As it extended, the arm curved, and when it was pulled out all the way, the bulb lighted. McKenna slid the arm back to its nested position, and the bulb turned off.

"You're a reader," Murray said. "The clips keep your book open, and now you can read in the dark." For a brief moment, his face was alive again, excited, exactly as McKenna remembered from when she was a girl. She hadn't dreamed this part of her life after all.

McKenna was crying without knowing why. It wasn't happiness. It wasn't sadness. It was something relatively unpleasant, like shame.

Murray had turned his attention to the dirt under his fingernail.

McKenna wanted to speak—a joke, a gush of appreciation, anything—but her mind was caught in a persistent loop, a needle skipping again and again on words spoken ten minutes earlier:

You two are sort of alike. You might enjoy yourself. You probably have a lot to talk about.

The questions, the questions. A swarm of bees in her head. A thousand minds, chaos, but all working together. Please don't sting me.

"I'll move out tomorrow," McKenna said.

49.

The curl of night. Sunken. Low breathing underwater. Rising to the surface, pursued by a shark. Its jaws filled with popcorn. Or marbles. Teeth grinding marbles (cat's eyes, jumbos, swirlies, aggies) the ones she used in grade school with Toby and the neighborhood boys. Toby who cheated; the boys who didn't dare speak up. Marbles rubbing together, a clacking squeak.

McKenna opens her eyes to the black cliff of a bureau looming in the dark beside her head. The drawn curtains, sewn by Grandma Pencil from heavy burgundy bath towels, are outlined by silver moonlight. McKenna climbs from the bed. The wood is cold under her bare feet. Her throat is dry. The heating vent pumps acrid air. She can hear Snoodles yelling to her, "Mac! Mac! MacMac-MacMac!" But why does he sound so far away?

The digital clock reads 1:45 a.m. The wind brushes the chimes on the back stoop, a sprinkling of holy water for the ears.

The clock switches to 1:46. The dream noise returns—a slow breaking, a clack, a faraway but sharp sound. Perhaps Misty is in the kitchen, cooking dinner.

But Misty is dead, isn't she?

Careful to lift the knob so it doesn't protest, McKenna opens the door. She pads down the hall, past Mom and Dad's room, Audrey's room, the bathroom. At the top of the stairs, McKenna stops. Looks back to where she's just walked. Shadows are wrong. Confused. That's not Audrey's door. It's Grandma Pencil's room.

That's not Mom and Dad's door. It's the bathroom. That's not the bathroom. It's a closet.

But the crunching—the hollow turmoil of destruction inside a mouth—*is* down there. At the bottom of the stairs. This is not a dream.

November.

50.

Lollapalooza brought Audrey fame, fortune, and feet. It didn't make her a household name—not yet—but she gained a rabid core of followers who bought tickets solely to see her performances. The majority of her fans were the so-called slackers and Gen-Xers of the early-to-mid-90s—the un-generation, the un-colas, those cool-in-their-uncoolness readers of beat literature, computer manuals, and eastern philosophy who pumped gas for $4.05 an hour. Those questioners of everything whose questions asked nothing. Those anti-corporateers with hoop rings through their noses, onion rings in the backs of their vans, dirt rings in their bathtubs. These were the vast majority of Audrey's fan base, and yet she had nothing in common with them, not even the adoration of herself and her gift. To the bitter end, she was disgustingly humble.

However, there was one exception to Audrey's slacker followers—Herr Essenalles, the notorious German "eatist."

Their first meeting took place on July 2, 1996. The stately, salt-and-pepper-haired Essenalles, sporting a pinstriped silk suit and a thick mustache, attended a Jim Rose Circus Sideshow in Portland, Oregon. He was so impressed that he sent Audrey a bouquet of Casablanca lilies and a $5,000 bottle of Gewürztraminer, with a note reading, *After we drink together, we shall eat together—From an Admirer.* Audrey, along with the rest of the United States, had never heard of Herr Essenalles, but after he bribed his way back-stage that evening, she accepted his invitation to dine at the illustrious Chateau de Spree, where they spent two hours in intimate conversation, the exact content of which has never been known, but which shall nonetheless be recreated here:

"You eat your soup so daintily," he purred, his accent dripping onto the table. The candlelight flickered in his narrow eyes. "Not at all like your vaudeville routine."

"What the fuck is vaudeville? I'm from Grand Rapids."

"Ja, of course." A pleasant, guttural chuckle that shakes the table. "What I mean is that you are like an animal on that stage. You have—what should I say?—*impulsion* in your gaze. No joy."

Audrey belched into her hand. Under the table, she lifted her leg to massage her right stump. Her knee bumped his. They exchanged bashful grins—his toothy, hers teethy.

"You are not such an angry person," Herr Essenalles said, wiping his mouth with the burgundy napkin. "It is acting, exactly as I had hoped. A persona for the stage. Such a kaleidoscopic beauty could not have the monster's heart that they say."

"I killed a doctor," she said. She raised a butter knife to her lips, bit it in half and swallowed. "How do you know anything about my heart?"

He stared in wonder as she gulped the rest of the knife. This simple act alone would have taken him twenty minutes. The nerves in his chest and groin came alive.

Beneath the table, her hand grasped his knee.

"I've had a shitty life," she said. Her teeth flashed again, this time not a smile. "Only one person really cared about me, and now she's in Hell."

Essenalles's lip itched. He wanted to wipe the perspiration, but he was unable to move, unable to breathe. Sitting here in her grip was intoxicating agony. "History," he managed to rasp, tears welling, "puts a saint in every dream."

* * *

Audrey, with the approval of Jim Rose, allowed Herr Essenalles unrestricted backstage access for the next five shows, after which the fifty-two-year-old German gave an effusive interview to the *Los Angeles Times*. He praised Audrey Mapes as a "biological miracle," "living evidence of evolution," and a "window to the future of mankind." The gist of his argument was that our century-long dependence on industry, chemicals, and artificial environs had created a new breed of human, one who could subsist entirely on man-made materials.

The article caused a minor stir in the United States, but a major stir on Moriarty Street. It inspired Toby to break a lamp with a karate kick. Murray got drunk on Maker's Mark and sobbed through three "sick days" in front of the television. Grandma Pencil prayed her entire 1932 sterling silver rosary, a gift from the St. Monica nuns.

It was clear from the article that the unctuous kraut was smitten. Audrey's family knew, simply from the words he used, that Audrey had slept with him. This didn't sit well, but there was nothing they could do about it.

McKenna ate a banana for fourteen hours, but it had nothing to do with Audrey's skeeziness. What was everyone so upset about? Audrey had never been a Pollyanna, never been pure. In ninth grade, she'd gone down on Bobby Merrick at the Comstock Park fireworks. In tenth grade, she'd lost her virginity to Markie Gearing. But oh yes, nobody knew about these transgressions. Nobody but McKenna, who actually cared enough to read her sister's journal and find out what kind of girl was living under their roof.

51.

UC Berkeley funded a team of doctors, medical students, and physiologists to examine Audrey. She participated willingly. Both her agent and The Jim Rose Sideshow, Inc., said it would be great for publicity. The only contractual stipulation was that Audrey should never eat any "non-food" in front of the research team. Not a bite. Her Lollapalooza performances would continue, but she would wait four hours before going to the lab.

The tests were rigorous and lasted an entire month. First, the researchers acquired Herr Essenalles's medical records to use as a model of an exceptionally vigorous digestive system. Whereas his sphincter and stomach lining were unusually thick, and his mucus, hydrochloric acid, and pepsin were especially prolific and potent, Audrey's tests revealed nothing abnormal. Her teeth, mouth, throat, stomach, small intestine, pancreas, liver, gallbladder, biliary tract, large intestine (including ascending, traverse, descending, and sigmoid colon), rectum, and anus—all of it looked and acted "textbook." The eggheads scratched their chins and wondered, as did everyone: "Even *if* you concede, hypothetically, that she eats this stuff . . . which is of course ludicrous . . . Where the hell does it *go*?"

They examined her stool. They sliced it, diced it, blended it, smeared it on slides, and read it under microscopes. They tested its chemical makeup, protein level, electrolytes, sugars, fats. They kept their eyes peeled for undigested hunks of glass, stainless steel, timber, sawdust, plastic, cardboard, Plexiglas, concrete, suede, leather. They found nothing of the sort. They'd been given a list of all the materials Audrey consumed during her stage show. Her poop confirmed none of it. There should have been high levels of some very toxic elements. The picnic table, for instance, made of pressure-treated wood, would have contained enough arsenic to kill ten people. And yet her waste revealed only the tracest amounts (approximately 0.010 parts per million), consistent with natural arsenic levels in California tap water. The researchers did find evidence of a chili dog, French fries, green grapes, a chocolate shake, apple juice, macaroni and cheese, and real dairy butter.

So Audrey was receiving nourishment from actual food. Ah ha! Not surprising to the researchers. More surprising if you'd grown up with her, in which case you knew that she ate so-called "real" food only sparingly. Perhaps she needed food to live, perhaps not. The family never checked. Maybe she was being social. Maybe she didn't want to appear rude when the co-freaks asked her to hit Denny's after a long day of grossing out the masses.

They sampled her digestive fluids. Drew blood. Charted her breathing, heart rate, cholesterol level, blood pressure, and body mass index. Measured her brain, arms, legs, fingers, hands, skull, chest. Sampled hair and skin. Performed throat cultures, counted antibodies. Completed a gynecological exam. They requested and received her entire medical history—birth records, hospital records, height and weight charts, vision tests, hearing tests, dental records, scoliosis screenings, immunizations. They tested her coordination, balance, reflexes, spatial sensitivity. They assessed her IQ, EQ, math and verbal skills, and personality type. They snapped photographs of everything—in close-up, wide shot, and shots for perspective and scale.

Normal, normal, normal. Maddeningly normal. Excruciatingly normal. Audrey was the human equivalent of the center of the center yellow line. In every area, she represented the statistical mean, to within a fraction of a decimal. Disgustingly representative. Putridly unremarkable. Rancidly ordinary. None of the researchers had ever seen anyone so normal. Her only abnormal feature was her missing feet, but even this turned out to be a dead end. Congenital birth defects were almost always accompanied by some additional aberrance—a weakened heart wall, poor circulation, breathing problems, brittle bones. But for Audrey, the defect appeared to be anomalous, affecting nothing.

She was unnerving; this run-of-the-mill, standard, fence-sitting girl. She was living, breathing par. They checked and rechecked their data. Tested and retested. They pulled out their hair. They hurled books. They couldn't sleep, couldn't eat. One despondent young man called a suicide hotline and checked into a safe house. The chances of a person being so statistically average in so many areas? Simply calculating those odds would require three or four calculators taped together.

With tears in their eyes, they pleaded with Audrey to "eat something crazy" under rigorous scientific observation. Viewing this process, they were certain, would expose her uniqueness.

"Do you really want to be *average?*" they asked, grimacing, as if merely uttering the word made them angry.

"Everyone is special," they goaded. "Didn't you ever watch *Sesame Street?*"

They positioned bowls of sparkling test tubes, like shiny candies, on the counter. Then they exited the lab to "answer an important call." (Could they have known how this image, the snack food in a bowl, turned her stomach?) They tempted Audrey with handmade mahogany chairs. They "accidentally" ripped their lab coats on the corners of desks: "Whoops. That's a shame. Now I'll have to throw away this perfectly delicious garment." Long, slow walk to the garbage chute. "Too bad there's nothing else we can do with it." Disappointed, wistful glances as they slunk out the door.

Audrey never budged. The researchers were allowed to attend

her Lollapalooza performances, so every day they scribbled in their notepads, pushed their glasses to the tops of their noses, whispered to one another, bobbed and weaved behind towering slackers to get an unimpeded view of Audrey's mouth, throat, and chest as the items went down.

When the month expired, the elaborate, costly study was deemed "inconclusive." That's what they wrote in the literature, anyway.

In person, the exhausted, demoralized researchers didn't hide their "humble" opinion:

Audrey Mapes was a goddamned hoax.

52.

The public debate began. Audrey was profiled (usually a couple of paragraphs), in local newspapers along the Lollapalooza tour. She received minor mentions in *Rolling Stone, Spin,* and *Modern Woman.* In Grand Rapids, Murray snipped every article and videotaped every TV reference. He and Toby pored over the clippings at the dinner table.

Ripley's Believe It or Not aired an eight-minute segment, consisting mostly of low-budget "reenactments" of her stage act. Four of Toby's muscle-bound buddies came over to watch the episode. They scoffed, "That actress isn't half as hot as your sister, dude."

(Did they realize that the pigtailed young woman squashed on the end of the couch, watching the show with them, was also Toby's sister?)

McKenna collected the articles, too, on the sly. At Grandma's house, these were considered contraband. McKenna hid them beneath her mattress and studied them by moonlight.

The famous magician duo, Krebs and Jenner, known for comedic and gory (yet intellectual) illusions and for debunking anyone who claimed to have psychic powers, appeared on *Later with Greg Kinnear* in early September. It was a tense moment for the Mapeses when Greg asked, "So what do you think about this Lollapalooza girl who, like, eats trumpets and scuba gear?" (Audience laughter.)

Ponytailed Krebs, in his pinstriped suit, one leg crossed onto the other, stroked his chin beard and insisted glibly, jovially, smugly: "It's a trick, Greg. A good trick, but just a trick."

As proof, his mousy partner Jenner produced a sledgehammer and obliterated a pile of coconuts. Then, in front of the live studio audience, Jenner ate the sledgehammer.

After the commercial break, Krebs revealed that the hammer was made of hollow milk chocolate. The real sledgehammer had been slid into Jenner's pant leg through sleight-of-hand, which Jenner then demonstrated. The audience whooped.

Murray erased that tape.

Out in the real world of Middle America, folks gave their two cents to the local news: "There's no way she's eating this stuff!" Others declared with equal passion: "She *does* eat it! I saw her in Denver! I don't know how it works, but it's true." A small minority said, "Who cares if it's real or not? It's damn good entertainment."

Audrey never gave an interview. She would have done so if she'd wanted to. No one was controlling her; no one was telling her what to do (as some have suggested). Jim Rose, however, definitely fueled the fires of mystery. To him, silence was gasoline. At every turn, he advised Audrey to keep quiet while the debate raged. Let our publicist do the talking, he said. A personal interview will kill business. You're an enigma, he said. A conundrum. A bugaboo. Let people pay full price and judge for themselves.

To this end, cameras were never allowed under the tent. Jim Rose warned against doing TV appearances, which would allow scrutiny of every move in painstaking detail.

Even without interviews or TV appearances, Audrey's fame grew. For this, I credit her cover-girl good looks—the innocent face, the porcelain skin, the curved lashes, the Farrah Fawcett hair, and the liquid eyes haunted by a touch of sadness. Men like the troubled beauty. Men also like a girl with an appetite, especially one who keeps quiet after she eats. Her footlessness was rarely mentioned.

Kalamazoo took pride in "Lollapalooza's Eating Girl," whom they touted as "locally born." They welcomed every roving reporter who happened into town. City officials gave guided tours of The Caboose and provided names and contact information for all of Audrey's arty high school/college friends and the professors who'd taught her during those two months. Eventually, newshounds sniffed their way north to Grand Rapids, to Moriarty Street.

Murray wouldn't answer the door. Toby dropped water balloons from the roof. Faithful old Snoodles, not long for this Earth, yapped and pawed at the living room window. McKenna and Grandma Pencil drank tea on Grandma's back patio, looking up the street, watching the white vans come and go.

Lollapalooza was only a summer tour, but when it ended in September of 1996, Audrey didn't return to Moriarty Street. She didn't notify her family of her decision; she simply didn't show up. Three months passed. At Christmas, Murray received a collect call (jab) from Germany. Audrey was living with you-know-who. That's what she said: "I'm living with you-know-who." She wouldn't even say the guy's name. Over the following year, the Mapeses received two postcards with nothing written on the back except *Audrey*.

In the summer of 1997, she signed on with Lollapalooza again. She performed for full crowds, but this time around, the novelty had worn off. The shock value was gone. When the tour ended, she flew back to Germany with Johann, and the Mapeses wondered if they would ever see her again.

But then, one month later, in October of 1997, Audrey returned to Moriarty Street for the first time in seventeen months. She strode up the cracked walkway. Strode. As in, without crutches and without hesitation. Speed-walker, almost. The design of her new artificial feet made her resemble a Greek God—specifically, Pan. Half goat.

Whatever the Jim Rose sideshow paid, it must have been good. Her new feet cost more than the house she entered.

53.

Muscle Dysmorphic Disorder (known as Bigorexia)

It's a messy name, nonsensical. A Latin-English mutt. 1997, co-incidentally, is the first year it was coined. But people, some of them very specific people, have exhibited symptoms of this disorder since the early 1980s.

Think of it as reverse anorexia. Anorexia strikes the women, bigorexia is for the fellas. Anorexics can never be skinny enough; bigorexics can never be big enough.

Not fat, mind you. Muscle. This is a stud's disease. These guys scope themselves every time they pass a reflective surface. Mirrors and windows, obviously. Also car bumpers. Mud puddles. Dead television screens. Black patent leather shoes and tinted sunglasses. Fifty, sixty times a day, they gawk at their maleness. Always scoping their sizes. Flexing as they appraise. A calf here. A tricep there. Gluteals. Pecs. Always mentally measuring themselves against other dudes, and yes, even other women—and always coming up short.

Bigorexics are trapped in a world of incurable puniness. Their own. (Despite what they insist to the contrary.)

Like anorexics, every day is a quest for the perfect body. They'll do anything and everything to reach the unattainable goal of looking like Arnold Schwarzenegger in the opening scene of *Commando* (except *better,* dude!). They'll skip their sister's choir performance. They'll bully their sister into doing their chores and homework. They'll feign illness and stay home from school so they can eat raw eggs and squat a couple hundred thrusts. On the job, they'll call in sick or late, trying to squeeze in one more work-out. Or else they'll get to the job on time but be written up for bench-pressing bags of kitty litter in aisle eleven.

They'll monitor every meal. They'll never eat at a friend's house. Eating at a restaurant by choice is rare. They'll dine at home only. That's where they can control what goes into the food. They'll want to see it being prepared. They'll count the calories. They'll get furious, red in the face and spraying flecks of spittle, when a sufficient carbohydrate isn't represented on the dinner table. They'll order Mom to microwave a plate of frozen Ore-Ida's. *RIGHT NOW.*

They'll step on a scale eight times a day. They'll put a morato-rium on masturbation because it expends energy that might be saved for "feeling the burn." They'll eliminate excess sleep, sur-viving on five or six hours to allow more time for free weights. They'll jump out of bed in the middle of the night to do pushups and jumping jacks. They won't care if it wakes up the girl on the other side of the curtain.

The exercise will be an end unto itself. It will be about the Way rather than the Goal. But they won't know this; they'll still believe in the Goal.

The Goal, in fact, doesn't exist.

And because they're doomed to feel inadequate, they'll be inadequate.

With every blink, every gulp of milk, every lathering of shaving foam, they'll know the crush of emptiness, the misery of unfulfillment.

And you'll try your best not to laugh.

54.

Rumination Syndrome

From the Latin word *ruminare*: to chew the cud.

One bite can last hours. Ruminators swallow food, then regurgitate it back into the mouth. Sometimes it's conscious, sometimes not. No invasive methods are required. No fingers down the throat. No gagging, no heaving. There's no unpleasant taste, no sourness, no bitterness. A gentle burp is all the ruminator needs to re-visit the morsel. It's virtually effortless. So easy, so natural.

But how do they do it? How do they swallow food and barf it back into their mouths?

No one knows for sure. Some research suggests that the lower esophageal sphincter must be relaxed—through learned, voluntary methods or otherwise—and that the abdomen must be compressed in order for stomach contents to be returned into the mouth. Others speculate that ruminators have altered their belching reflex to such a degree that it creates enough gastric distention to relax the lower esophageal sphincter.

So a few mysteries remain. While graduate students with no social lives will continue to investigate how and why the ruminator does her ruminating, the most important point is this:

The ruminator doesn't bother anyone.

Every epiglottal teasing is private. Every ride up the pipes, every re-mastication, goes unnoticed. Ruminators aren't out for attention. They aren't vain. They don't need to check the mirror or step onto the scale for an affirmation of their human value. They aren't haunted by a fantasy image that they can never become. They aren't jealous of waif-like magazine models, or even of their own more feminine, curvaceous sisters.

Ruminators want nothing. Except to savor. Again and again. In this way, they are exemplary human beings; they crave *enjoyment* of the world they inhabit.

Sure, their ranks have been infiltrated by anorexics and bulimics who use the method for ill-advised, egocentric purposes. But these are a minority, and they normally don't remain ruminators for long. The pure ruminator has a healthy self-esteem. She is an equal-opportunity regurgitator. She'll ruminate a meal she hates just as often—and for just as long—as a meal she loves. It's not the taste of the food that she cares about. It's the dwelling, the oral loitering.

It's the flex of the throat muscle that the ruminator enjoys, the ability to bring it all back into play. Encore, encore!

It's the tickle she feels as the remnant returns, altered.

It's the reshaping. It's the melding of her saliva with the food.

Her body wants to break down this food, make it disappear, but her mind won't allow it, not without a fight.

The ruminator hates saying good-bye. The ruminator hates to lose things forever. The ruminator can't even imagine forever. Forever is not a palatable concept. Forever cannot be pondered.

There are drawbacks. There's the halitosis. Even though it doesn't taste bad to the ruminator, the vomit leaves a distinct odor that has been described by boys as "like a sewer" and "like a dog's ass." The ruminator may develop a complex about this, may stop kissing boys altogether, may have to reprioritize. The ruminator suffers chronically raw, chapped lips. Indigestion raises its gassy, burny head. The ruminator's tooth enamel may erode, to a degree. The ruminator will lose weight. She will question her arms and legs, question their ability to perform basic functions. She will wonder when and if her thinness will be noticed by her friends, her family. She will stare in fascination at her sunken eyes, puffy skin, angular body. She will draw in her stomach just to gasp at the teeth of her ribs. Her breasts will stop growing. Now and then, vomitus will appear on her lips, chin, and shirt. She will be teased by her classmates but will be too tired to respond. She will find it difficult to concentrate on things like schoolwork, dating, and personal relationships.

The ruminator expects each upchuck, each fresh tango with that bite, whether it's the fourth or the fortieth, to yield something new and surprising. Another layer. Something she missed the first thirty-nine times. The ruminator believes that the "true" flavor has eluded her. That if she can just give it one more try, one more swish around the mouth, then she'll *know* it, know this thing, really *know* what she is about to swallow.

The ruminator may want to believe in God. The ruminator may try to pray.

Part Three

My City Was Swallowed and
All I Got Was This Lousy Shirt

55.

There was no grand announcement of her return to Mall City. No trumpets hailed her arrival. No palms tickled the hooves of her donkey. No brass band *thrump*ed as a welcoming committee adorned her neck with wreathes. No sash-wearing public official led a boisterous crowd in a prayer of thanks.

Not yet.

Audrey wouldn't have wanted that sort of attention, anyway. Of course she wouldn't. Everyone knows how humble, how unselfish she was—"the accidental Messiah," I've actually seen written. Standing out from the crowd was never something she sought, even though her unabashed footlessness, her cultivated movie star good looks, her decision to hit the road with Lollapalooza, her coy flirtations, her Porsche, her romance with an international eatist older than her father, her unrelenting drive to remain, above all else, *mysterious*—these might *seem* like attempts to push herself into the spotlight.

But don't be fooled by the facts. When Audrey drove that lonely, flat stretch of US 131, she didn't know where she was going. She was guided by an impulse she didn't understand. When she saw the exit signs for Kalamazoo, she followed them. When she arrived, she simply parked her bright red Porsche in an abandoned lot near the railroad tracks, then walked five blocks west to the downtown Radisson, pulling a suitcase much like

193

McKenna had done through the Kalamazoo streets nine years earlier (with wheels, minus the harness).

In Audrey's head, there lived no dreams of glory. There lived no plan.

There was anger. There was resentment. There was sickness, the need to be filled, the sick to be a vessel for something larger than her own insignificant self.

In Audrey's head, there was probably no Toby. Probably no Murray. Maybe some McKenna? She must have had room in there for big sis, right?

The Radisson's rate was $140 a night. When the hotel clerk asked, "How many nights?" she answered, "Whatever this can get me," and dropped three thousand in cash on the counter. She registered under Grandma Pencil's real name. She spelled it, "Pencilochski." Make of this what you will. When she entered Room 1022, she tipped the bellhop handsomely. She unpacked her suitcase, arranged her toiletries neatly on the bathroom counter, hung her dresses in the closet (she always was a girly-girl, more Misty than Grandma Pencil), put her unmentionables, socks, jeans, and other informal wear into the bureau drawers, and settled in for a long stay.

Her lip had stopped bleeding somewhere around D Avenue, twenty minutes outside of Kalamazoo. The balled handkerchief in her purse bore a dozen red splotches. She tossed it in the trash can beneath the desk. She cracked the plastic lock on the refrigerator and drank two whiskey sours while watching *Headline News*. She removed her new feet, which, when viewed without legs attached, looked nothing like human feet. They were thin bands of a space-age fiberglass; imagine a yardstick bent into thirds. In profile, they resembled the letter "Z."

Audrey was nervous and didn't know why. Her stomach felt bubbly and uncomfortable. She lay on the bed, thinking that her whole life had been a series of unrelated events that had nevertheless worked in concert to bring her to this precise moment. Her indigestion felt like the tip of an iceberg, hiding an immense, heavy shadow that had been inside her, unnoticed, for years. She was on the cusp of something spectacular. She knew she was going to eat something in Kalamazoo, but she didn't know what. She tried to sleep. She couldn't. Her arms tingled. She wondered if she was having a heart attack. She resisted the temptation to call Johann No one should know where she was. Not yet. They would know soon—this was unavoidable—but not yet.

It was 2:30 a.m. when she sat up in bed. Why wait until morning? she thought. Why not start right now?

She dressed in the dark. She folded her hair into a bun and put on the 1996 World Series baseball cap that Johann had bought her. Opting for the crutches, she donned her stump covers and headed downstairs, via the elevator, into the night. The streets were empty of pedestrians, and a cool wind bore down upon her. Traffic lights swayed.

She looked about her, momentarily overwhelmed. All of this, she thought, could be hers. Could be inside her. She salivated.

But it was too much. It was impossible. No one would understand. A streetlamp here and there, sure, but *everything*? They would arrest her. They would toss her in prison. If she was lucky. More likely, somebody would shoot her dead.

Now and then a car purred down Main Street. A teenager in baggy jeans and a sideways Detroit Tigers cap approached, sauntering by, flashing a gold smile, looking Audrey up and down with glassy eyes.

After he passed, Audrey felt a brief and terrifying urge to chase him, leap upon him, and devour him. What would he taste like? What would he do? Would he scream? Would he have time to grasp what was happening as he slid down her throat? Would he appreciate, even for an instant, the historic gullet he was entering?

Would he fill her?

Wasn't this, after all, what her horrible gift was building toward?

Had she been put upon the earth not to consume concrete, glass, and steel, but flesh, bone, and blood? Was she evil, like Grandma said?

No. Eating this kid would give no satisfaction. She thought of McKenna's hand halfway down her throat. She could have inhaled her sister like a spaghetti noodle. But the taste was wrong. It was the flavor of alive, and it had made her queasy.

She crutched along Rose Street. Two blocks ahead, she could see the intersection of a main road, and beyond that, the Amtrak station where her family had disembarked the train nine years ago.

She tried to recall that visit but could only envision a great, tangled ball of barbed wire, ten feet high, hundreds of pounds, thundering down the sidewalk, rolling on top of her, pinning her, puncturing her, a thousand tiny holes, a thousand streams of red.

She stopped abruptly. On her left was a parking garage, untended and dark. On her right, a row of parking meters. She approached the nearest one. She opened wide.

She became a vampire, staving off sunlight with the heavy Radisson drapes, sleeping until 4 p.m., the *Do Not Disturb* sign a permanent presence on the door handle. Nights, she allowed herself one or two parking meters, but never two on the same block.

A week passed. She didn't hear from anyone—her family, her agent, her ex-fiancé. This was both a comfort and a source of anxiety. Even if they wanted to, how would they contact her? She hadn't told anyone where she was going. She was a big girl now, a grown woman. She'd told Johann she was going to America, to Moriarty Street, for a few days, maybe a few weeks. He was under strict orders not to telephone her. She knew that even if she hadn't made this clear, Johann wouldn't call. He wanted his space.

Only an hour into her visit, she'd stormed out of her childhood home with a bloody lip.

When she had arrived and opened the front door, she'd expected noise—a big shout from Toby, a bear-hug, maybe even some tears. Instead, McKenna and Murray stood in front of the staircase, arms crossed, frowning at her new feet. Two years and not even a smile. They said, "Hi, Audrey." They acted nervous. Murray's beard was entirely white, and he wore a hearing aid.

Stiff embraces were offered. McKenna suggested they "catch up" in the living room. Toby, she said, was in Detroit for a body-building competition. Audrey collapsed onto the recliner, exhausted from the trip. McKenna, employing a volume that suggested someone was sleeping in the next room, asked about the flight and the weather in Germany. Audrey answered the questions politely. Murray blinked. Audrey recognized her surroundings in a detached way, like she'd entered a museum exhibit. The furniture, the paint, the carpet—it all looked exactly as it had seventeen months ago. Her sister and father were slightly more wilted, but otherwise the same. Kenny sported her trademark braids and bad complexion. Dad fidgeted with his bootlaces and didn't make eye contact. But as familiar as they appeared, they were strangers now. They communicated to each other with gestures and facial expressions that Audrey didn't want to understand.

Audrey's mouth was dry; no drinks were offered. She didn't even feel she had the authority to walk to the kitchen for a glass of water.

Then Kenny pointed at Audrey's hand and asked, "Where's the ring?"

After that, a blur. What started as an inquisition about the breakup with Johann turned quickly to other things—dead people who acted alive, alive people who acted dead, unhealed wounds, journal entries, betrayal, cradle-robbing, and so on. Voices rose into shouts, heads heated.

Then Murray said, "I don't hate you. I hate the idea of you."

More shouting. Audrey spat out cruel words about her sister and father. She called them "pointless air breathers." She said she couldn't wait until this rotten house was bulldozed. And when she saw that her bullets were bouncing off or missing their targets altogether, Audrey aimed the big gun: "No wonder Mom didn't want to live with you losers."

Audrey felt a punch in the face. So she left. In a hurry.

Some families would be concerned by such an exit. It was possible that Murray, in a few days, might contemplate picking up a phone. Might contemplate calling Johann and, after learning that Audrey hadn't flown back to Germany, alert the police. Without a doubt, Murray might contemplate such actions. Might contemplate them into paste. The worker bee (the streaked gray hair made Audrey think of him this way) was a master contemplator. He'd contemplated himself a nice little life—a shabby house, a dysfunctional family, a job that crushed his spirit, an abandoned passion, and a wife driven to madness, despair, and suicide.

After she thinks this, Audrey says it aloud, as a fact, to Room 1022: "Mom committed suicide."

The phrase is sickening on her lips. Vulgar, like saying "cunt." Still, she takes a deep breath and repeats it: "Mom committed suicide." She pauses. "Mom killed herself."

At 8:38 a.m. on the morning of her sixth day eating Kalamazoo, alone on the bed, beneath the covers, buoyed by a half-dozen pillows, Audrey accepted—Audrey *knew*—for the first time that her mother had intentionally swallowed too many Fluvoxamine tablets. Misty had washed them down with three glasses of gin. It was, quite suddenly, a fact. Nothing frightening. This was Real. This was Truth, stripped of its garment of mystery. And after saying it ten times, the phrase tasted like sugar.

The hotel room—bedcovers, desk lamp, drapes, striped wallpaper, bureau—shone with sharp, blinding detail. Clarity and precision surrounded Audrey, and she saw a message written not in words but in *furniture*, in objects. This message was Misty. Misty was speaking to her. She was infusing her life force into every square foot of carpet, every reflective inch of mirror, every glowing cathode ray, and every plastic component of the Mister Coffee.

Her mother was everywhere, and Audrey felt warmed. All of the anger caused by not-knowing, the confusion of wondering *why* her mother might—even in theory—do such a thing . . . all of these feelings drained from Audrey's body in a pleasant rush.

The questions no longer mattered. What mattered was the answer. And the answer was to swallow. The answer was to *be* the machine she was born to be—the monstrous, wondrous, evil, beautiful, freakish, glamour-girl machine. Mother had withdrawn herself from this life not to punish anyone, not because she was sad about something her family had done, not because she felt un- loved. She'd done it to show Grandma Pencil what a Mapes girl could do when she put her mind to it. To show Grandma that you didn't need a book, a ridiculous book written by white men pre- tending to speak for God. You didn't need ten rules carved in a rock to know how to live forever. Religion was a safety net for the indecisive. It was the coward's way of facing eternity. Even dopey atheists like Murray and Toby were more courageous than McKenna and Grandma Pencil.

Misty had known the secret. This was why she'd always worn that beguiling smile. She knew that men had invented religion because they are weak. They are incomplete. They bear a *lack*. Misty understood that a woman carries eternity with her every day, that a woman bleeds eternity fifty days a year, that a woman is a small link on grand chain, a chain connecting her to her mother, her mother's mother, her mother's mother's mother, to every other woman in her family, womb to womb to womb.

Men. Men like Murray and Toby. Above all else, they needed to prove that they could *create*. As grown adults, they still needed mommy to clap for them, to squeal her approval. Make a bell that rings throughout the house! Make wings out of Sporks! Make an arm that's thick as a fire hydrant! A neck that can crack walnuts!

Even Johann. He worked so goddamn hard just to get a coffin

down his throat. He worked and worked. For the glory. For the *craft*, as he called it.

Men are watchmakers; women are forces of nature.

That's why the nuns were the true freaks. They'd forsaken their place in the chain to live as sexless beings in service of an all-powerful Father. They were dead. McKenna, too, from the look of things, was heading down that path.

Yet Audrey herself had broken from the chain. Not by choice. Her womb was a desert. She'd learned about her infertility two weeks before flying to Grand Rapids. She and Johann had been trying to get pregnant for two years. Now their relationship was over, and it was his fault. His gift, his Chlamydia, had made her this way. His past haunting her, ruining her. She wasn't average anymore.

Audrey climbed from the bed. She balanced awkwardly on her stumps, steadying herself by holding the mattress. She moved from the nightstand, to the table, to the easy chair. At the window, she pulled the cord, and with a dramatic rushing sound, the curtains parted. Daylight flooded the room. From the tenth floor—the hotel's highest—she saw Kalamazoo stretching to the horizon. Truthfully, it didn't look like much. A dozen low-lying buildings spilled together like toy blocks. To the north, street after street of two-story houses as grim and worn as the graduate students and blue-collar workers who lived there. The northwest showed part of Western Michigan University's campus, where Audrey had taken, or tried to take, classes. Bronco Stadium, the recreation center, the running track. She could see West Main snaking up the hill, past the spot where trees had been cleared— Mountain Home Cemetery. She remembered that cemetery. She remembered Grandma kneeling on the grass, oblivious to the heat, the wind, the world.

In the window, Audrey's reflection hovered above the city. Like tenth grade English class, the movie version of *Jane Eyre*. Orson Welles's gigantic face in the sky: "Jaayyyynnne . . . Jaaayyyynnne . . ."

She would haunt them like she'd been haunted. She would make them ask *why*. She would make them see that they were dying so they could see that they were living.

Once she was committed, it took Audrey two nights to eat every parking meter in the downtown area. She did it on a weekend, so nobody noticed right away. By noon Monday, every local news channel and the *Gazette* scrambled to write leadoff pieces. As you might expect, the headlines were uninspired, falling back on the vagaries of the interrogative: "Parking Meters Stolen?" and "Vanishing Meters?" "Meters Being Replaced?"

Late Monday night/early Tuesday morning, Audrey walked east on the deserted Main Street to the edge of downtown—six blocks distant— where she'd spotted an empty one-story building. On the large plate-glass window, a white placard read *Available for Commercial Lease or Sale*. The building had been a coffee shop for eight months, followed by a bicycle repair shop for five, so the flavors of grease and espresso beans saturated the glass, drywall, cement, copper wiring, plaster, brick, ceramic tiles, fiberglass insulation, and steel. She ate it in less than four hours, and she was proud of herself, especially the way she'd accessed the roof by way of the dumpster in back. This place didn't have a ladder like The Caboose.

The sun was rising. A couple of drunks reposed on a loading dock across the street, watching as Audrey appraised the now-barren concrete lot. Who knows how long they'd been there? Audrey waved at them, and they crossed themselves.

She felt tired, but in a good way, like she'd put in a solid day's work. (She'd never put in a solid day's work, not ever. But did she contemplate this fact? Heck, no. Not her thing, contemplation. That's precisely what she once said to McKenna: "Thinking about myself isn't really my thing.")

Her stomach did not feel full or satisfied. It growled. She ate a *Begin One Way* sign. There was an all-night gas station a hundred

yards up the street. She purchased a Gatorade from a woman
seated behind bulletproof glass.

She drank the Gatorade at the Kalamazoo River. Her stumps
were aching from the new feet. Standing on the bridge, she peered
over the rail. She searched for her reflection in the black water.

That's how it began. After a few more sneaky nights of gobbling
abandoned buildings, Audrey was caught. The cops handcuffed
her and put her in the cruiser. They radioed ahead about who they
were bringing. The officer behind the wheel couldn't stop gawking at Audrey in the rearview mirror. At the station, conversations
went silent, the clicking keyboards died. Everyone turned to
see—officers, secretaries, custodians, pimps and whores, perverts,
crackheads, petty thieves, and even the two homeless drunks
from the other morning. All the riffraff and boys in blue stood as
equals when she entered the room; all were held motionless by her
spell. So striking. Such a cute nose. She batted her eyes, flashed
the "aw, shucks" grin, blew kisses.

They treated her "special" this time. Her own holding cell.
Fresh coffee whenever she asked. The next day, faces appeared
constantly at her 10″ × 10″ door window. Faces that beamed when
she caught their eyes. Cops brought lemon squares that their
wives had baked. Lawyers gave her their cards. Clerks offered
Band-Aids for her stumps, which were still adjusting to the feet.
(Even MIT eggheads cannot fool the body, it seems.) She signed
autographs but politely refused to be photographed.

The press caught wind of her return. The *Gazette* ran a front-
page piece, "Caboose Eater Returns for Another Taste of Kalamazoo." The article reads more like entertainment puffery than hard
news. A sample:

> Audrey Mapes, that golden haired enchantress who worked
> the alternative music crowd into a frenzy at the Lollapalooza
> festival the last two summers with her jaw-dropping 'eatis-

try' was apprehended in a barren lot on the corner of Portage and Vine at 5:20 a.m. Thursday morning. The lot wasn't barren the night before Mapes's arrival, however. A two-story building had resided there. Until three weeks ago, the ground floor had housed Purple Pete's Aquarium Supplies, and the upstairs had been The Lock Shop. Both businesses had moved out, and the building was empty. The property is owned and managed by Dale Wermer of Hotspots Commercial Leasing, Ltd. He tells the *Gazette*, "I got a call from KPD this morning. It felt like someone kicked me in the gut. This girl just came out of nowhere, for no reason, to my property, and chomped it to bits. I'm overjoyed. Things like this don't happen to me." Wermer says he has no intention of filing charges against Ms. Mapes, but he hopes that she will consider eating his home garage so he can build a new one.

And so it went. The owners of the other abandoned buildings came forward. They skipped the legal system and leapt in front of the cameras, practically bursting out of their skins to show off the gutted foundations, grinning hugely while holding up a plywood scrap missing a U-shaped bite. "I'm putting this on eBay!"

No one pressed charges. No one complained. Each property owner, citing various reasons, said she'd done them a favor: free publicity; removing a blight they couldn't afford to remove; collecting insurance; providing them a deep, spiritual reminder of their past selves, before they became money-grubbing real estate tycoons. One man said, "The way she gobbled my building . . . I realized that's exactly what I've been doing, gobbling up properties. No reason, no joy. I'm out of this business, as of this moment. Look out, culinary school!" Even Car Park, the notoriously reptilian company whose meters she'd consumed, laughed off her act of vandalism: "Half of them were jamming quarters, anyway." They giddily proclaimed that next month (October) would be "Audrey Mapes Month," which meant free downtown parking, ALL DAY, EVERY DAY (except Tuesdays and Wednesdays 8 a.m.–5 p.m., and Fridays from 12–4 p.m.)!

Audrey accepted Dale Wermer's invitation to eat his garage. Her only stipulation was that no cameras record the event. To help achieve this, she ate at night. Still, a crowd of three hundred locals surrounded the house. A few cameras flashed, some videotapes rolled, but it's doubtful they caught much. When she finished, the Wermers let her sleep in their guestroom.

The Wermers' telephone rang all through breakfast the next day. Audrey received thirty requests: Other people wanted her to eat their roofs, sheds, or front porches so they could rebuild them. City managers wanted her to eat blighted houses with deadbeat landlords. College students wanted her to eat a dunk tank for charity. A distraught man wanted her to eat his philandering wife's clothing. A ska band wanted her to eat their instruments while they rocked in front of a live audience. An elderly woman wanted her to eat the mental ward where her husband was receiving care.

And meanwhile, for the first time in history, every resident of Kalamazoo woke up excited. Whether it was at the crack of dawn or the crack of noon, they kicked off their sheets and phoned friends and family. They talked to each other. At the breakfast joints—The Flame, Sweetwater's Donut Mill, The Corvette Café—at the bars—The Green Top, Waldo's Tavern, Bell's Brewery—at the laundromats—Duds 'N Suds, Norge Village, Ye Olde Laundromat—all around Kalamazoo, strangers chatted. High school kids and retirees gabbed across bus aisles. Janitors and accountants chuckled warmly, sipping coffee together. Phlebotomists and plasma donors high-fived. Barber shops, classrooms, libraries, dealerships, factories, gas stations, hobby shops, supermarkets— any place people could gather, they gathered to talk about the Incredible Eating Girl. They asked questions: Why had she come back? Why *here*? What would she eat next? Was it all a trick? Was it a publicity stunt? Was she human? Was she good? Was she evil? Was she single? Was she actually seven different people with power tools? Where did she come from? What was her purpose? Were they being tested? Was it a government experiment? Had the water supply been dosed with LSD? Was there any limit to what she could eat? Would she start charging a fee?

Speculation raged, theories abounded. Young and old, black and white, gay and straight, rich and poor, flat-chested and buxom, hippies and jocks, nymphomaniacs and the frigid, appliance repairmen and appliance breakers, swimmers and joggers, the bold, the shy, the fat, the skinny, the hirsute, the bald, the sociopaths, the Celtic musicians, the CEOs, the soccer moms, the depressed, the terminally ill, and the glue-sniffers—all felt united by their common humanity. They finally had something to share, in the name of love for their sweet city.

It's too bad Audrey never cared about them.

She accepted a few of the requests. Not all. Not the ones that asked her to eat for charity or in front of a crowd. In the pitch of night, she devoured. The families gave her a place to sleep, let her watch videos, knitted sweaters for her. Gave her the love she never got on Moriarty Street. She played the part of the waif pretty well, with the wide eyes and crutches and all. The pre-dawn air became a percussive concert of splintering lumber, tinkling glass, operatic metal. Crowds gathered. Requests poured in. Too many requests.

One night, at a residence where she was supposed to swallow only the roof, Audrey kept going. She ingested the whole house, including furniture, appliances, tchotchke.

The family didn't protest. They climbed out of their camper— Mike and Judith Crawford and their two sons, Mike Junior and Pete, ages eleven and thirteen—and stood like towheaded zombies: mesmerized, awestruck, speechless. Everything was gone. Their entire life had been reduced to a billowing cloud of dust.

They joined the gathered crowd in raucous applause.

Sheepishly, a rotund man stepped to Audrey's side and tugged her shirtsleeve. "Excuse me, miss," he mumbled. He cleared his throat, twisting the nightcap in his hairy hands. The applause

died down, and someone handed Audrey a damp cloth. Audrey
said thanks. The rotund man waited patiently while Audrey
toweled drywall powder from her cheeks and forehead. When she
finished, he said, "I'm Jim Logan, from next door? I run the pet
store downtown. Um, if you aren't busy, like, tomorrow, do you
think you could, I mean, would you mind doing that to our
house?" Behind him, huddled in nightgowns against the cool October morning, stood his wife Monica and three daughters.

The Logan girls looked to be ages six through ten. The youngest clung to the middle one's arm, and the middle daughter's
stance and expression suggested she was wary of Audrey and prepared to defend her little sister should this savage blond lady decide to turn that pretty set of chompers on them. The girl's brow
was set firmly, stern and uncompromising. At only eight years of
age, she was her sister's keeper; she would claw out the eyes of a
grizzly bear if it stepped too close.

"I'd be happy to eat your home, Mister Logan," Audrey said.

People underestimate the seductive power of Audrey's gift. To
witness everyday objects disappearing into that mouth was like
seeing Jesus jog up to the house after being crucified and say,
"Stick your finger in *this* hole, bub." For the Mapeses, Audrey had
been a gradual buildup over many years, but by the time she got
to Kalamazoo, she was darn good at what she did. And what she
did was impossible.

All they could do was stare. It was shocking, deeply unreal.
Physically numbing. A narcotic. It was a fairy tale played out before
their eyes. Violent, horrific, grotesque, and at the same time it
seemed, for lack of a better word, *expected. Comforting.*

Of course, their blown minds said. *Of course there is a shapely
woman with the face of an angel standing in my living room, gorging
herself on my coffee table. Why wouldn't there be?*

The snaps of teak so bombastic you have to cover your ears.

Her grunts wet and vulgar. Her face animalistic; twisted and unseemly. To watch for more than a few seconds is difficult. Because
of the tingling sensation it evokes, it feels embarrassing. The impulse is to squint, flinch, peek. And yet you want to be near it.
Like a fire. You need to be close. Scorch your arm hair. Sting your
eyes with its smoke. Throw yourself on the flames.

People asked for it. The reasons? Neighbor envy. Desire for attention. Curiosity. Sexual turn-on. The search for a spiritual
awakening, a mystical communion with the divine. To have a
good story to tell at the next family reunion. Just because. Name
your reason.

Inevitably, the neighbor asked for it, too. And every neighbor
has a neighbor has a neighbor has a neighbor.

The national media caught wind. White vans crowned with
satellite dishes flowed into the city. Reporters flooded government
offices and restaurants, brandishing power suits, smiles, and lap-
tops. They offered hard cash for information about Audrey's
whereabouts. They rarely looked anyone in the eyes. The insincer-
ity in their voices cut into the locals like piss cuts snow.

Kalamazooans were onto them. They knew these big city folks
meant trouble. They knew that Audrey hated (claimed to hate)
the spotlight. But all it takes is one mouth—as Sister Maximillian loved to say, "Loose lips sink ships." Media crews soon discov-
ered Audrey and attached themselves to her like barnacles. They
camped on the lawn of the house she was slated to eat. The family,
the Polegas, had packed their clothing and stood in the foyer
ready to go stay a few months at a relative's house (that's the pro-
tocol that fell into place) when they noticed the sea of cameras,
microphones, and stiff hair waiting outside.

"Is she in there? Is she in there?" Seventy-five voices. A gust of
perfume, choking.

"Has she started yet?"

"How does it feel?"

"Aren't you afraid she'll swallow your children?"

"Does she snore?"

"Does she sleep in the nude?"

"Is she a Satanist?"

"Can she come to the window with a blender in her mouth? I just need one picture, dude."

Audrey wouldn't eat crayon one until they all disappeared. It took three weeks for the last van to vamoose. Those news corporations have deep pockets, but no story equals no money.

This particular episode inspired The Plan.

The citizens of Kalamazoo have been called many things. Boring. Unadventurous. Unfashionable. Narrow-minded. Jealous (of Ann Arbor, of East Lansing, of any place with regular helpings of sunlight).

Never have these simple, hardworking people been called *geniuses*. Well, let these scribblings be the first to claim it, loud and proud.

In October of 1997, when a police cruiser's spotlight illuminated an abashed Audrey Mapes with a four-foot section of PVC pipe protruding from her mouth, the citizens of Kalamazoo immediately recognized that they had something special. Their freak had returned. Out of all the cities in these United States, she'd chosen this one.

Knowing that Audrey was special isn't what made them geniuses, though. Recognizing her gift was one thing; doing something with her gift was another.

After the national media swept into town and were laboriously swept back out, the Kalamazoo City Council met for an emergency closed-door session. Two days of round-the-clock meetings ensued, and with the help of Audrey's agent and publicity manager, both of whom had flown in when the story broke, the council emerged with a proposal, *The Mapes Initiative: For a New 'Zoo*, which was presented and voted on by the citizens in a hastily organized election. The proposal, approved by an amazing 99.8 percent of the voters, was then ratified by the mayor.

The first half of the legislation laid out strict ground rules for protecting Audrey from the media. It dictated a "comfort radius" of two hundred feet. It stated that no direct questions should be asked to Audrey (no such consideration for her family in Grand Rapids). The council was smart about rules regarding videotaping. They knew she preferred to eat in the dead of night, so filming her in action was allowed so long as reporters respected the comfort radius and didn't disturb the neighbors with "bright lights" or "loud noises." This made it effectively impossible to get usable shots. Additional provisions restricted the distribution of any footage or photographs without Audrey's permission.

One glaring omission in the *Initiative*—no limits were placed upon artists' renderings of Audrey Mapes. This was Kalamazoo's ace in the hole.

That's all fine and dandy. But the second half of the proposal contained the genius. Section 11.1 decreed that "Every structure and object devoured by Audrey Mapes will be re-made to resemble exactly, in as fine and minute detail as humanly possible, the original structure or object." In other words, as Audrey ate, the city would rebuild. Once she finished one structure, the people would gather to reconstruct it. And "reconstruct" is the precise word.

Painstaking care, for instance, would be taken to ensure that an olive green house with forest green trim would be repainted just so, using the same type of lumber, the same layout of windows, the same thickness of window glass, the same number of bricks constituting the chimney. A three-bedroom home with one-and-a-half baths and a stairwell with an oak banister would be reborn *identically*. Whenever possible, they would consult original blueprints. As a backup, they would take pictures of everything as documentation. If necessary, they would amass old photographs, journal entries, home movies, piles of store receipts.

They would interview family and friends, home repairmen, furnace servicers, and the like.

In the case of a business, lavatories would house an identical number and brand of toilets, sinks, hand dryers, wastebaskets. Cubicle walls from the same manufacturer would be assembled to reflect the original pattern. Meticulous measurements would be taken. Desks, computers, telephone lines, fax machines, window blinds, carpets, potted plants, water coolers—all exactly the same as before.

Using every available resource, each new structure, inside and out, would *be* the structure now residing in Audrey Mapes's bottomless belly.

It took dedication. Teamwork. Camaraderie. Respect. Money. Patience. Kindness. Empathy. Compassion. Discipline. Pride. Love. Heart. Brains. Stomach.

Daily life continues pretty much as normal for most citizens, except everyone you see—your coworkers, the gas station attendant, the mailman, your kids' teachers, the congress of teenagers skateboarding in Bronson Park—looks ready to burst into song. The air is lighter, crisper. The radios play jangly pop songs around the clock.

One night, you awake to a distant noise. A faint buzzing. Like a plane or helicopter, but more ragged, more staccato. You swat at your ear. Half-asleep, you realize that no, it's not a fly. It's nothing, you tell your husband. No reason to get excited. Go back to sleep.

Two nights later, your children appear at your bedside. The digital clock reads 3:24 a.m.

"Audrey's coming," your youngest says. Her front-tooth gap is so cute you want to smother her in kisses.

"Come here, Mom and Dad!" your twelve-year-old son says, "It's true!"

Your husband throws open the window. You sit up. Your heart

races. Your breath comes short and hot. You knew for months that this day would arrive, but still, now that it is here, the rush is pure and overwhelming. You clutch your daughter's hand. Both of you are suddenly giggling. She's coming! She's coming!

Up and down your street, windows are lighted. Men and women step out onto porches, pinching bathrobes at the neck. Word spreads: She has arrived.

The next morning, unable to control your smile, you tell your coworkers the news. They make an announcement on the hospital P.A. All day, doctors, nurses, administrators, and patients—an equal mix of friends and strangers—congratulate you.

Your children can't concentrate on their schoolwork, but that's okay. Chances like this come once in a lifetime. Math, spelling, science projects. You try to help, but time feels short. There's so much to do. Soon you give them the answers, to get it out of the way.

You spend every spare moment packing clothes and making arrangements. You're on the phone constantly, lining up relatives and friends who can put up your family. You take photos of all your belongings, careful to document the positions of every item in the house. You are near frenzy trying to finish. You snap at your husband. He snaps back. You dig up receipts and instruction manuals so you can remember brand names and models. You call Consumers Energy, the cable company, and the phone company, approximating a shutoff date.

Every night, the sound grows louder, until it is impossible to sleep. Your street is alive with people twenty-four hours a day. Your exhausted family huddles together under one blanket, shivering in anticipation.

One night, the noise is deafening. It rattles the walls, drops pictures to the floor. The children tremble, clutch at your neck. "Are we going to die, Mommy? Is she going to eat us?" You try to answer, but your throat is thick with dust.

When you awake the next day, it is a miracle. You are still
alive.

Then your doorbell rings.

She moved from house to house, business to business, school to
school, church to church, park bench to park bench, street lamp
to street lamp, stop sign to stop sign, traffic signal to traffic signal,
telephone pole to telephone pole, swing set to swing set, mailbox
to mailbox, parking ramp to parking ramp, picket fence to picket
fence, basketball hoop to basketball hoop, fountain to fountain,
church to church, library to library, viaduct to viaduct, gazebo to
gazebo. Every manmade structure came down, with a few notable
exceptions: Sidewalks and roads were ignored; so were vehicles
(she did chomp the occasional canoe in someone's garage, an ATV
here and there); so were cemeteries.

People were kind to Audrey. Warm and giving. They welcomed her into their homes, treated her like family, fed her,
bathed her, knitted her scarves in the winter, gave her a bed where
she could sleep through the day. When night fell, they ate one last
meal with her, maybe played a couple games of euchre, and then
left her to her business. At sunrise, exhausted and covered with
soot, snow, insulation, what-have-you, she went to the next house
and pressed the doorbell.

Through 1997 and 1998, morale was high. Kalamazoo was
united. Everyone felt special, everyone had a purpose. Unemploy-
ment was virtually eliminated. Construction companies were
always hiring, and suppliers—for lumber, concrete, piping, wiring,
paint, glass, insulation, furniture, appliances, electronics, books,
CDs, toys—were swamped with orders. T-shirt companies, novelty stores, and trinket manufacturers kicked into high gear:
twenty-four hours a day, they cranked out souvenirs of the momentous occasion. Shirts (*My City Was Swallowed and All I Got Was
This Lousy Shirt*); coffee mugs (*Audrey Can Eat My City Anytime*);
pins (*Audrey for President*); baseball caps (*Kalamazoo Says—EAT*

ME!); bumper stickers (*Honk if a Gorgeous Blond Just Ate Your House*). There was the Audrey Mapes nutcracker; the Audrey Mapes lunchbox; the Audrey Mapes alarm clock; the Audrey Mapes toothpaste/toothbrush set; the Audrey Mapes Halloween Mask; the Kellogg's breakfast cereal (*Audrey-O's with Marshmallow Homes*). Orders poured in from around the globe. The city became a whirling dervish of economic activity, a parade of semis streaming in and out all day and night, every month of the year. Even in the harshest January snowstorms, construction continued. Neighbors helped neighbors. Families and friends went to live with one another; they bonded into the night over extended meals, discussing the trivialities of their lives, but also the big things—death, love, hope, fear, sanity, depression, God, the future.

Kalamazoo became a worldwide phenomenon. The media returned, of course, mere weeks after they were first ousted, but this time, they played by the rules. After all, nobody wanted her to *stop* eating. Jesus, they'd be out of jobs. They treated her like a rare animal on protected national land, respecting her nocturnal feeding habits and being as minimally invasive as possible. Reporters and camera operators donned camouflage, used night vision technology, whispered into their microphones. Like nature show hosts, they caught spooky green footage of a shadowy silhouette with glowing eyes and a flowing mane of hair squatting in a corner, munching.

This took more effort than it was worth, though. Mostly, they left her alone and stuck to capturing audio recordings of her chomping, before/after shots of buildings, and interviews with local residents. So many interviews. Suddenly, everyone's opinion mattered. They tracked down classmates from college, cops who'd arrested her, the lady who sold her the Gatorade. They descended upon Grand Rapids and staked out the house on Moriarty Street. Getting no answers there, they located Sheenie the midwife, who was happy to discuss Audrey's birth in sticky detail. They found North Park teachers, nurses from Dr. Burger's office, high school boys she'd blown.

Maybe it was all the toxins in the air. Maybe it was the general bubble of goodwill that Kalamazoo had become. Whatever the case, the media used the interviews not to tell a story of freakish Audrey Mapes and her mouth but to tell a story of human beings. Of a once-depressed city, a bleak, gray, middle-American burg where smiles were once as rare as rainbows. Now, however, there was light. There was hope. Women's Groups championed Audrey as evidence that there was nothing an unmarried broad couldn't accomplish. Physical Disabilities support groups said the same thing about people with limb loss. B.A.B.E. (Blondes Are Better at Everything), Children of Factory Workers, Atheists Unite!, The Southpaw Society—all claimed Audrey as their own. Memberships skyrocketed. Kalamazoo had died and been resurrected. This was the triumph. This was the moral. Heaven was right here on Earth. Heaven was the mouth-breathing bag boy at the Jewel-Osco; it was the shell-shocked WWII vet at the halfway house who dressed like Uncle Sam; it was the single mother of two who'd just earned her master's degree; it was the president of WMU; it was the out-of-work guitarist singing for two bucks a day to an empty sidewalk; it was you and me.

Jealousy grew in other cities. They wanted to be Heaven, too. Grand Rapids was livid—Audrey wasn't even *from* Kalamazoo! On Moriarty Street, hate letters filled the Mapes mailbox. The outlying communities were especially green. Portage, an adjoining suburban community, had fought for years, and recently won the right, to be recognized as an autonomous city. Now this decision was biting them in the ass, hard. They petitioned Audrey. They sent videos of their overachieving schoolchildren singing "We Are the World." They offered money, lots of money, for Audrey to ditch Kalamazoo and eat their city instead. If she didn't want the cash, they reasoned, she could give it to her favorite charity. Heck, they would start a charity in her name, maybe one for babies without feet? When every attempt failed, they wrote a letter to the Mayor of Kalamazoo, pleading: Let us rescind our cityhood! Absorb us back into Kalamazoo! This was all a big mistake!

Finally, they grumbled. It's BS, they said. Discrimination. Who does that girl think she is, anyway? They printed their own T-shirts: *Portage—Too Rich For Audrey's Blood.*

No matter how wonderfully life is treating us, it's human nature to get antsy, to want more. Jesus understood this. He spread his miracles out. Even the sensational turns bland after a while. Supermodels can't keep their husbands' eyes from wandering. Professional baseball players demand raises. The flawless Jamaican beach becomes "too sandy." That's why Heaven is an unimaginable concept, why we envision it in childlike terms—hanging out with dead relatives, reuniting with our dogs, trading licks with Hendrix. We envision happiness in the most generic sense, transferring our everyday, pragmatic needs and pleasures to a place with clouds for a floor. We can't really, truly, wrap our minds around the idea of perfection. It doesn't exist. Perfection, if we're honest, sounds like death. *At rest.* It's *boring.*

A frenzy cannot be sustained. No one has the energy. The girl herself was hardly ever seen, so Audrey faded into the background. She continued grazing on the city. In fact, her pace increased dramatically, to five, ten, fifteen structures a day. The construction crews dutifully rebuilt. They had it down to a science by this point. Imagine barn-raising by Amish pill-poppers. Families, businesses, and churches dutifully moved back into their new dwellings and ordered identical versions of everything they'd lost.

They stuck to the plan. They would remake their lives. To a person, the Kalamazooans had a vested interest in making it work. They'd voted on it, all except the children and the institutionalized—an amazing show of solidarity, an unheard-of level of support. By following the proposal to the letter, they believed there could be freshness in familiarity. Originality in a copy. New in the old. Change without change.

Of course, they soon realized what the Mapes family already knew: Such dreams are more impossible than swallowing a city.

Your three-year-old's primitive drawings, the autographed photo of Ray Bolger, the deck of cards you bought in Paris when you were eighteen, love letters written to your ex-sweetheart, porno tapes you couldn't admit to having, the half-ounce of weed in your bottom drawer, the flattened penny you placed on the tracks in 1957, the one poem you've ever written, penciled on a napkin.

No one had calculated the value of these possessions. They hadn't thought it through. They'd been caught up in the heat of the moment. Sure, a few people undoubtedly secreted away their most cherished tokens before Audrey came calling. But most didn't. As time passed and they settled into their "new" lives, they felt a nagging incompleteness, an unnamable sensation of loss. Something wasn't right. They squirmed in their recliners.

"I don't think they gave us the same one we had before. This thing puts my ass to sleep."

"Honey, give it time. That old one was broken in, remember?"

"Humph."

Discomfort turned to annoyance.

When the local news went to its nightly "Audrey Watch," they grabbed the remote. Switched to CNN. MSNBC. Fox News. On every channel, the millennium was approaching. Computers weren't encoded properly. Y2K loomed on the horizon.

The family gathered in front of the TV, shivering.

56.

In 1999, McKenna rented a car and drove to Kalamazoo. Like most Americans, she had earned her license on her sixteenth birthday. Unlike most Americans, her fourth time behind the wheel came at age twenty-seven.

She preferred public transportation. McKenna rode the bus to the Old Kent on Plainfield where she worked as a full-time teller. The twenty-minute trip allowed her to read, think, and write before she had to turn off her mind and deal with customers for eight hours. Every day, she sat in the same bus seat—third row, left side. When someone happened to be in her spot, she took the nearest one available, but this always soured her mood and meant that she would have a bad day.

She had worked at the bank for four years, since earning her B.A. in philosophy and English from Aquinas College. Murray had long ago stopped asking if McKenna was going to "use" her degree, as if an education was a screwdriver.

One year ago, she'd completed her conversion to Catholicism. She and Grandma Pencil attended weekly mass together at St. Monica's. The two were tall and lean, of identical height, with severe cheekbones. No makeup. Their shoes were low-heeled and closed-toed. They favored conservative, loose-fitting dresses, earth tones or navy blue, sometimes with a subtle floral pattern. Occasionally, they wore each other's clothes. When entering and exiting the church, arms linked, people asked if they were mother and daughter.

Driving on the open expressway, McKenna was overwhelmed. She felt vulnerable. She'd never been naked in front of anyone, not since she was a baby, but this is what she imagined it would feel like. Her flaws were on full display. Every person in every car whizzing past was witness to a petrified lady gripping the wheel of a tin can, and they laughed at her. She was drifting over the center line, driving too slowly, sitting with improper posture.

She refused to speed up. Rolling along with nothing but a thin layer of metal between her and the pavement? Fifty-five was fast enough, thank you. McKenna knew about metal. Kalamazoo knew about metal now, too. Metal was a joke.

Despite the pleasant June weather, she kept the windows closed. Too noisy, that wind. The radio on, but very low. Air conditioner off. She heard it used up gasoline, and she was not going to be stranded out here. Just in case, she'd made certain there was a gas can in the trunk. And flares and a first aid kit. And a crowbar on the seat next to her. She nibbled daintily at the Hershey bar her father had given her.

Neither Murray nor Toby wanted to come along. If they had, she wouldn't be driving, that's for sure. She wouldn't be so tense. She had asked. Pleaded. Laid a guilt trip.

"Almost *two years*, Dad. Don't you even care how she's doing?"

"I can throw a rock and hit someone who'll tell me how she's doing. I don't need to go to Kalamazoo for that."

"She hasn't been on the news in months. She could be sick."

Toby came through the front door and immediately closed all the living room blinds. "Watch the windows. There's a blue Saturn out front. Probably some goddamn freelancer snooping around."

"*Please*, Dad. I'm officially begging."

"Sit down, Kojack. That's McKenna's Saturn."

"Kenny's?" Toby chuckled. "My bullshit meter's going off."

"Don't call your sister that. It's stupid. Grow up."

Toby had gotten his own apartment in 1998 and was now a supervisor in the Outdoors Department at Lowe's Home Improvement. He could really talk awnings. On the weekends, he flexed his oily wares for regional bodybuilding competitions. Murray still put in his forty at Hanson Mold, still bought five Lotto tickets a week, still bore the white beard he'd grown after Misty died nine years ago. He lived alone and no longer cracked Catholic jokes.

"Okay, Mr. Discipline," Toby said. "Whatever you say." He dropped into the recliner, which groaned. He looked at McKenna. "So why'd you rent a car, Ken?"

"To see Audrey."

The playfulness drained from his face. "Are you fucking *crazy?*" On his temple, a pair of veins bloomed. His knee bounced. "Tell me you're kidding. Is she kidding, Dad?"

Murray, eyes closed, hands folded, gently rocking, didn't answer.

"Why would you do that?" Toby said. He was on the verge of tears. "Oh wait, let me guess. You're a *Christian* now. You want to save her soul. Did Grandma put you up to this?" His searched the room for something inexpensive and dramatic to smash, so he could make his point without using these pesky words. Finding nothing, he sputtered, "Can't that old bag leave Audrey alone?"

Murray opened his eyes. "Cool it, sport. Annabelle's recovering, remember. And she's still your grandma. You better hope you never end up in a hospital."

"Grandma has nothing to do with it," McKenna answered. Her heart was in a sprint, threatening to snap her chest like finish line tape. Her voice, however, sounded relaxed and steady, and she was proud of herself. "She's my sister. She's family."

"Those reporters are going to eat you alive. Look at you."

"Are you scared of something I might say?"

"Everything." He shook his head. "Anything. Fuck."

She understood Toby's concern. The media blitz had only recently ebbed to a tolerable level. From October of 1997 until May of 1999—nineteen solid months—legitimate reporters and paparazzi alike had been daily presences at the house. From the beginning, Murray, Toby, McKenna, and Grandma Pencil had sworn a solemn oath to never say a word to the press. Whenever possible, they would avoid being photographed. Since this was inescapable, however, Murray bought everyone huge sunglasses. He also suggested wearing hats and engaging in unabated nose-scratching whenever stepping outside.

"Why don't you come, Tobe?" McKenna said. "We'll rescue Audrey together."

He thought about this, trancelike. A small vertigo nested in his eyes. At last, he seemed to wake up and see the living room, his father, McKenna. He drew a deep breath through his nose. "I think she needs to rescue us."

57.

Audrey wasn't tough to find. She had arrived downtown. Main Street was closed. A circumventive detour connected the east and west sides of the city. Traffic was heavy everywhere, and frequent blocked lanes exacerbated the problem. Construction workers held *STOP* and *SLOW* signs, allowing only one stream at a time to pass. New power lines, new street signs, new bus stops, new homes and buildings.

Drivers were ornery. They mouthed obscenities, tapped the roofs of their cars, threw up their hands, punched their steering wheels.

As McKenna was pushed along with the flow, not knowing where to stop, the radio DJ began talking. She turned up the volume.

"If you are *tired* of Chopin, then by all means, drop by the studio and donate any of your classical records or CDs. Anything! And by 'studio,' I refer of course to the reconstructed basement of my parents' new-but-not-new house, our temporary WMUK base of operations. Official word, again, from the powers-that-be, is that it was administrative 'oversight' not to preorder even *one* of the records Audrey was planning on turning into *dinner* . . . Whew. But bygones and all that. Here we are. One hundred watts of power from a five-hundred dollar transmitter kit, generously donated by the fine folks at McDonald's, where good food equals good times. I'm playing selections from *Chopin's Greatest Hits* if you missed the first eleven times I've pointed this out. This one's for you, Audrey. A big fat *thank you*, Audrey! Good luck eating the Radisson this weekend. Why the hell not. And bite me, FCC. This is your campus public radio, WMUK."

McKenna found a parking place on a residential side street. She walked to Rose Street and followed it four blocks north. Downtown Kalamazoo looked like a war zone. Fire trucks and ambulances. Vacant lots gutted by excavators. Lots planed by graders. Herds of yellow machines roaming the streets like dinosaurs. Pile drivers, front loaders, cement mixers. Thick-armed men unloading bricks from flatbeds. Construction workers in orange vests smoking on the curbs, dozing off, leaning on their shovels. Towering mounds of dirt everywhere. Jackhammers clanking, ripping through pavement. Cops posted on every corner, hurrying the occasional dazed citizen around open sewers and pyramids of aluminum pipes. A haze of dust stung McKenna's eyes and coated her tongue.

"You'll need one of these, ma'am, before you go any farther," a woman said. She stuck a filter mask into McKenna's hand. McKenna strapped it on and took a dozen steps before she realized that the woman had been a nurse.

McKenna arrived at the corner of Rose and South. The traffic light wasn't functioning, and no cars passed along the roads, but she stopped anyway. She recognized Bronson Park on her left. Grandma Pencil had started the war there. McKenna felt a dull ache through her body, like the beginning of a fever. This place, that moment, had made her what she was today. Turning to her right, she expected to see the library. Nothing. Years ago, they'd vacationed along this road. Three pairs of Mapeses. Mom and Dad holding hands. Mom two years from dead. There should have been a row of brick buildings on both sides of South Street—a pastry shop, a dentist office, an eyeglasses store, a coffee shop, a bar.

But now, shaved scalps. That's what was left. Two rows of shaved scalps, each one cordoned off by yellow tape. Lonely, tidy piles of swept rubble all that remained of the businesses.

McKenna's view extended two blocks, all the way to the walking mall, where the buildings remained intact but no one walked. The entrance to South Street was blocked by orange barrels and manned by a pair of police officers. When they saw McKenna gawking, one of them spanked the air, *keep it moving*.

The next intersection was Main Street, which was also barricaded and could not be crossed. The end of the line. One block east, the Radisson hotel—what was left of it—stood in plain sight. Once the tallest building in the city, it was now half its original size. The top had been sheared off at the fifth floor, jagged like a broken bottle.

"Are you lost?" someone asked.

It was another police officer. Even partially hidden behind a filter mask, he was quite handsome. His eyes were the same soothing brown as the Hershey bar McKenna had just brought back into her mouth for the seventh time. Wavy hair, lightly dusted. Kind wrinkles encircling his eyes.

And what if she answered, "Yes, Officer Mitch. I *am* lost."? What then? Would a dimple form on his cheek? Would his eyes sparkle? Would he lift and carry her, like Toby used to carry Audrey? Would he whisk McKenna past the barricades to the scarlet horizon, into a new life? Would he teach her, at last, how to be a woman?

"This is a restricted area," he said. "Want me to call you a cab?"

"My sister is eating your city," McKenna answered. "And I need to speak with her."

Two hours later, she was issued a hard hat and a pair of earplugs and escorted to the Radisson.

They had scrutinized her driver's license, then contacted the police chief, who contacted the Executive Director of The Mapes Initiative, who contacted Audrey's legal representatives, who

contacted Mayor Bowman, who contacted the Executive Director
of The Mapes Initiative, who contacted the police chief, who contacted the foreman of the Zone 12 construction team, who sent an
envoy in a telehandler to drive McKenna to the hotel.

"You're really her sister, huh?" the envoy said. "Let me guess—
older? You don't look like her." He was barely more than a kid.
Lean and rangy, with unconvincing stubble. Wearing a sleeveless
orange vest and a hard hat. His right shoulder sported a black tat-
too of Audrey, a bust. She looked like a Hollywood starlet, with
pouty lips, heartbreaking lashes, flowing locks.

"You're a fan?" McKenna asked.

"Me personally, hell yes," he said. "Don't have to worry about
college for my boy. Last two years there's been more work than I
can handle. I don't see the family much, but I've saved a buttload,
ma'am. A buttload."

"Do most people feel like you?"

"Sure," he said. "Why not?" He coughed, and then hacked a
ball of phlegm out his window. "I hear griping, definitely. More
lately. I think people are tired of it. Some ain't been paid in a
while, either."

"I thought she saved Kalamazoo. That's what the news said."

"I don't know about that. Tons of money from all the merch,
that's for sure. Went into the rebuilding, right into our pockets. I
guess it saved us for a while. I'm going to drop you off right up
there."

"So what changed?"

He stopped the vehicle. "Who knows? I mean, she *has* been
breaking the rules lately."

"What rules?"

"She's supposed to go in order, right? They made a whole plan
for her to follow." He drew a circle in the air with his finger. "Start
on the outskirts, work her way in, a spiral. That way, everyone
knows when she's coming. Companies have their 'Audrey's At the
Door' shindig, pack up the personals, get out nice and calm. She's

also supposed to eat at night. This wig shop down that way?" He pointed vaguely. "Don't tell anyone about this—they're trying to keep it hush-hush—but Audrey's not supposed to touch anything on the mall until next week. On Wednesday, she comes charging in at nine in the morning, starts chewing. All the wigs, the mannequins. Freaked the shit out of the customers. Owner tried to shoo her out with a broom. She ate the broom, almost took off the guy's hand."

"Go figure."

"Talk to that gentleman over there," the kid said. "He'll take you to Audrey."

"Thanks for your help." McKenna stepped out of the telehandler. Before she closed the door, the kid leaned toward her.

"Oh, and tell her 'Hi' from Chet," he said, winking.

58.

1991.

"This is unacceptable," Grandma Pencil said. "I should file criminal charges."

"Of course you should," McKenna said. "It's a robbery. It needs to be reported."

Grandma stood on the hearth, studying the empty space on her fireplace mantle. When she looked at McKenna, her eyes pulsed with rage. "Don't get smart with me," she spat. "I won't have two traitors in my family."

She stepped down, clumsy in her Adidas sneakers. She'd purchased new shoes two days earlier because her other pair vanished. Now, her Pope John Paul I Commemorative Plate, made of porcelain and inlaid with gold, was missing.

The week before, it was an antique Royal Bonn vase. The week before that, the framed photograph of herself with her father, standing beside the tracks of the Kalamazoo train station. This one particularly stung. Once Grandma realized that it was gone—really gone, not coming back—she had wept on the sofa for nearly an hour. McKenna comforted her, reassured her that it had just been misplaced, that it would turn up eventually.

Grandma had composed herself, and then telephoned Murray. "That beast," she said, "is eating my personal property. Tell her I will be watching. I won't sleep. I lived on two hours a night for four years. I will catch her, and when I do, I will not hesitate to use force."

Whatever Murray told her had placated her for the moment. A few days passed, and she began to question her own perceptions. "Was that the original photograph? I think it was a copy, wasn't it?" The next day: "I wouldn't have kept such an important picture on the end table, would I?"

"There *are* bowls of food everywhere," McKenna agreed. "I don't think you would have risked getting crumbs on the original."

"But it *was* out here, wasn't it?"

"There's a lot of pictures in this room, Grandma. Honestly, I couldn't say."

Then came the commemorative plate. Afterward, Grandma stayed awake for three full nights. She sat in the recliner, motionless, shrouded in darkness, waiting for an invader who never arrived. During the day, she slept like a log.

This was the next phase of Audrey's war. This was the retaliation Grandma had brought upon herself after Misty died.

It would continue for nearly four years. Her good silver. A brooch. Her toaster. Her wedding dress, dragged downstairs from its box in the attic—the empty box left boldly on the kitchen table. On more than one occasion, all the snack bowls disappeared. Family photo albums. The solid silver rosary, a gift from the nuns.

Not all at once. It followed no pattern. No way of predicting it. There were gaps—days, weeks, even months would pass. But it always started again. At first, Grandma almost lost her mind. Her daughter had died. She'd been exiled from her daughter's house. Granddaughter McKenna had moved into the spare bedroom and now they shared bathroom, refrigerator, TV, everything. Grandma became jittery. She couldn't keep food down. She took lots of hot baths and stopped drinking her beloved tea. McKenna would come into the kitchen to find Grandma supine on the floor, hands clasped in prayer, her face lined with anxiety and sorrow. The nuns visited. They cooked dinner, led her in hymns, told her to tough it out. They assured her that nothing the monster ate could affect her core self, her spiritual self.

McKenna also tried to help. She held Grandma. Prayed with her. Voluntarily stayed awake all night and watched the house. She told Grandma she'd reported the robberies and that the house was now under police surveillance. If Audrey *was* the perpetrator, McKenna said, she would be caught. She would be punished. "But honestly, Grandma," McKenna said, "I don't think even Audrey would be capable of this."

The police never caught her. Nobody did. Nobody could prove Audrey had anything to do with it. Doors and windows never showed signs of forced entry. Footprints in the snow were too numerous and jumbled. Murray insisted again and again that Audrey didn't leave the house at night—"For Pete's sake, she's fourteen!" He even sent big, strong Toby to stay with Grandma and McKenna for a week. It didn't help: During his visit as a guardian on the sofa, Grandma's coffeemaker vanished.

Grandma sunk so low as to suspect McKenna. "This all started right after you moved in!" she screamed. "Why don't you go? You bring trouble. Get out!"

After a heated discussion, during which Grandma collapsed in tears on the bathroom floor, McKenna said, "I forgive you, Grams." They hugged. McKenna smiled.

59.

She heard it as soon as she stepped out of the fifth-floor stairwell: the lovely, aching song of Audrey trying to fill herself.

McKenna thanked the foreman—a white-haired, stocky guy named Merle, whose moustache might have been pilfered from Mark Twain's lip. He told McKenna to be careful. "Sometimes she doesn't look where she's eating. And she moves pretty quick. I'll be right here if you need me."

McKenna walked down the hallway toward Rooms 501–520.

"Hey!" Merle called. McKenna turned around. "Tell her she don't have to finish the whole city if she don't want to." He tried to grin. "If she don't want to, that's all."

McKenna rounded a corner. The sounds of crunching fell silent.

She stopped in her tracks. She couldn't grasp what she was seeing. On her left side, it looked like any hotel—a row of numbered doors.

On her right was a surreal scene. McKenna stood facing a bizarre diorama—a string of ten hotel rooms and bathrooms stretching for two hundred feet. No walls anywhere, except the exterior wall. It looked like a department store display. Everything in its place. Beds made. Television cabinets closed. Writing desks clear of clutter. Wastebaskets empty. Shower curtains draped regally over tubs. Freestanding toilets and sinks. A dollhouse. Everything peaceful beneath a snowy blanket of dust.

The curtains were drawn, but sunlight poured in. A humid breeze touched the top of McKenna's head. She looked up. The ceiling was gone. Mist enchanted the air, an ethereal glow.

Maybe this is Heaven. Couldn't I make it so? Climb into one of those beds? Sleep here forever.

"You look like I feel," a voice said.

McKenna stepped into one of the "rooms." She squinted through the toxic fog, grateful for the filter over her mouth. On a queen-sized bed, Audrey reposed.

She hadn't bothered to clear the drywall and sawdust before lying down. She didn't wear a mask. She watched McKenna approach. Her lips pulled histrionically at a cigarette. She blew a column of smoke toward the sky.

"That's always been your problem," McKenna said. "If you felt how you look, you wouldn't be eating a city."

Audrey considered this. She shrugged. McKenna dragged a chair from the writing desk and sat beside the bed.

Audrey scooted herself into a seated position against the headboard, grunting as if making a great effort. She was dressed in a brown WMU sweat suit. Her expensive feet were nowhere to be seen. Not even her padded socks. Just bare, exposed stumps. Didn't they get cut by glass, splintered by wood? Where were her crutches? Did she crawl around the floor and eat things? Like she'd done with McKenna when she was a baby?

Maybe this was what Audrey longed for, a return to the days with McKenna, days of joy and crayons. It was a pleasant idea, and McKenna held onto it.

"You're the first one to visit me," Audrey said.

"Johann says he tried a few times."

"Oh, him. He tried. He failed."

"I thought you were in love with him."

"Who said I wasn't?"

"Are you?"

"Is there a rule that says people you love should get better treatment than everyone else?"

"I thought so."

Audrey shrugged. "News to me." She took a drag. The ember sizzled a stray hair. She flicked her cigarette into the bathtub ten feet away. "Two points!"

McKenna waited.

"Look, we had no future. I cut him off a long time ago. End of story."

(It's a lie, but did McKenna know it at this moment? Or was it only years later, from reading books, when she learned that Audrey couldn't bear Johann a child, so he'd sent her packing? Sent her back to Michigan, back to her destiny.)

Here comes that Hershey bar again.

"Chet wanted me to tell you 'Hi.'"

With her fingers, Audrey flung the hair off her shoulders, did a head shake. A familiar move, whenever boys were mentioned. "Really? He's sweet."

"He's got a kid."

"Why are you here, exactly?" She rolled off the bed on the opposite side from McKenna. She came up with crutches under her arms. She looked gaunt and hollow-eyed. Her hands were skeletal, the skin papery and transparent.

"You don't have to keep doing this," McKenna said. "Some people don't want you to—"

"Oh, let me guess. You're here to boss me around. Because you don't have a goddamned life of your own."

"Come home! Or go somewhere! Do something."

She blinked. "You really are saying this? *You*?!"

McKenna stood from the chair. Audrey crutched to the bathtub. She leaned over and with a primal scream rent an enormous chunk of porcelain with her teeth. McKenna plugged her ears. Audrey took another bite, and another, and another. It was quick

and brutal, her head whipping back and forth, a bedlam of oblit-
eration mixed with the wails of a dying animal.

Fifteen seconds later, the tub was gone. Audrey sat on the floor
and quietly slurped the shower curtain into her mouth, followed
by a handful of plastic rings, which she ate like donuts while
speaking.

"They wanted me, Kenny," she said, chewing. She stood with
difficulty. "I know you don't like to hear it, but it's the truth. I
know most of my family hated me for being what I am. Hid me
away, treated me like a disease. Listen, Kalamazoo *needed* me. This
was *their* idea. They made the rules. They can't just *stop* now and
say good-bye. They can't just be tired of me. That's not how it
works. I won't allow it. I WON'T ALLOW IT!"

McKenna startled. Audrey burst into that same aggressive guf-
faw she'd used on Grandma Pencil, but this time, her voice was
wheezy and thin. She stopped. Her breathing was labored. She
rested on her crutches, her eyes closed.

"I'm sorry I punched you," McKenna said.

Audrey didn't open her eyes. She swayed in place, her stumps
padding on the floor in a delicate dance, her head bowed. She
wanted to melt, dissolve into this nightmare domestic space she'd
created. At last, she whispered, "I forgot all about that."

The Hershey's slid back and forth along the inside of McKenna's throat.

Audrey opened her eyes. "Did you apologize to Grandma?"

McKenna made a smiley face in the dust with the toe of her
shoe.

"Of course not," Audrey said. "You and those pigtails. Still a
child."

"Grandma's sick, if you want to know. She's in the hospital."

"Oh." She raised her left leg, picked a couple chunks of porcelain off her stump and ate them.

"She had a stroke."

"Oh."

"And by the way, she took back what she said."

"Took what back?"

"That thing she said about Mom."

Audrey gave her sister a hard sidelong stare. "Bullshit."

"Honest. That's why I came to see you. She said there's no pas-sage in the Bible that calls suicide a sin. Nothing explicit, anyway. I worked on her. Maybe it's because . . ." McKenna paused, feel-ing the Hershey bar drift back down, the final time. "Anyway, I thought you should know."

Audrey wiped her mouth. Blinked. Her eyes were watery and red from the dust. "Well. I guess our plan worked, then." She coughed wetly. "I'm glad you told me."

McKenna felt the urge to step in closer, perhaps touch her sis-ter on the shoulder, but she couldn't be sure of the outcome. "Re-member how I used to feed you?"

The sun climbed from behind a cloud and brightened Audrey's hair. Sounds of machinery, of repair, rumbled beneath Audrey's voice: "I don't remember."

"You weren't even a toddler yet. I smuggled crayons, soap, what-ever you wanted. I can still see your face, so happy." McKenna felt a rising sensation inside her, as if her blood were being drawn toward the sky. "And now I'm here. When nobody else is."

Audrey's jaw tightened. She pursed her lips. She seemed to be fighting to keep the words in her throat from escaping her mouth. When she looked up at McKenna, her eyes appeared scarred by the glaring sunlight. She nodded as if they'd come to a mutual agreement about something.

Then she brought a cigarette out of the pack and lit it. "I'm still going to finish eating."

"Of course."

"These people love me," she puffed. "They do."

"Of course. We all love you."

60.

It was a crisis of calculation. Kalamazoo thought they could fund the reconstruction of an entire city with the profits from tacky celebrity merchandise. The plan worked for the first year. But the famous face never showed her famous face. She granted no interviews. She lived like a bat. She hated cameras. She didn't speak publicly, didn't smile. In many ways, and especially to the outside world, Audrey never *was*. She existed only as a name, a concept. At best, she was a caricature, a cartoon figure. At worst, she was a Freudian nightmare—the cherubic, fair-skinned girl-next-door with the mouth that might swallow your head.

Most importantly, though, Audrey stopped capturing hearts and imaginations because people didn't believe in her. How many T-shirts can you sell of a fraud, a cheat? Ask Pete Rose. Ask Milli Vanilli. Ask Jim Bakker. Ask Tonya Harding.

To millions, she was a hoax. Conspiracy theories abounded. There is no Audrey Mapes, they said. Kalamazoo bulldozes their own buildings in the dead of night so we'll think they're hot stuff. We've done the math: She'd have had to wolf down fifty buildings a day to finish in two years. Sure, there's a girl named Audrey Mapes. A shyster who faked her way through a sideshow performing; tricks any third-rate magician can do. She just "happens" to be gorgeous? With a *handicap*, no less? UC Berkeley did a comprehensive study in 1995, and they *proved* she couldn't do what she said. But you didn't care about that, did you, Kalamazoo? Slap a drawing of the pretty cripple on a bumper sticker; sell it for ten bucks. Instant attention, instant cash. Add computer effects to some grainy night-vision footage and boom—a modern-day legend!

Don't you want to buy an oven mitt?

Yes, pretend you've been chosen, Kalamazoo. Pretend you matter. Exploit the world so you can find an identity. Shame on you, Kalamazoo. We knew you were desperate, but geez.

Of course, millions of believers remained, all around the world. Audrey received fan letters from Argentina, Zimbabwe, Russia, Malaysia, Mexico, India, Iceland. Families saved money to pilgrimage to Kalamazoo in hopes of catching a glimpse of the "Miracle Mouth of Michigan." Unable to actually see her, they did their best to elicit stories from the locals. Most every Kalamazoo resident had met Audrey. She'd slept in their beds. She'd played "Simon Says" with their children. She'd taken coffee with them, kissed their babies good-bye. But no one was talking anymore. They were all talked out. Even the most destitute refused fifty bucks for an anecdote of their encounter with the eternal. That's how badly they wanted Audrey gone. She'd become a bad dream; they wanted to wake up, or at least move on to a different dream. Travelers inevitably left Kalamazoo with a few dozen photographs of construction vehicles, a profound sense of disillusionment, and a souvenir tennis visor.

The merchandise stopped selling. The cash dried up. Construction crews went weeks, months, without getting paid. Flatbeds bearing lumber were turned away due to lack of funds. Businesses and homes couldn't be reassembled. Campus dormitories lacked walls. Church parishioners waited impatiently for Italian marble altars that never came. A waiting list was created. By August of 1999, the backlog was one thousand strong. An emergency meeting was called. Taxes were raised. Undocumented laborers were shipped in to speed production. Shoddy materials saved the city a bundle, but now and then a house caught fire.

People stopped helping one another. They noticed each other's
crooked teeth, love handles, double chins. The imperfections sick-
ened them. They elbowed each other in the pews, if they were
lucky enough to have pews. They no longer kicked off their sheets
in the morning and rushed out to gab with their neighbors. Instead, they huddled under the covers and cursed Audrey. Out of a
job indefinitely. All those lucky assholes that got their houses
eaten first. Who came up with the stupid spiral idea, anyway?
Rich people, probably. Portage was probably behind the whole
thing.

Some people actually moved away. Most didn't. But they talked
about it.

Audrey ate through it all. Protesters gathered. Unruly crowds
waved crude messages—"Mapes Rapes the 'Zoo," "Audrey Can
Eat Shit For All I Care," "Beelzebub Called, He Wants His Appetite Back," "Bite on THIS, Mapes!" and "Last Time I Checked,
Gluttony Was a Sin."

The friendliest *Gazette* editorials commanded her to leave town
and never return. The others called for a criminal investigation.
Local television news ignored her. The evening "Mapes Watch"
was replaced by the "West Michigan Golf Course Spotlight." Ac-
tivists organized; petitions were circulated. Twenty-five thousand
signatures for Audrey's immediate ouster were presented to the
mayor.

Mayor Bowman stood firm. Not much longer, he said. We
need patience, he said. We need to stick to the plan. No one said it
would be easy.

It was October 1999.

Security forces were doubled. Two dozen rent-a-cops guarded
the downtown structures Audrey ate: the courthouse; the Michigan News Agency, which hadn't missed a day of business in thirty
years; Jiffy Print; a parking garage.

One night, three angry, unemployed men carrying handguns
snuck past security into the dry cleaners Audrey was ingesting.

The men emerged five minutes later. Their faces were bloodless. They surrendered without resistance.

One of them said, "I never expected it to move. Jesus. Was that *her?*"

Another one said, "I think she's alive."

The other one didn't speak for a month, until after Audrey was gone.

Even as she fed on the machinery of civilization, she wasted away.

Even as she consumed the muscle of society, she shriveled.

Even as she chewed cinder blocks the size of Buicks, she shrank.

In darkness, she drifted through corridors. Outside every window hung a moon she could never swallow. Clouds she could never wrap herself in. Stars that twinkled, stillborn, into her eyes.

Icy wind crept into her lungs, swirling.

Her flesh withered. A veil shrouded her eyes, turning them to ink. Her bones screamed softly, and her hair fell out, slow and gray, in the moonlight. Her once-enchanting glow faded. Her ribcage yawned.

She ate her own teeth, and then she ate no more.

Nobody held her. Nobody came running when she finally cried out, her ragged voice indistinguishable from the machines on the streets, the earthmovers.

She relived the baths, the tender hands. She splashed diamonds in the sun.

She was my sister.

She shivered on a concrete floor that smelled of gasoline.

61.

McKenna chews.

Alone in the house on Moriarty Street.

From her bedroom, she watches unshapely tourists come and go.

They point. They snap photos. They bang the metal porch door with their umbrella handles. "Hello? Hello?" They ring the bell once, twice, three times. They cup their hands and peer into basement windows. They chisel hunks of cement from the front steps and stuff them into their purses. Then scurry to their minivans.

At night, McKenna watches television. She drinks tea. She prays. Writes. Prays. Chews. Writes. Prays. Writes. Chews.

She talks to Grandma Pencil on the phone. She talks to Murray on the phone. She talks to Toby on the phone. She tells them everything here is fine. They never discuss Audrey.

A new millennium has dawned. The world remains unended, for now.

What's left of Audrey resides in a plot next to Misty, at peace. She might eat her way out of the coffin. Then they'd believe. Then she'd get that statue.

Except Audrey is ash now, so this would truly require a miracle.

She died on the last Christmas Eve of the twentieth century. No one knows how or where.

One morning, her body was seen blowing down the middle of Main Street like an empty plastic bag. At least that's what some people say.

Some people had honestly believed that nothing could kill her. Some people wrote books about her immortality.

What's certain is that there was enormous pressure from all sides to perform an autopsy. Huge sums of money—seven, eight figures—were offered for her body. Everyone wanted to take a look. Everyone wanted to put her in jars.

Murray has recently relocated to Arizona. Put himself up in a modest house with a view of a butte or two. Audrey's death hit him pretty hard. He hadn't expected it. The only other girl in his life, snatched away. Maybe that's how he saw it. He never said it in so many words, but it's worth thinking about.

McKenna was never much of a girl, never the daddy's girl a daddy likes to fawn over. McKenna knows this. She accepts it.

Early retirement from Hanson Mold pays some of Murray's bills. He also lives off Misty's life insurance, which has grown in a mutual fund for ten years.

Toby lives in the south side of Grand Rapids. He still supervises lawn furniture at Lowe's and frets about his puny muscles. His steady girlfriend Amber, plucked hot and steaming from the cradle at nineteen years of age, manages his fading bodybuilding career.

Grandma Pencil did suffer a stroke in 1999. McKenna hadn't lied to Audrey about that. Grandma recovered, mostly. She sold her house and most of her possessions and was taken in like a stray puppy by the geezers.

The stroke put half of her face to sleep. It also wiped out half of her memories. A happy occurrence, really. Some experiences are better left forgotten. She doesn't even remember what Audrey did to her, how for five years Audrey took away everything she treasured, including her will to live. How she'd had to resort to the same mental numbness that had allowed her to survive internment camp and the agonizing mystery of her father's fate. How she'd learned to view all of her possessions as temporal, insignificant, *already gone.* How she'd learned that loving *things* was always a dead end.

Grandma doesn't remember these valuable lessons, so there's no immediate need for McKenna to apologize for unlocking the back door, for letting the monster inside every time.

A confession wouldn't hurt, though. Next week.

62.

In time, the tourists stop coming.

2005.

McKenna celebrates her thirty-third birthday with a bowl of instant pudding. Tapioca. She doesn't need much. Canned soups, bread, eggs, milk. She makes everything last. She turns the thermostat as low as she can stand it, spends evenings curled up in Misty's old quilt, fills pages by candlelight. Her hand cramps.

When Grandma sold her house and moved in with the nuns five years ago, McKenna lugged all of Murray's inventions back here, stored them in the attic. Sometimes she goes up there and picks through the boxes, reconnects with something. Murray doesn't know she has these things. He'd be embarrassed. They phone each other every month, although both of his ears are quite deaf now, and he hates his hearing aids, so conversation is awkward. He calls to make sure she got the check.

Her faith has deepened. Some days, it feels like she really is in harmony with her creator, like she has given herself, body and soul, to Jesus. She knows she must serve Him. She knows, in fact, that she is blessed with the chance to serve Him. He will forgive her sins. Even when she confesses that she deceived Grandma for so many years. Even when she confesses that her last words to Audrey, her words about Grandma's change of heart, were a lie meant only to fester like an open sore. Jesus will forgive her when she confesses.

Other days, McKenna is certain God will never love her. Not until she changes. Not until she stops destroying the temple. Her teeth are sensitive, stripped. Her throat is hot agony. Dark green welts form on her thighs from the slightest stove bump. Her menstruations have stopped. She is officially not a woman. The nuns visit, pray with her, urge her to seek help. The ones McKenna grew up with—Sister P.V., Sister Max, Sister Juliet—all of them are gone now, but fresh ones, young ones, some younger than McKenna, have taken their places.

If you won't see a doctor, they say, at least change your lifestyle. The Dominicans, they say, are a good order. They are always looking for new sisters. Your silence, your reflectiveness, will be put to a divine purpose. This house is unhealthy, they say. It is killing you.

One morning, Sister Pauline comes by. Her knock is softer than usual.

"Annabelle went to be with God last night," she says, taking McKenna's hand. "She's at rest."

McKenna smiles. Swallows.